W9-AOH-071

By _____

THE WRATH
OF CON

No Longer the Property of
Hayner Public Library District

DANIEL
YOUNGER

HAYNER PUBLIC LIBRARY DISTRICT
ALTON. ILLINOIS

OVERDUES 10 PER DAY, MAXIMUM FINE
COST OF ITEM
ADDITIONAL $5.00 SERVICE CHARGE
APPLIED TO
LOST OR DAMAGED ITEMS

HAYNER PLD/ALTON SQUARE

This is a work of fiction. The characters, incidents, and dialogue are drawn from the author's imagination and are not to be construed as real. Any resemblance to actual events or persons, living or dead, is entirely coincidental.

THE WRATH OF CON © 2016 by Daniel Younger

All rights reserved. No part of this work may be reproduced or transmitted in any form or by any means, electronic or mechanical, including photocopying, recording, or by any information storage and retrieval system, without permission in writing from the author.

Cover illustration by Ben van Duyvenyk

Avast! Mutant Panda heeds no scalawags 'n takes no prisoner. Copyright infrin'ement be punishable by law. Take from us 'n ye'll be punished. ye've be threatened. Come aboard at mutant-panda.tumblr.com

Also by Daniel Younger:
Delirious: A Collection of Stories
Zen and the Art of Cannibalism: A Zomedy

Get in touch with Daniel:
danieljyounger@icloud.com
@YoungerDaniel
danielyounger.com

ISBN-10: 1533488363
ISBN-13: 978-1533488367

3461033

For David Sturgeon

THE WRATH OF CON
OF CON

PART I
SOME ASSEMBLY REQUIRED

"An art thief is a man who takes pictures."
— George Carlin

CHAPTER 1
JUST DESERTS

As kidnappings went, Josh Harlan thought he could do a lot worse than the trunk of an Audi. For one thing, it was spacious. Just enough room to bang your elbows any time you struggled with the zip ties. Also, it smelled nice—carpet cleaner, nylon and a touch of perfume. It was cool and dark, and the steady hum of the tires on asphalt created a sort of sensory-deprivation chamber. Sure, he was on his way to almost certain execution, but Josh couldn't help but doze.

He barked his elbow as the car drifted onto the shoulder. They came to a stop. Doors slammed. Gravel crunched, and the trunk opened, searing Josh's retinas with high-noon sun. The vast shadow of a man named Tiny loomed above.

"I swear to god I wasn't napping," Josh said.

The goon yanked him out and draped him over his shoulder like a rolled carpet. They were in the desert, about a mile west of the Hoover Dam. Tiny hauled him over to a pre-dug hole and plopped him on the ground. Gavin Whelan followed, working a crease out of his blazer methodically.

"Where's the diamond, Joshua?"

"Really, Gavin? Desert execution? Here I thought you were an original-type guy."

Whelan shrugged. "Some things are effective."

"Right. Theatrics."

"I asked you a question," the tycoon said, patiently. This was the single most irritating thing Josh had ever found in the guy's character. Here he was, about to kill him, and still reserved as a Catholic blow job.

"And I didn't answer. Now, are you gonna shoot me or talk me to death?"

Whelan produced a mean-looking .45 from the back of his slacks and crouched in front of him.

"That's up to you. Where is it, Josh?"

Josh hung his head. This guy was a tool. Putting aside the fact that he'd captured him, drugged him, and was probably about to kill him, he still had no idea this was exactly where Harlan wanted him. "Have you tried retracing your steps? Think of the last place you saw it. Go ahead, I'll wait."

"Boss, mothafucka's not sayin' shit," Tiny grumbled. "I say we pop him."

"There's an idea," Josh beamed. "Put me out of my boredom, already. This sucks."

Tiny growled like a dog poked with hot iron.

Whelan waved him off. "I'm going to give you one last chance, Josh. The—"

"Will this sentence end with a bullet? I've got nothing to tell you, Gav. You took me out to the desert before my team could even call. Plus, even if I *did* know, I probably wouldn't tell you."

Tiny produced a Desert Eagle .40 and racked the slide. "Hell, I'ma put a hole in him myself."

Josh gave the goon a once-over and chuckled. "Tiny?"

"Yeah?"

"Get a real name. We're not here to kill me."

"…We're not?" Tiny gave Whelan a look, as if to ask: *…We're not?*

"Nope," Josh said.

Whelan sighed, the gun falling to his side.

Tiny's brow stitched with confusion. "Well then… Why we out in the desert, next to the hole where I'm planning to bury you?"

"Intimidation." Josh smirked. "Not really the smartest ploy when you're dealing with a con artist, but here we are."

Whelan rubbed the bridge of his nose. "Tiny, if he answers for me one more time, you can shoot him."

"Gavin, dearest, are you cracking? Is it the heat? Do you need air conditioning?"

"On second thought, I'll do it myself."

Perfect, Josh thought. "See, Tiny, when you're not a henchman, you do all kinds of things that might threaten a fella into talking. One of which is showing him imminent death."

"'Cause we gonna kill you?" Tiny said, brightening.

Josh sighed. "Mister Brawn, do keep up. I know something Gavvy here needs to know. If you kill me, he's humped. But, you hurt me the right ways and ask the right questions… Well, you just might frighten me into telling."

Tiny straightened up here. "I like that last part."

"Here's the thing. You messed up. You caught me early. Now all the things I could probably tell you, I don't know, and this whole deal is a massive waste of time."

Whelan sighed. "You really don't know, do you?"

"Honestly? I'm starting to feel like a broken record here." Josh tried to shrug, but his restraints made it more of a wriggle.

"Well, then I suppose this is goodbye." He cocked the hammer of his .45. "Sorry, Josh."

Aw, crap, thought Harlan.

CHAPTER 2
HIGH-HEELED ROBBERY

Las Vegas: Six Nights Earlier

Three-thousand slots machines blipped like a spazzing Nintendo game while Brie Cassiday sat at the disc-shaped bar of the Olympus Casino, thinking: *How quickly can I get this guy's room number?*

She was thirty-one, with a spray of freckles and a tangle of crimson curls tied in a loose chignon. She wore an aquamarine minidress and a bloodred scarf, paired off with fuck-me pumps that made her heels hurt. Hence the urgency.

"Thirteenth floor," slurred the guy next to her. He was early forties and well-dressed, with an avalanche of salt and pepper. His name was Ben Connolly. "They say it's unlucky. Well, I showed them!"

"You haven't crossed any black cats tonight, have you?" Brie said, removing her scarf. She twirled a lock of her hair and sighed; her breasts rising and falling in the way she knew would captivate him.

Clockwork. Ben's gaze latched onto her cleavage like a remora. She finished her drink just in time for him to say, "Want another?"

"So he's lucky *and* he's got good timing? Sure."

"Pfft! I don't need luck. I've got *per diem*. What d'you need luck for when you're riding someone else's cash?" He signaled the bartender, who returned with fresh hootch. Ben sloshed his martini and chuckled, continuing. "I can't go wrong. Even if I lose, it's company dime."

Brie leaned in, finding her hook. "So, how much do you want to tempt fate?"

"Fate?" Connolly spat a chunk of olive across the bar. "Fate! Ha! I'll take fate out to the playground and beat it up. I'll fist-fuck fate with the iron glove of confidence. I'm on the thirteenth floor, in room 1313, and I don't give a gilded shit what superstition says. Fate?!"—and here he made an impressive raspberry—"I'll take Fate to lunch and skip on the bill!"

Brie chuckled. *The winners always think they're invincible.* "I guess we'll let it ride."

Ben took a long breath, his gaze wandering up to a terrible idea on his left. "You should come back to my room. We can celebrate."

"Sure, that could be fun."

"Good," Ben slurred. "Meantime, I gotta wet the puck." With that, he slid off his stool and swayed a beeline to the bathrooms.

"Showtime." Brie grabbed her bag, headed over to a wide bay of elevators, found one, and hit the button for the thirteenth floor. A door opened and closed. The elevator whirred. It dinged. Brie grinned and strutted down the hall to 1313, passing a maid's trolley on the way.

She reached the door, produced a dry-erase marker wired to a small chipboard, and shoved the end of the marker into the bottom of the lock. Generally, you could hotwire electric locks using the power bypass. She pressed a button on the device, waited, and it bleeped twice. The small LED light on the board went red. She sighed. She'd been using it a lot lately, and worried the charge had dulled.

Three tries later, Brie hated the color red.

She decided to gamble and headed back to the room service trolley to look for a key, but only found rolls of toilet paper and hopelessness. She sighed, undoing the chignon and running her fingers across her scalp. Then, she produced an electric drill from her bag and started working her way around the aluminum edging of the cart.

Three seconds later, she pulled the metal off, straightening it, then created a hook on one end of the six-foot length. She went back to the door and bent a right angle at the opposite end from the hook. She crouched, snaking the metal under the door. She fished a little, found resistance, pulled, and the door's latch opened from the inside.

She slipped into the swank lodgings, did a three-sixty, and headed for the bedroom. The Grand, the Venetian, and Caesar's Palace all had safes in the bedroom closet; why should the Olympus be any different?

Brie ripped open the sliding door and discovered an entire wall of shoes. Without giving herself the moment's envy, she trudged over to the wall, where she met her reflection in a mirror. She sighed, brushing her hair out of her face before wrapping her fingers around the glass.

Three seconds later, she'd found her safe.

The Olympus was only three-weeks old. Typically, en suite safes have a staff override code of *0-0-0-0-0*. She punched in the code, and the safe swiftly failed to open.

Not bad, she thought. *Most casinos never change it.*

She produced two six-inch pieces of metal shaped like chopsticks and found the keyhole. She jammed them in and jimmied until the safe's lock spun freely. Then, she tilted the second prong upwards, pushed, and with a heavy click, the safe swung open.

There were stacks of bills—mostly hundreds—wrapped together like green bricks. Brie unzipped the front of her Fendi backpack and started scooping them in.

That's when suite's door opened.

Ben Connolly spilled into the room, tossing his keycard on the table. He kicked his shoes the full length of the suite. There was a built-in bowling alley off the living room, and his first shoe followed an arc that landed behind the pins.

"Fuck," he sighed. He was just about to hit the minibar for a nightcap, when he turned on the lamp and caught a woman's nude silhouette in the bedroom. "What the—"

"Room service?" Brie beamed, patting the spot beside her on the bed.

Ben blinked, as if this entire situation was some alcohol-fueled delusion. "How did you…?"

"The maid let me in," Brie said, flinging the covers. She patted the spot again. "Join me?"

Connolly didn't know what to think. On one hand, he really doubted the maid would've let her into the room on her own. Also, he did have a girlfriend back in Boston who'd relieve him of his testicles if she could see this situation. On the other? Well, she was really naked over there, and really hot. He was in Vegas, right? Wasn't this the national capital of adultery? He swayed on the spot, lust, booze, and indecision pumping through his veins.

"Air," he said. "I need some air."

"Well don't mind me getting offended over here."

Ben threw open the door leading to his balcony. The Strip

glimmered like a string of Christmas lights below. He breathed the desert air and rubbed his temples. He wheeled back into the room and grabbed a mini bottle of vodka.

"You're not a hooker, are you?"

Brie narrowed her eyes. "And more with the me being offended."

Connolly drained the vodka and started pacing. "I'm sorry. I don't know. It's just you win a couple games of blackjack, meet a pretty girl and suddenly she's naked in your bed. It's too lucky."

"Exactly. Luck. Don't you want to get more lucky, sailor?"

Well, he did. He really, desperately did. Only…

"It's just—well—I… I've got a girlfriend…"

"And I've got no clothes on," she said.

Damn, she really did have him there. He opened his mouth and closed it a few times, trying to coax a response. "I'm sorry I called you a hooker. It's just—"

And here, a low growl came from behind. Something deep and predatory and vaguely feline. Ben went to turn when something heavy caught him by the solar plexus and knocked him to the floor.

When Ben got turned around, he screamed, and the claws slashed at his throat.

Brie scrambled back on the bed, wrapping herself in the sheet as the puma snarled and tackled the drunken businessman. It was the size of a vending machine, with jet-black fur rippling over cords of muscle as it pinned him to the floor. Its head was boxy and its tail described a whirling question mark, grumbling as Connolly struggled.

"Holy f—"

The big cat roared. Ben knocked it back with a kick. He scrambled to his feet just as the feline smacked its paws against the carpet and lunged.

It happened in snapshots: Ben staggering backward. The cat going airborne, catching him by the shoulders. A backpedaling shuffle—straight back, through the open door to the balcony and off the edge.

Silence.

More silence.

Thwack.

Brie scrambled onto the balcony and peered over to find the man and the puma splatted against the concrete below. Already, tourists were circling the slash of red painting the sidewalk. A twelve-year-old spooled the film in his disposable camera.

Before anybody could look up, Brie swept across the room, put on her dress and bounded over to the safe, where she began stuffing bills into her cleavage. She bolted around the bed looking for her Fendi, but it had been swept up in the scramble to get naked and under the covers before Connolly had entered the room.

Fuck, fuck, and triple-fuck! No time. Sirens wailed down the Strip. The sound of rescue vehicles skittering over the curb dopplered up the casino. She gave the room a final sweep, tried and failed to catch her breath, and hurried out of the room with her pumps dangling in her hand.

By the time Brie hit the lobby, the scene in the casino's round-about had escalated to full-blown meltdown. An ambulance straddled the curb. Two EMTs stood beside Connolly and the cougar, scratching their heads at how to proceed. Meanwhile, an unmarked sedan screeched to a halt beside them, and a rumpled-looking man in his late forties heaved his considerable frame from the car.

"Don't you fucks touch anything," he barked. "Pictures, chalk, crime scene tape. Leave the rest."

"You don't want us to try to revive?" said the younger EMT.

The cop gave the kid a deadpan expression. "What are you, the fucking Wizard of the West or somethin'? Pictures and tape, fuckwit. Go."

He turned to the growing throng of onlookers and held out his hands, the messiah of dead dudes. "Okay, assholes. Back it up. He might not need the breathing room, but I sure as shit do. Vanish!"

As the crowd loosened off a little, the cop lit a cigar, hunching over Connolly and the big cat. "Fuckin' vultures."

The older EMT wiped his brow, removing his plastic gloves. "We've got blunt force contusions, multiple fractures—"

"And a bonafide man-cake. They give you scrubs a course on stating the obvious, or is it just your personal flair?"

The EMT shot him a tired smirk. "Catch you at a bad time?"

"It's Vegas, scrub. It's always a bad time." The big cop rose, a cloud of smoke hanging around him like a halo. "My, this *is* a first. What d'ya reckon? Murder/suicide? Cat didn't like the treats this guy was feeding it?"

The EMT chuckled. "Gonna need some ID before I comment."

The cop flipped him a badge and his middle finger. "Either of these work for you? Ferret, homicide."

"Well, Detective, all we know is they came off the balcony and they're both disco-dead. You might want to talk to the vultures."

"Blue-perfect shit," snarled Ferret, wheeling around on the onlookers. "Any of you jackals see what happened?"

Brie tried to slip into the crowd, but the sleuth caught movement from his periphery and turned.

"You. Redhead. What about you?"

Brie shrugged. "I'm just on my way."

"Yeah, but did you see it?"

She shook her head, going for *upstanding citizen*. "Sorry."

"That's bullshit!" said a squeaky voice from the crowd.

Ferret and Brie both wheeled around looking for the source of the voice. Nobody came forward.

"Really, officer, I didn't see anything. Now if you'll excuse me, I've got a date."

"She was talking to him at the bar!" the voice came again.

Ferret swooped around, puffing his cigar with a satisfied grin. "That a fact?"

"It is, actually," Brie said. "You can check my text messages once you get that warrant thingie. I've seen *CSI*."

The detective gave Brie an appraising scowl, stalking forward with his hands on his hips.

"She probably did it!"

"One more from the peanut gallery and I'll crush you into the jar myself," Ferret called over his shoulder, his gaze staying on Brie. "What's your name?"

"Fiona."

Here, the cop gave Brie an unquestionably sleazy once-over. "Okay, *Fiona*. You wanna tell me why you've got what I guess is a few grand in your top?"

Brie looked down to find the ruffled green corners poking out of her cleavage. Traitors.

"It's a casino. I just won it."

Ferret smoked, squinting as his gaze moved up the building. "See, I kinda had a different notion."

"Well, then I'll leave you to it." Brie started away and the cop caught her by the bicep.

"Actually, I think you'd better come with me."

CHAPTER 3
COPS AND ROBBERS

Every time he landed in Vegas, Josh Harlan was taken with the overwhelming vibe that someone was plotting to kill him. He felt this way because usually, with only the rare exception, someone was.

"…Murder," said the agent.

"Huh?"

Max Reyes sighed, running his hand through his graying hair. "I said traffic's gonna be murder."

McCarran Airport: a sea of tourists in Day-Glo shorts and Hawaiian shirts, drifting from terminal to baggage claim over tracts of psychedelic carpet.

"Cheer up, Max. It's not the end of the world."

The agent wagged a threatening finger. "Harlan, what have I told you about apocalyptic idiom?"

"That it makes you nervous and sweaty, and under no circumstances should I use it?"

"Exactly."

"So… what was the problem?"

Reyes sighed. "We're doomed."

"Now who's working a double-standard?" Harlan gave the agent an affectionate grin. "Hey, cigarette stand!"

"Harlan…"

"Oh, lay off it, Agent. You might've quit smoking, but I just got out of the joint. That stand is gleaming decades of currency. Besides, I've been on a plane for three hours."

Before the agent could give an exasperated sigh, Harlan was across the terminal and swapping cash for cigarettes. He came back to Reyes, who was hanging his head—the overtired parent of a rambunctious toddler.

He slapped the agent's back. "See? No muss, no fuss."

Reyes hung his head. "This was a terrible idea."

"Max? Trust, remember? The foundation of all healthy relationships is trust."

"Yeah, but when your partner's a con artist, I think that skews things a little."

Josh grinned and gave Reyes a side-hug. "See, partner? We're already making progress."

Max just groaned. "Can we please go to the baggage claim?"

"Can I smoke first?"

"You can't smoke in here."

"Well, can we make it snippy so I can go outside and smoke?"

Max Reyes didn't understand how he got himself into these things. He'd taken the job at the bureau thinking white-collar crime would be a welcomed change of pace: lower stakes, less trouble. More paperwork, sure. But fewer shootouts, sweaty basements, and tweakers than a life undercover affords.

When the file for a crooked-seeming casino magnate named Gavin Whelan landed on his desk, he thought he had duck soup: Make a few calls, scour the books, find the spot where the tycoon had cooked them, and send it up the ladder with a bow. Problem was, the guy's files were airtight. He couldn't touch them and the DA wouldn't issue a warrant. So, he started talking to all the people who might have dirt on Whelan.

It was here Max found himself in a room with the conman. Harlan had been nabbed by the local P.D. for an attempted heist on Whelan's estate. He was looking at twenty-five to life, and made it clear he had no intentions of serving that time.

"I'm too pretty to rot in prison. What do you say, Agent? Scratch-each-other's-backs-type thing. You get me out of here, I'll help you."

"Help doesn't get you out of prison, Josh."

"Good thing I've got that spoon and the portrait of a naked lady waiting in my cell. I'm talking about a deal, Max. It's mutually beneficial."

Reyes couldn't help but be amused. "Do tell."

"I have a plan," Harlan said. "But first, you gotta get me out of here."

"Let's hear the plan and I'll think on it."

"You don't understand, there's a four-hundred pound Aryan named Shelly who said he wants to ream my ass with a meat rocket. I don't know what it means, but I'm very certain I'd rather not find out."

"I hear Shelly's a very sensitive lover," Reyes said, grinning.

Josh lit a cigarette, blew smoke in the agent's face, and stood. "Fine. Best of luck, Agent."

"Wait, wait." Max sighed. He hated how this guy knew it was his only option. He didn't trust him, but what choice did he have? "Sit. Talk. At the very least, I'll get Shelly transferred."

Harlan grabbed his chair, flipped it around, and plopped down with his elbows on the table.

So here they were, in a lineup for cabs stretched around the block. Reyes sighed, slumping on his luggage while Harlan patted himself down, a cigarette dangling from his mouth.

"I need a light."

"Well, don't look at me."

Harlan rolled his eyes. Sometimes, his patience for the agent wore thin. "I'll be right back."

"No, Harlan, don't—" but before he could finish, Josh was out of the line and heading over to the cadre of limo drivers in front of McCarran, smoking, chatting, waiting for the high-rollers to exit the terminal.

Josh closed in on a driver slouched against his Lincoln Continental blowing smoke rings. "Got a light?"

The driver nodded, producing a gold Zippo with the name *Wynn* etched into it. "You a whale?"

"Excuse me?"

"You know, a high roller."

"No," Josh said, lighting his smoke. "Not a whale."

"Oh."

"I'm a shark. The name's Ignatio. You're my driver?"

The guy pitched his smoke and started scrambling to straighten out his jacket. "My mistake, Mister Ignatio. Apologies."

"No biggie," Josh said as something caught his periphery. "S'cuse me."

The man holding the sign was enormous. Early forties, rough and muscular. He looked like Ving Rhames. Sunglasses worked into his brow as if they'd been surgically implanted. He was holding a bristol sign that read: JOSH HARLAN.

Josh walked over and nodded. "You've got my name on your sign."

The big guy raised his chin. "You Harlan?"

"…And you've got my name on your sign."

The big man crossed his arms. "Mister Whelan wants to speak with you."

"Can you take a message? I'm kinda busy tonight." Josh eyed the guy, assessing. No, there wasn't any escaping this besides confusion.

"He said you'd say that… Said to tell you 'no.' "

"Fine," Josh replied. "But maybe I don't want to see him right now."

"Maybe I wasn't asking."

Here, a hand landed on Josh's shoulder.

"He's got prior engagements," Reyes said.

The goon removed his sunglasses and glared.

"I will break you," he said. "Clean in two."

Josh felt the agent's grip relax and said, "You got booze in that tin-can?"

The giant looked back at the town car and shrugged. Then, before anybody could protest, he grabbed Josh by the collar, tossed him in the back of the cab, and peeled off into the night.

"Hey, he stole my lighter!" said the other driver.

Midnight. The Las Vegas Municipal Police Department was like the Island of Misfit Toys for degenerates. Vegas nightlife brought all forms of entertainment, and the precinct was no exception.

Here you found a homeless guy wearing a decade's patina of grime and sweat, in for trying to beat up a dumpster (and losing); a street performer coated from head to toe in metallic spray paint, caught trying to fondle a nine-year old; two Elvis impersonators of the pudgy era, apprehended in the midst of a fistfight over who was the real deal (tidbit: one of them was); and a gaggle of drunks in a holding cell, all in varying stages of undress—one of whom wore only a traffic pylon on his head.

Officers whirred around the puke-green bullpen with pan-icked efficiency: answering phones, taking people in, processing them, and shipping them to Clark County Detention Center as fast as the ink dried on paperwork.

Brie sat in front of a desk that looked like a tsunami had hit it while Ferret scribbled his report. She tried to work out the best way to keep her money and keep herself out of County. There was enough trouble in her life already—she'd rather not add *robbing the cops*, or *breaking out of prison* to the list.

"You know, you can't keep me here on a hunch."

Ferret deposited the paperwork on one of the mounds dress-ing his desk. "I've got a lot more than a hunch, sweet-cheeks. For starters, let's talk about the witnesses that put you talking to the deceased at the bar before he took his tumble."

"Oh, what? A twelve-year old and a bunch of drunks? You'd get the same story from the clowns in here."

Whistling and cat-calls erupted from the drunk tank.

Ferret threw his trashcan at them. "Keep it fuckin' down, or I'll make you jailbait before you can suck off a breathalyzer." Then, to Brie: "There's also the part where the guy's safe was empty, but staff have footage of him winning three grand"—he produced the bent-up piece of maid's cart from behind his desk —"And this was used to open the suite's door. Clever." He contin-ued, replacing it with Brie's Fendi. "And we found this in the room."

"And I haven't seen any of this stuff before," Brie said. He was fishing. Just a nosy cop, trying to be clever. All of his evidence was circumstantial. He didn't have shit.

"Well, you say that. But then there's the five grand you had stuffed down your top."

"I told you, I won it. It's a casino. Kinda where that happens." Brie wanted to rip her Fendi out of this guy's grip and brain him with it. "I didn't have a bag, so I improvised. That's not a crime."

"Here's what I think." Ferret crossed his arms and leaned back. "I think you were there. I think you looted the guy's safe. I think he stumbles in and you toss him off the balcony before he can call security."

Brie rolled her eyes. "You're right. You caught me. I'm a panther trainer who taught it to maul people when they catch me mid-robbery—"

"Cougar," said Ferret.

"Huh?"

"There aren't any panthers in North America. Panthers are from Africa. It was a cougar."

Brie wagged her head. "Uh, whatever? And whatever you think, I was just in the wrong place at the wrong time."

"No," Ferret grinned, resting his hands on his belly. "Getting creamed by a falling piano is wrong place, wrong time. You got caught, kid. I don't know how I'm gonna prove it, but I know."

And here, she had him cornered. "So, you mean that currently, you can't prove it?"

"I, like you, am not sayin' shit," the cop grumbled. "But let me make it perfectly fuckin' clear. I'm going to slam you for this."

Brie leaned in, planting her elbows on her thighs. "So, what you're saying is, I'm not being detained?"

The cop's expression wilted like month-old arugula. He didn't have cause, he didn't have any direct evidence—she was free.

"Now wait a fuckin' minute," Ferret growled.

"Of course," Brie said. "I'll give you three while you give me my money back."

Here, Ferret brightened. "Oh, no. I'm keeping the money."

"What?" Brie felt acid rise in her stomach. "You can't. I need that money. It's—"

"It's fucking evidence, is what it is," Ferret snapped. He pushed his chair back, slamming his fists on the table. "I'm taking a break. You are decidedly not free to go. I've got more questions."

With that, he turned and headed down the hall, shaking his head.

It's about goddamned time, thought Brie. *But what about the money? You can't walk away from five grand! Not now, of all times.*

Too late. It was as good as gone. Time to cut her losses and get out of here. She snatched the Fendi from Ferret's desk, thinking, *If he really knew who I was he wouldn't leave me alone for five seconds. Tool.*

Not even the drunks noticed her slip out the front door. Cat burglars are sneaky like that.

Detective Jack Ferret slipped into the morgue and lit a smoke, longing for the days where all it took was a taste for violence and a drinking problem to be a sleuth. He looked at Ben Connolly's corpse on a slab next to the cougar and sighed. Four hours ago, he'd been on his way home with a grease-stained bag of Del Taco, but a detour on MLK put him on the Strip, and now, here he was. He exhaled, lamenting the cold and therefore unsatisfying dinner awaiting him.

At least he had the cash. The fucking bitch was stonewalling him. He knew it. He could almost taste it, but he had no way of proving it. He was tired. He was hungry. He was frustrated. So he smoked, eyeing the corpses with passive interest.

No matter the situation, Jack found the presence of the dead calming. Inevitability: One day, it would be him on the slab. The ultimate retirement. No more problems, no more questions— peace. Remembering this helped Ferret think. He weighed out his options.

He could lean on her. Maybe with enough pressure, Fiona Mills would crack. On the other hand, he was pretty sure she'd given a fake name. She wasn't carrying any ID to prove it, but he knew. The broad was slippery; more crooked than he was, and the second he let her off the hook, she'd disappear like all his off-hours wagers.

"Fuckin' broads," he mused. He dragged on his cigarette and eyed the bodies.

Something just didn't add up. Why the cougar? How did it even get in there, on the thirteenth floor of a casino that hadn't even officially opened yet? A casino that didn't even have animals on its entertainment roster, no less. It was an annoying fucking conundrum for a cop already as overwrought with bullshit as him. Far better to call it a night, eat his cold burritos and gamble until morning.

He sighed. Fuckin' broads, indeed.

It was here his gaze fell on the big cat, just in time for it to start moving.

"The fuck?" Ferret puffed his smoke as the cougar undulated, its limbs slapping against the slab. He took a step forward, then froze as the feline's shape began to shift—limbs elongating, tail curling inwards. It stretched into the figure of a woman: sharp-featured, jet-black hair, an hourglass physique. Before he could even blink, Ferret was looking at two corpses... One significantly prettier than the other.

He stood, gaping. The woman got up, arched her back, and wagged her head, sticking out her tongue as if she'd just eaten a ball of dust. She coughed, then slid off the table and strutted over to the cop—who, despite the situation, had already removed his trench coat and draped it over an outstretched arm.

The woman took it. Then, she plucked the cigarette from his lips and kissed him on the cheek.

"Thanks, pumpkin."

With a wink, she threw Jack's coat around her shoulders and strutted out of the morgue, a trail of smoke hanging in her wake.

Ferret blinked. He'd already forgotten why he'd come to the morgue in the first place.

CHAPTER 4
STICKY FINGERS

Josh thought the creepiest aspect of Gavin Whelan was his unflappable calm. The way he never raised his voice, never let his tone waver; that he was relaxed, polite, and affable—even when he was threatening you… Well, it gave Josh the willies.

Knowing what people were thinking, playing their emotions, that's what cons are about… Pushing people's buttons. Whelan was the only mark Josh had met whose buttons he couldn't find. Four million dollars in art, all he got was a smile before the cuffs were on him.

Tiny escorted Josh off the elevator and across a posh waiting area. He winked at the secretary while the goon dragged him to a pair of French doors, knocked twice, and shoved him inside.

Josh sized up the place. Glass shelves lined the wall to his right. On the left was a huge painting, depicting a man chained to a rock while an eagle chewed out his liver.

Whelan sat in a leather chair behind a desk you could hold a banquet on. "Hello, Josh."

"Gavin," Josh replied.

The tycoon stood and motioned to the chairs in front of his desk. "Have a seat."

"Maybe later," Josh couldn't take his eyes off the painting. "What *is* this tragedy?"

Whelan moved over to the wet bar and poured single malt in a tumbler. Josh couldn't help noticing they had the same taste in scotch.

"Prometheus. He stole fire from the gods, and was punished by having his liver eaten out by the bird for eternity. Drink?"

"Sure. Moreau, right?"

"Eighteenth century original." Whelan handed Josh a glass. "It was appraised at over three-million."

Josh strolled over to the painting. He wasn't looking at the composition, which was rigid and tacky; he was looking at the brushstrokes, the weave of the canvas, the pigments. He'd taken up forgery in prison and knew all the tells. Any schmo could nail composition, it was the details that mattered.

"Hmm." He sipped. "Fake."

He grinned at Gavin, who shrugged. "If you say so."

Josh wandered around the office, eyeing all the trinkets on the shelves: an onyx carving of the Sphinx, several old and expensive-looking pendants, some brassy junk, a diamond the size of a fist on a purple cushion, and a brass telescope sitting on a wood stand.

"Nice digs. Lot better than that broom closet at the Bellagio."

"Baby steps," said Gavin.

"Right. *Kudos.*" Josh headed over to the telescope and picked it up, examining. The tycoon didn't argue—which was disappointing, since he was only trying to get a razz out of the guy.

He extended the scope and pointed it at the window behind Gav. He brought it to eye-level, then paused. "I'm not going to get one of those pirate circles, am I?"

Whelan chuckled. "You're the prankster, Josh. Not me."

Josh looked through it, then acted as if something was obstructing the lens. He collapsed the scope and pretended to wipe, slipping a device that looked like a black ladybug on the lens. He put it back on the stand, pointing it at the desk, and sighed. "So what's this about?"

"What are you doing in Vegas, Josh?"

"Obvious, isn't it?" Harlan put his drink on the shelf. "A little gambling, maybe a show... Is *Cats* still playing?"

Here the tycoon sighed, which Josh saw as progress. "You don't really expect me to believe that."

"Nope. But I figured some foreplay would be friendly. I'm here to rob you, obviously." He waited for a stammer, a steely glare, anything...

"Oh?" The tycoon straightened his cufflinks.

"Ya-huh," Josh said. "It'll be tricky. I mean, now you know. Plus, I won't be able to use any of my usual contacts since you'll spot them a mile away, and I can only assume your security is a frog's ass."

Gavin sipped his drink, contemplating. "I don't suppose you'll indulge me with your plan."

"Mhmm, basically, you're gonna let me do it. That's all I've got for now. But trust me, it'll happen."

"Okay, Josh," Whelan sighed. "Well, this is the part where I say if I see you again, I'll have to kill you."

Harlan grinned. "Don't worry. You won't. I'll show myself out."

He slipped through the tycoon's door, thinking: *That went well.*

Well, that sucked, Brie thought. She stared out the window of her cab as they pulled off the Strip into Downtown. The cabbie stayed as far away from Fremont as he could, barking at other cars in Spanish between rants about Old Vegas.

"I remember when this neighborhood was where it was at. Now it's all pushers, hookers and bums. Fucking shame."

Brie wasn't listening. She'd lived in the area her whole life, and while it was one of the rougher neighborhoods, you got used to it. Downtown left its people alone. Sure, you had to dodge the odd crackpot or gun-totting gangster, but when you're a professional cat burglar, that isn't a problem.

There had only been one time she'd ever dealt with it. It was late, and she hadn't been able to catch a cab after a job. Brie walked with her hoodie pulled tight around her ears, head down, when someone caught the strap of her backpack.

She turned and found a guy in baggy jeans and a T-shirt. He was tweaker-thin, with a Lakers cap pulled low so you couldn't see his face. The smell of sour sweat and stale bong hits came off him in a tidal wave. About a block away, the shadows of six more guys waited. Gang initiations. She'd heard of this; all the newbies had to rob someone while the crew watched.

"Yo, bitch. What's in the bag?"

"Tampons," Brie said. "Want some?"

The guy pulled a gun from the back of his jeans. "You fuckin' wit me? You know who I am, you fucking *punta*?"

He wagged the gun, yanking Brie backward. The men surrounded her.

"The guy who'll be screaming 'Oh god, my wrist!' in about three seconds?"

"Huh?"

This is why you never walk alone, she thought, slipping an arm free from the bag. She grabbed the robber by the wrist and snapped back. The guy screeched like a mashed cat, dropping the gun as he crumpled to curb.

"Oh god, my wrist! Oh fuck!"

She took her bag, the gun, the guy's wallet—then kicked him in the ribs just for fun. She eyed the guys surrounding her. "It's been kind of a long night. So if we could just get on with this, that would be great."

Without words, they scurried back into their alleys.

"Aw, fellas, don't take it personally! I'm just tired."

After that, nobody fucked with her. Still, she'd learned her lesson: taking a cab was better for everybody.

Now that she was home, the weirdness of the night hit Brie like a sack of bricks. What was the deal with the cougar? Who brought wild animals into a casino? How had it gotten loose? Why did it go straight for Connolly? Even for a town as quaint as Vegas, a blood-thirsty puma stalking casino halls was a new level of strange.

She'd never seen someone die before, and thinking back on the man's fall drove a chill up her spine. *Shake it off. You've got bigger problems, kiddo.*

Two days until the debt was due, and the five grand was gone. She considered her options: she could hit Circus Circus, or the Grand, or Caesar's…

Sure, she could break in easily enough. But without an exterior camera or attaching a bell to the mark, there was no guarantee the same thing wouldn't happen again—well, the cougar part was probably doubtful, but aside from that.

Normally, the risk of getting caught was a thrill. It was half the fun—like having sex in public. The rush was its own reward, but this one wasn't for her. It was for her family, and with the deadline looming closer every minute… She couldn't risk it.

Brie threw on a record and cracked a beer. She slumped on the couch in her living room and stared at the ceiling, willing her mind to problem-solving. What she needed was a second pair of eyes: someone to work the lookout position. Brie hated this. She liked working alone. Alone, there were no loose ends; no people to get in her way or get greedy.

She sipped her beer and snatched her phone off the table. She scrolled through contacts, bobbing her head to *Sticky Fingers*. Who owed her a favor? Who could she trust? Then she landed on Jimmy Wok's number and a grin spread across her face. She dialed.

"Jimmy," she said. "How fast can you get a suit?"

CHAPTER 5
FREM**ONT**

If you're looking for good Mexican food in Vegas, you go to the Arts District. Jonesing for stupidly overpriced jeans or a rhinestone T-shirt? The Fashion Show Mall has you covered. How about some quiet contemplation over that lost trust fund? Lake Mead's your man. Maybe getting stabbed, shot, or beaten to death is your thing, so head on up to North Vegas. But, if you're looking for a snapshot of city history, a reasonably affordable libation, and the rare sensation of getting squeezed through a kaleidoscope's poop chute, then you can't beat Fremont.

The promenade was awash with tourists, taking in the sights while a massive canopy above played thirty-one flavors of acid trip. The smell of cigarettes, beer, and a dozen perfumes mingled on a soft breeze.

"Alright, gather round, everyone. Gather round," called a man behind a fold-out table. He was late-twenties and slim, with a greasy mane and a tattered vest. A sandwich board beside him read: THE KING OF CUPS. "Now, watch very closely."

Josh threaded through the crowd as the magician produced a pin cushion and a glass of cranberry juice. "Wait a tick, something's missing." He hitched up his slacks and came back with a fifth of Jameson's.

The crowd laughed.

He uncorked the bottle and splashed three fingers into the glass.

"Better. Although, I think it could have a bit more bite. Agreed?"

Here, he began plucking needles from the cushion. He placed them in the glass, added a piece of thread, and took a deep, meditative breath.

"Now there's a drink." He raised it, grinning. "Cheers."

With that, the magician dumped the contents back. He swallowed hard, then made a face as if to say: *Oh, bollocks. I've just swallowed a bunch of needles. Bloody idiot, I am.*

The crowd gasped. Some of them went to help, but the King of Cups waved them back.

He gulped. Then, he closed his eyes and reached into his mouth. He came back with the thread, puckered his lips, and pulled. A needle popped out, dangling by the eyelet. Then another, and another, and another…

When he finished, the crowd clapped. The magician bowed.

"Thank you. Much obliged." Above, a couple whooshed by on a zip-line running the neon canopy. "Now, who'd like to see me make those lovebirds disappear?"

The crowd cheered, but the King of Cups held out his hand. "Well, I can't really do that." He turned his palm up, waved the other hand in front of it, and an apple appeared. "But who's got a twenty?"

"I do," Josh said, producing a bill and planting it on the table. "How about that trick, Hasselhoff?"

"Alright! An American twenty, ladies and gents. Taken from what I can only presume is a very rich man. Now—"

He rolled the bill, blew into his hand and the money disappeared.

"Huh. Now where could that've gone?"

He rubbed his short sleeves, scanned the ground, rooted around the table. He sighed, perplexed. "Well, I guess it's vanished. Now, I must confess… I'm something of a stress-eater. And we all know how losing money feels."

He produced a pocketknife and stabbed the apple. Rather than making a slice, he sawed the fruit in half. Where the core should be was the rolled-up twenty. "Ah ha!"

Above, the zip-liners came rushing back toward them. At the exact moment they passed, the King of Cups tossed the halved apple into the air and it exploded in a rain of confetti.

The zip-liners vanished.

A collective gasp. The magician raised his arms in glory. "I may've been lying about making them disappear."

He clapped his hands, and the couple came whooshing back in the opposite direction. The audience roared, and the King of Cups grinned.

"Thank you. I'll gladly accept all your money, now."

A half hour later, Quinn "The King of Cups" Donovan was in the basement of the Double Down Saloon, thumbing a deck of cards across from Josh Harlan. They were surrounded with splashes of technicolor graffiti. The Clash thumped through the floor while the magician shuffled.

"I have a fair bit of cash."

"For now," Harlan mused. "Deal the cards. Let's see how long it lasts."

Quinn snorted. "You sure you wanna make that wager? I *am* a magician."

"Yep. And you're wearing short sleeves. I already told you, I've got a lot of money. Deal."

Quinn tried to read Harlan, but figuring him out was like pulling teeth sober. "You're not nervous?"

"Nope. You're drunk. Deal the cards."

Quinn sighed, eyeing the half-emptied bottle of scotch. "You *are* nervous," he chuckled, wagging a finger in what he hoped was Harlan's direction. "One quip about magic and you don't trust me. I'm hurt."

Harlan lit a smoke. "You're loading the deck. You're wasted. And I'm ninety-percent sure you're Irish—tell me, why *would* I trust you?"

Quinn thought about it. The man had a point—well, several. "Because you like my accent?"

"Whatever. Gimme the cards."

"I haven't been cheating—"

"Gimme the cards. Let's find out."

The King of Cups sighed and handed over the deck. "And how exactly are you the trustworthy one? For one thing, I don't know you from a hole in my sock. And, knocking off a casino? It's—"

"Seventy-two million dollars."

"You're my best friend."

Harlan shuffled and dealt. "I need a sleight of hand guy. You're the fastest I've seen. I'm on kind of a schedule, and well, you heard the take. Are you in, or what?"

Quinn took his cards, thinking. "And you presume I won't go running to the feds—why?"

"Because you're greedy."

The magician chuckled. "You really *are* my best friend. Which place?"

"The Olympus."

"Never heard of it."

"It's the new giant phallus next to the Tropicana. Word is, they're filling it with whales for First Friday."

Quinn sloshed his drink. "You wanna rob a casino, in two weeks?"

"Yep."

Quinn wasn't sure. Knocking off a casino? In this town? The mobsters might not run Vegas anymore, but nothing said a businessman wouldn't put you in the ground if he caught you trying to take his money.

"You still need to convince me I won't wind up fertilizing cactuses if this goes tits-up. Have you got a plan?"

"Tell you what," Josh said. "You beat me, I'll tell you."

"Brilliant," Quinn said, slipping the cards he'd lifted back into his hand. "Got any threes?"

"Go fish. Got any sevens?"

"Wanker." Quinn sighed, throwing his cards on the table. Nobody ever caught him cheating at Go Fish.

The woman sat at the bar, swirling a frosty tumbler, watching a young man work his slot machine like a feeding trough. She was playing a game: every time the guy pulled the lever, she'd flick her fingers in his direction. Two times, he'd come up winning. On the third time, he'd bet big, riding his streak, and this was when he'd lose and she'd take a drink.

The guy swore, slapping the machine and dumping another stream of quarters into it. Ah, youth: Never knowing when your luck's run out. Never accepting you've had too much. Always chasing that next bet, that next lay, that next drink. Just one more, and it'll get you there. It was charming, really.

Usually she'd be by his side, flirting, working him; driving his hope up just to watch it go splat when he lost—slowly driving him batshit. But, considering only a few hours ago she'd been a cougar, and was still working the kinks from her neck after her own splatter, Jezebel decided that sitting at the bar and messing with him was good enough.

She'd traded the detective's trench coat for a silk cocktail dress: a plunging neckline, a frilly hem. Enough to draw attention, but not enough to get badgered by drunks looking for a hookup. Besides, the way she carried herself, she knew they were too intimidated to try.

The guy pulled again.

She waved her hand, striking off an invisible checkmark in the air.

Blip-bli-bli-bli-bli-blip! Bloop. Two bananas and a lemon.

"Motherfucker!" he screeched, grabbing the kiosk like a vending machine that had eaten his last quarter—which, in a way, it was.

Before he could land a wild haymaker into the plexiglass, two goons in suits dragged him off his stool and out the front door. She grinned, emptying her tumbler and signaling the barkeep while she picked out her next victim. As if on cue, the air beside her shifted.

"I wish you wouldn't do that," Gavin Whelan said.

Already, she'd chosen an elderly woman two rows over. "And I wish I'd never taught you to teleport. Looks like we've both got our burdens."

Whelan sat beside her as the bartender came back with a bottle of top shelf. "Of all the ways you could've done it... A cougar?"

Jezebel shrugged. "It got the job done, didn't it?"

"It created a spectacle."

"I know. Lovely, wasn't it? Tell me you got it on tape."

Whelan sipped his drink and sighed. "I need you to keep a lower profile."

Jezebel was thinking, *Give granny a heart attack, or not?* She turned and gave the tycoon a mock-innocent pout. "But sweetums, I thought you needed him dead?"

"What I don't need is a crowd of onlookers or a detective or newspaper articles about the freak cougar incident."

"Well then, you should be more specific." *Way to be a party-pooper,* she thought. "If it's any consolation, I've still got a wicked hairball. I'm sorry, I didn't see you jumping off a balcony tonight."

"I'm still trying to follow why you decided that was a good idea."

"Irony," Jezebel grinned. Falling off the thirteenth floor had a certain pleasing aspect to it—but having Connolly fall off the thirteenth floor at the paws of a giant black cat? She was proud of herself. "Keeps things interesting, don'tcha think?"

"It was reckless."

"Darling, what do you want from me? I can't help my nature."

"No, I guess you can't." Whelan rubbed his upper lip, deep in thought.

"So, what's next, boss?" Jezebel flicked her hand and the old lady's pacemaker gave out. She flopped on the floor, sputtering.

Whelan didn't flinch. "I have someone I want you to keep an eye on."

CHAPTER 6
FAMILY VALUES

Baby Cluck Cluck's was a greasy spoon on the west end of Paradise. It was fifties-cute: all red vinyl and checkered linoleum. The diner buzzed with coffee-guzzling truckers, off-shift go-go dancers, and the three surviving members of the Cassiday clan.

It was a sort of tradition. Every Saturday, Brie, her younger brother Kevin, and their foster father Paul grabbed a booth, ate, and swapped stories from the week.

Paul: fifty-three, keg-bellied, salt and pepper—made entirely of tough exterior and teddy-bear stuffing, shuffled a deck of playing cards. "What's the count?"

"Plus fourteen." Kevin, twenty-five, freckled and lanky, slouched beside Brie, nose-deep in his iPhone.

"It's plus-twelve, dummy." Brie forked off a chunk of his pancakes.

"She's right," Paul said. "So, what do we do, kids?"

Kevin sighed. "Paul, buddy. We've been doing this for years—"

"And yet the prodigal son so swiftly manages to fuck up the count," Brie said around a mouthful of flapjack.

"Practice keeps you from getting sloppy, Kev-o," Paul said.

"Which, little bro, you definitely are. You wouldn't last five minutes against a five-deck shoe."

"Yeah, well, you're… fat."

Brie narrowed her eyes. She loved him. She knew she loved him. Yet so often—especially when he opened his mouth—Kev could be improbably annoying. She turned to Paul, knife dangling in her grip. "Can I kill him, please?"

"No. I expressly forbid killing at the breakfast table." And here, Paul took his own chunk of Kev's pancakes. "So, big guy—what do we do?"

"Is everybody going to eat my food?"

Paul shrugged. "Never order a plate you can't finish. Win the bet, you get mine. Deal?"

"Fine, but you're keeping the fruit."

"I'm taking the fruit," Brie corrected. "How 'bout if he loses, I get to kill him? Now those are stakes."

"No, but an argument can be made for injury. What d'you say, Kev?"

"Oh, I *love* you assholes." Kevin rolled his eyes and returned to his phone.

Brie snatched it out of his grip and pocketed it, giving him a look that said: *Dare you.*

"Fiiine," he grumbled. "It's plus twelve, so I raise."

"Very good, broheim." Brie eyed her cards. "Hmm. I'm gonna stay."

Paul bounced his brow. "Sure that's a smart move?"

"Come on, Paul. Live a little."

"Do I get to kill her if *she* loses?" Kevin said.

"Nope, but I'll give you this back." Brie dangled the phone and feigned curiosity. "Who's your girlfriend?"

"Nobody."

Paul slurped his coffee. "Now I wanna know. Who's your—"

"Nobody! I'm not texting a girl."

Brie grinned. "It's a brave new world, Paul."

"Shut up." Kev snatched his phone back like a lizard eating a fly. "I'm texting Jones."

"Not helping your case, kiddo."

"Deal the cards, Paul."

Paul dealt. Kevin won. Brie lost.

She shrugged, taking another hunk of Kevin's pancakes. "I did that on purpose."

"Maybe you should tell him what you *didn't* lose on purpose."

"Twerp!" Now, this was the part she'd been avoiding.

"Harpy."

"Hey, I might be a cagey harpy who uses her feminine wiles to steal money from drunk dudes—but I don't need to tolerate you calling me one."

"Kids—play nice," Paul said. "What's this?"

Brie took a long breath. "It's kind of a long story."

"She got caught last night," Kev said.

"Well, longer than *that*."

As she told them, Brie was relieved to see them both as confused by the story as she was—but less relieved by which parts they focused on:

"Freak cougar accident," Kev said with a grin.

Paul tried to put it together. "Well, was it his wife or something? It happens."

"No, I mean it was a literal cougar. I tried to leave with the cash, but this dick caught me and arrested me."

"I'm sorry. Cougars? Dicks? Are you sure you're being literal?"

"I mean a literal cougar and a detective. Yeesh, you guys have complete gutter-mind. Anyway, I'm headed out again tonight. We'll have the whole thing cleared up by morning."

Paul gazed into his coffee mug, deep in thought. "No."

"What?" Brie said.

"I second that—what?" added Kev.

The great man sighed, glancing out the window. "I'm sick of you running around being a criminal on my behalf."

"I'm totally fine with being a criminal."

"I know that." Paul wagged his head. "Listen, honey. You have done more than your fair share of cat-burgling for this family."

"She's never even stolen a cat," Kev said.

Paul waved him off. "I'm an old man. Old and stupid. That's not your fault. You keep at this long enough, you'll get cold and jaded, and I'll be gone. You might even end up hating me for it—and I'd rather die now than have that happen."

Brie took his hand, squeezed. "You don't need to worry about us hating you, ever."

"We'll hate each other first," Kev offered.

"Change," Paul said. "It's time for change. Got a free afternoon coming up? We can swing by your parents' old storage locker, see if there's something worth hocking."

Kev finished the remains of his food, checking his phone. "Crap, it's noon. I gotta work."

"And I've got a date with Ruby," Brie said. "One o'clock tomorrow work for you, big guy?"

Paul pushed away his plate and signaled the waitress. "Sure does. Hop to it, squirts."

"I'm still going out tonight," Brie said as she and Kev slid out of the booth. "Argue and die."

"Haven't enough people died around you lately?" Kev asked.

"Gee, I dunno. You're still breathing."

Paul stared out the window while he waited for the check. Too long. He'd been letting the debt hang over him for too long. Using his kids, having them steal—hell, he was lucky he'd come this far without facing the music.

He sighed, feeling like a week-old bag of dog shit. Sure, Brie said she didn't mind robbing people for him, but he did. She should be out there, living life and robbing people for her own damn benefit. It would be so easy to let it all go. One phone call, and the whole thing went away. Problem was, if he did that, the kids would find out what the debt was really about.

And that—well, he couldn't have that.

He heaved himself out of the booth and slipped through the diner's door. *It's inevitable,* he thought. *No matter what you do, luck always runs out.*

He crossed the parking lot toward his car when boot heels clicked behind him. The hairs on the back of his neck stood up.

"Hiya, Paul."

He turned to find a woman in black skintight jeans and a leather jacket. She was bone-pale, her hair pinned up with a pair of ebony chopsticks.

"Jezebel," he said.

She grinned. "Got a sec?"

Larry the Werewolf slouched in a salon chair, smoking a cigarette while scissors whizzed around his mane. He yawned a remarkably doggie-like yawn as Billie Black worked. She was twenty-nine, dark-skinned, frizzy-haired, and desperately in need of a catnap.

Inside of Black's FX was a rainforest of severed limbs and prosthetic stage pieces. Monster heads hung above the counter like trophies in Van Helsing's living room. You couldn't turn without elbowing some relic of Creature Feature: giant slugs, ghouls, mutants and aliens—even a life-sized unicorn. Billie's paradise.

Larry's head lolled forward with a snore.

"Shit. Stacey? This guy needs an espresso, stat."

"What I need is a caesar," the werewolf grumbled. "Do you guys do caesars?"

Billie's assistant, Stacey, came back with a steaming demitasse and shoved it under Larry's snout. "What he needs is a twelve-step program."

"Do not." He pouted (which was impressive, considering the mask didn't move).

"I don't want to hear it, Larry. We're sending you to AA. Nobody likes an alcoholic beast of the night."

"I thought all alcoholics were beasts of the night," Stacey said.

"I'm *not* an alcoholic!"

Billie smacked the back of his head. "Bad wolfie. Now hold still. We've got another twelve of you to do, and I swear if you puke in my mask, I will ram a can of Coors through your chest my-own-self."

The werewolf brightened. "Beer?"

"Silver bullet," said Stacey.

The phone rang. Stacey disappeared through the salon's curtain.

Larry lifted the espresso to his snout and sighed. "How am I supposed to drink in this thing?"

"Hasn't stopped you yet," Billie said, snipping. "There. Finished. Go forth and get sober."

Larry shuffled out of the studio, growling at Stacey as she came back with the cordless.

"It's Gus. He sounds pissed."

"He's always pissed." Billie sighed, grabbing Larry's cigarette from the ashtray and took the phone. "Hi, Gus."

"Rent's late," said the gruff voice of her landlord.

"We talked about this. I'm waiting for the check from Planet Hollywood to clear and—"

"I don't care, Billie. Your bills become my bills. You've got a week or I'm evicting you."

This is what I get for being nice to people. Bille took a steadying breath and said, "Go fuck yourself, Gus. I'll pay you when I pay you."

She hung up the phone and tossed it on the salon chair. "Dick."

Stacey brought her a latte. "We're behind."

She was right: they were doing costumes for a new show at the Circus Circus called *Werewolf Bimbos of Rising Moon*. Opening night was tomorrow, and the shipment of fake fur had only arrived yesterday.

"We've done more with less. When's our next victim in?"

"No, I mean we're behind on rent, on inventory, electrical. Finically we're—"

"Stacey, Stacey." Billie waved her assistant off. "Chill, okay? We'll work something out."

" 'Kay... What?"

"I dunno."

" 'I dunno' isn't something."

Billie raked her hands through her hair and mashed the cigarette in the tray. Stacey meant well, but sometimes her concern for the business was frazzling. "I could fire you?"

Stacey sighed, sweeping up the clippings of Larry's mane. "We're fucked."

Before Billie could answer, the door buzzed open, and a handsome man in his early thirties entered. He was wearing jeans, a blazer, some fancy sunglasses and a Sabbath T-shirt. He looked around the shop, grinning.

"You guys do disguises?"

The Flamingo Casino is a slice of Vegas legacy. It's kind of where it all started. With a reputation steeped in infamy, it's the place tourists go hoping to spot some vestige of the mafia in the glitzy city. And time after time, they go in, poke around, and come out saying: "Well that's totally not what I expected—hey look, naked bronze chicks!"

The Rose Garden, the Flamingo's cocktail lounge is all red velvet and mahogany—something you can hit in Vegas with little more than a sneeze. But they do make a really good piña colada—which is why Brie and her best friend Ruby Cobb were here.

"I've heard of guys falling for cougars before," Ruby said. "But that's kinda literal." She was twenty-three, platinum blonde, and small enough to fit into most carry-ons.

Brie sighed and took a gulp of her drink. "It doesn't matter. I'm out the cash and have two days to hit the deadline. I—"

"Sound like you need a job?" Ruby offered.

"No. Ruby, no. We talked about this…"

"Aw, come on. I know of like four big jobs on the Strip, even as we speak. Let the criminal liaison do her thing and liaise."

Ruby wasn't a thief, but she was insanely well-connected. Brie thought of her as a sort of criminal matchmaker: getting the right people together for the right job. If you were a bad guy working in Vegas and you needed something, Ruby Cobb was who hooked you up.

Brie finished her drink. "I don't play well with others."

"Well, B. Sometimes you can't do it alone. And what about Jimmy? Does he suddenly not count as others?"

"Jimmy's my exception. We're hitting the Bellagio tonight."

Ruby sighed. "You know what you need?"

"Another drink?" Brie said, just in time for the bartender to replace her empty glass. "Ah, here we go."

"I'm only doing one more," Ruby said, scrolling through her phone. "Nobody likes a day-drunk hussie."

"Hey, give yourself some credit. You'll be a really cute day-drunk hussie."

Brie hoped beyond all reason that Ruby would drop it. She wasn't looking for help, talking about the events of last night—she was just letting off steam. But the little vixen was incorrigible.

"You should meet Josh Harlan. He's pulling some big thing at the Olympus. Payout's ten-million each or something bonkers. I have half a mind to get in on it myself."

"Woah, girl," Brie chuckled. "Remember your place, 'kay? You get the cons together, you don't play in their sandbox."

"I do what I want," Ruby said, chewing her straw. "Just take the meeting. You'll break bank and probably spend the whole job ignoring each other."

Brie wasn't having it. "Can we get the check please?"

Ruby insisted on paying. They got up and headed out through the casino. Brie could tell Rubes was trying to guilt-trip her, and if she hadn't already dug her feet so deep in the sand, it might even be working.

"You're not guilt-tripping me into a meeting, you know."

Ruby shrugged. "I'm not doing anything. Just think on it, B. Harlan's smart. A little self-absorbed, but he grows on you."

They passed a bay of slot machines just in time for them to all go off winners. The players gave a collective cheer. Brie rolled her eyes. "Grow on me like ew. I'm not feeling it, Rubes. There's not enough time."

"Suit yourself," Ruby said. "So what's this thing with Jimmy?"

CHAPTER 7
ROSEBUSH

Las Vegas, 1946

It seemed like Vegas had sprouted overnight the day Gavin Whelan stepped off the train. Everywhere, the sawdust joints were being swapped out with analogues for casinos—the scaffolding of progress. But looking around, Gav had to admit it was still very much a splatter of civilization next to the railroad—an accident, a fluke. Not an Eldorado.

A cherry red Chevy coupe pulled up to the roundabout and he climbed in. The driver was too scared to talk, and Gav didn't blame him. He was here from New York on mob orders. He was used to people being intimidated back East, so he welcomed the silence like an old lover.

The first person he met was Benjamin Siegel.

"But call me Bugsy," he said, squeezing Whelan's hand.

The two walked up the paved entrance to the Flamingo. The twenty-foot tower with the name on it was just being installed. It was about the biggest thing for a mile in every direction.

Gavin had been sent here to keep an eye on Siegel's spending habits. But, after six months, he came up with a better idea. One that was mutually beneficial

"So Gavin," Ben said, considering. "Who's side are you on?"

"Yours, Ben."

Bugsy waved him off. "Yeah, yeah. I got that much. You come up to me, speak honestly, offer a relatively smart alternative. I'm not exactly big on the 'equal shares' notion, but I can see you want to work with me. Tellya what. I'll give you a cut with room to negotiate."

Gavin shook his head. "That's not what I offered."

"I hear ya, kid." The mobster grinned. "But you're still a little wet around the ears. I'm not saying no, exactly. I'm saying let's ride it out, let you come up a bit, and if you prove your worth, you'll get what you're asking for... Once I know whose side you're on."

At a spry thirty-four, Gav couldn't see he was being played. "Your side, Ben. I told you."

Siegel grinned. "Eager ears misses the point. I'm not talking about that."

"What are you talking about?"

Ben brought them over to the bar, sat Gavin down, and grabbed a bottle of hootch. He poured them each a tumbler and dumped ice in the glasses. "I don't mean to be all condescending, but kid? Where you're at right now, you see the world as a lovely shade of gray."

Whelan chuckled. "Coming from you, I'm not sure how to take that."

"Take it as it is, Gav-oh. The point is, the little things of life— the *minutia*—look at them, what you see is gray." And here, the mobster waved towards the heavens. "But, the big picture's different. Look from a big enough scope and you see it."

"What?" Whelan sipped.

"There's only two sides, kid. You either want to make the world better, or you're here to make it yours. So I'll say again, which is yours?"

"Whichever makes me richer?"

Bugsy cackled. "That's the spirit. Richer is better, yeah? We start at fifteen percent."

So they partnered up. Bugs could never admit the difference Gavin made in management: costs went down, ratings went up, and then they had to close on account of running out of liquor.

After the mysterious closing, Gavin expected the turnout of their second opening to be crappy. People forgot about things in a small town, especially when that town had a railway headed west. But Ben had different expectations. This led to a five-month argument that went pretty much as follows:

"It's gonna suck."

"It'll be spectacular."

"Spectacularly empty."

"You and your negativity. Always such a Sour Sue."

Sixteen hours after the opening, they sat at the bar while the cleanup crew—one usually reserved for mob hits—finished mopping. Gavin and Bugsy got drunk on champagne.

"What'd I tell you?" Ben practically giggled. "What exactly did I say?"

Gavin's cheeks felt hot. "You gotta tell me how you did it. Think about how we could leverage it."

The mobster raised challenging eyebrow. "What makes you think I'm not already?"

"I know you are, but I'm curious. Shoot me."

And here, Bugsy produced a .45 snub nose from the back of his slacks. "Well, you see, I already considered that."

Gavin's blood went cold. Siegel stared him dead in the eyes, then grinned. "Kidding. Jeez, you are a tight-ass. It was just poking me and I thought it'd be funny."

They finished their drinks. Bugsy put on his fedora and said, "Hey. Show ya something?"

Gavin followed him out the exit through the kitchen. They cut across the horseshoe-shaped grotto around the pool and fell upon a garden. It was all roses, kept neat and elegant. The only light came from the moon, painting everything in blue shadow.

Bugsy took a breath and stepped into the thicket of roses. Gavin was just drunk enough to follow. The thorns scored bloody rivulets in his arms.

Ben continued along the invisible path, turning once. "Just a bit further."

As they waded through, Siegel took on a troll-like aspect, hunching and tearing at the brambles.

They reached a clearing, facing a large stone tomb in the middle of the rosebush. Ben stood, returning to being a head taller than Gavin, and wiped the blood from his arms.

Whelan nearly folded over with disappointment. "You dragged me all the way through that for a giant rock?"

"So to speak"—and here, the mobster cackled—"No, my friend. We're here to see my point of leverage."

He moved over to the stone, then started patting its backside. Gavin took a breath, noticing the engravings on the front: a triangle, a moon, and an upside-down cross. Before he could ask, Ben found what he'd been looking for, pressed, and the heavy stone lid popped open with a thud.

It slid away. Ben leaned into the case and motioned for Whelan to come over.

Inside was a diamond: a jagged teardrop, gleaming in the moonlight, brighter than any diamond Gavin had ever seen.

"I got here, there was nothing," Ben said. "I find this, I get an idea, and everything starts falling into place. This is why we did good tonight, kid."

Whelan tried to follow. "So it's your good luck charm?"

Ben chuckled. "Kid, you got this stone, ain't nothing you can't will into existence. Luck herself will be your tool."

"Sounds kinda hokey."

"Uhuh. Well, in a lot of ways, it is. But that's the world we've got, Gav. It's hokey. There's two sides. You got the diamond, you have both."

"You're talking about luck." Gavin tried to sound skeptical, but after all he'd seen, it wasn't so hard to believe.

"Bingo." Bugsy set the diamond back in the box and the lid slid shut. "All of this, came from that."

"Why would you tell me this? I mean, you really trust me that much?"

"Well, that's the thing, champ. I don't needah. The diamond keeps me from getting old, and it's excruciatingly hard to kill me. Plus, without the magic words, it's just a fancy stone."

Whelan sighed. "You really believe all that?"

"Gavin, kiddo. *Seeing* is believing. And I've seen shit that'd make you go wobbly-legged."

Gavin tried to be open-minded. He tried to wrap his head around what Bugsy was saying, but—well, it was just too batshit. "I'm sorry, Ben. It just seems a little nutso."

Ben just grinned. "Ya think that's weird. Lemme tell you about the woman."

Now, one-hundred and three years old, Gavin found himself trying to sweep up how weird the woman could make things.

"It's a mess, boss," said Steve Halverson, a lanky man, mid-forties and wiry-haired.

Phil Gibbons, thirty-five, bald and jocular, nodded. "The Gazette's pressing for answers. The SPCA, PEA, and PETA are all emailing."

"Not to mention the LVPD's called twice," added Halverson.

Whelan sighed. He'd been avoiding this as long as he could.

They were in the security wing of the Olympus, on the raised platform known as the Perch. Below, over thirty ex-spies recruited by Halverson and Gibbons watched the casino's comings-and-goings on massive video displays mounted across the wing.

"You can handle the press," Gavin said.

"Already done," said Steve.

"The official story is the guest in 1312 was a magician in possession of the cougar. He got drunk. It got loose. None of them survived," added Gibbons.

"So no questions," beamed Phil.

"No fuss," finished Halverson.

Gavin nodded, going over the scenarios in his mind. "I'm worried about the detective."

"Ferret?" Halverson chuckled. "He's as straight as a corkscrew. Our intel pegs him as a textbook gambling addict."

Gibbons nodded. "He'll know better than to snoop around a potential golden goose."

Gavin shook his head. "No. He's glimpsed the impossible."

"...So?" the marketing geeks chimed in unison.

"He won't remember it. He'll never be able to make sense of it, but that's the problem. He's a sleuth. It'll bug him until the day he dies. We can't risk it."

"You really think he could compromise us?" Phil said, wiping his brow.

"I think we can't risk it." Gavin massaged his temples. "We need to make sure he'll never talk again."

"He won't remember?" said Halverson.

"We need something untraceable," Gavin mused, padding around the Perch. "Something nobody could ever follow back to us. Something impossible to follow up on. We need—"

"An act of god?" suggested Halverson.

Whelan sighed. "I wish you wouldn't put it like that."

Steve and Phil looked at each other and nodded.

"We'll make a call," said Phil.

"Hey, that's my line," said Steve. "Asshole."

"Just get it done," Gavin said, walking off.

Suddenly, the floor stretched in front of him, then snapped back, knocking him off balance. He went to catch himself against the wall, and his hand appeared as a withered husk. Shriveled like a raisin. Dry, peeling flakes of skin. His breath caught in the back of his throat.

Whelan slumped to his knees.

"You okay, boss?" Hands helped him to his feet. Halverson and Gibbons, looking concerned.

"Fine," Gav waved them off. "Fine. It seems that killing off the candidates has its ill effects."

"No kidding," said Halverson. "You're looking kind of gray."

Whelan gave the agent a tired grin.

"Uh, literally," added Gibbons. "Boss? Consult a mirror, pronto."

Because the first gray hair Gavin had ever grown was sprouting from his scalp.

Superpowered jets shot pillars of water in a thirty-foot tango across the manmade lagoon while Brie strutted the Bellagio's foyer. She was in full-blown seduction garb: a bloodred chiffon that showed just enough leg to give men whiplash, ivory pumps and a splash of apple lipgloss to bring out her eyes. She was a huntress. A predator in a slinky outfit. She was out to turn heads.

She swept through the casino, passing a blackjack felt where six men threw out their necks trying to watch. She hit the bar and flagged down the bartender, who all but sprinted over.

"Ice water," she said. "Extra lime."

Normally, she'd have a drink or two in the scouting phase, but tonight the stakes were too high. She needed to be sharp.

Brie scanned the crowd, making note of the big players: A man in a Stetson with a handlebar mustache throwing chips at roulette, a sweaty guy in Saville Row drinking Patron like water playing craps, and a handsome man in a V-neck throwing twenties at his waitress like they were business cards at the baccarat table.

Watching the flow of cash, Brie was thinking: *Pay off Paul's debt. New car. A little Prada. Shopping. Trust fund for Kev. A fancy blowout. More shopping...*

"Hey, girl!" came a voice from behind.

Brie turned and found Ruby Cobb, done up in a cute black tutu with her bangs swept over her eyebrows. She flanked a horseshoe of dudes who looked like pot dealers dressed for the prom. She shook their hands, then came over and took the stool beside Brie.

"Ruby," Brie said. "Keeping good company, I see?"

"Coke folk." Ruby shrugged. "They can handle themselves. How's the thing going?"

"Just getting started," Brie said, gritting her teeth. This was not a good sign.

Ruby signaled the barkeep. "Scotch, neat."

"And a vodka tonic, extra lime," Brie added. Then to Ruby, "You're paying. I can tell this is a setup."

"I love paying," Ruby said. "And what do you mean, *setup?* I only do that with permission."

"I know what you're doing, Ruby Cobb. Where is he?"

Ruby looked perplexed. "He, who?"

"Harlan. Him Harlan, where is he?"

"You need to lighten up, B," Ruby chuckled. "I wouldn't do that. So lemme guess, you're thinking Mister Mustache."

Brie sighed. "How is it you always know?"

"Well, with that 'stache, you'd better be loaded."

Just then, a man in gray Armani with a burgundy ascot approached. "Excuse me, *madames*," he said in a thick Parisian accent. "Is this seat taken?"

Brie eyed Ruby, knowing the first to speak was the one who'd be stuck with him. She sipped her drink. "Which one?"

Armani shrugged. " 'Ow about this one?"

He sat next to Brie with a grin. The barkeep came over. Without breaking eye contact, Armani said: "Cognac, *monsieur*. I have won an excellent game of backgammon, and am in need of celebration. And, of course, drinks for my friends here—champagne perhaps?"

"Scotch," Ruby sighed.

"Vodka tonic," Brie added.

He grinned. "A scotch—neat, I think—and a vodka tonic, *supplémentaire* on the lime, no?"

Brie kicked Ruby under the bar and whispered, "Your doing?"

Ruby shrugged. "Blame your dress, hun. I think you might be lucky."

The bartender came back with drinks and the Frenchman grinned. "Ah, *merci*." He produced a hundred-dollar bill and handed it over. "Keep the change, *oui*?"

The barkeep went to argue, but Armani waved him off. "I am told it is customary in *L'Amérique* to tip. I must insist." Then to Brie and Ruby: "A toast. *Célébration*. To good winnings."

He raised his glass, and motioned for them to follow.

They looked at each other, shrugged, and raised glasses.

"*Santé.*" The Frenchman grinned, and dumped back his cognac. "My name is Miguel LaSoirée, and I am a filthy-rich industrialist from Monaco."

"I'm Madison," Brie said, taking his hand.

Ruby sloshed back her drink. "I'm going for a walk."

"But madame," said LaSoirée. "So soon? I have won many thousands of dollars, and don't mind to buy drinks for you both—and perhaps, we could make love later."

Brie was thinking: *Ferrari, escargot, maybe a micro-island...*

Ruby smiled. "Definitely going for walk. Monsieur, it was a pleasure. Madison? *Bonne chance.*"

With that, she was gone. Brie turned back to Miguel and shrugged.

"Your friend," he said. "She is—how you say?—a pistol, I think."

Brie chuckled. "You have no idea."

Miguel nodded. "You know, it is a lovely dress you're wearing."

"I know." Brie tossed him a wink.

LaSoirée stroked his goatee, contemplating. "Although, it would look better on my floor, I think."

Well, maybe this could work. Brie eyed him up. He was handsome, well-dressed and clearly loaded. Maybe she could have him take her to his room, get him drunk on the minibar and when he passed out, she'd take his cash. It could work. She pulled her phone from her clutch and texted Jimmy: NEW PLAN. TOMORROW. 7AM. DEETS SOON.

"That depends on what your room looks like."

"I have executive suite," Miguel said. "Very excellent carpets."

"Show me?"

"*D'accord.*"

She took his arm and they strode off through the casino.

CHAPTER 8
THE FLY

Detective Jack Ferret's peer-review files were colored with phrases like "Unethical"; "Morally bankrupt"; "Ruthless"; and "Meteoric attitude problem". One officer had even written "Ferret is biggest douchewad I've ever shared a cruiser with." He'd extorted witnesses, bullshitted due-diligence, and beaten the piss out of a dozen perps. He shot first, asked questions later, and shot again if he didn't like the answers. No matter who you asked, the answer was always the same: Ferret was an irredeemable bag of cat shit.

And he justified it all with the fact that he was actually a pretty good detective. Jack thought if you were a sleuth, you needed an edge. And if you didn't have one? You were a pansy. Plain and simple.

Bad guys had drug problems. Bad guys beat hookers. Bad guys lied and cheated, and did it all while guzzling bourbon like lemonade. If you wanted to catch bad guys, you had to be able to think like one. The easiest way to think like one was, well, to be one.

So when the comped visit to the Olympus landed in his inbox, Jack's mind lit up like a Fourth of July party. Sure, it was fishy—obviously a bribe to keep him from following the thing with the cougar—but Ferret loved bribes. Why not? Take the free shit and throw them in County when you'd had your fun.

He was rolling on a pinch of coke swiped from a pusher he found working Symphony Park on the way to the casino. It was Saturday, and Saturday meant it was time to blow his paycheck and slurp discount booze. He had the cash from Fiona Mills to supplement his spending, and was throwing chips around the table like they were breadcrumbs in a sea of ducks.

He slouched, eyeing his cards. "Hit me."

The guy next to him, a young Asian, shook his head. "Buddy, you should stay. The shoe's cold as a dead hooker."

"I fuckin' ask you, Jackie Chan? Do us a favor and keep your mouth to yourself, lest somebody smack it around a little—somebody meaning me."

"Whatever," the guy mumbled, tossing back his drink. "Prick."

"That's better." Ferret grinned. Then to the dealer: "I don't recall asking for dramatics. Deal the fuckin' cards."

Jack's strategy for blackjack was the same he used to solve homicides: Instinct. Guts. None of that counting bullshit you saw in the movies. Sure, it might be true that his guts had shit for brains when it came to gambling, but such it is. The dealer laid down the cards.

"Twenty-eight."

"Rusted cunt-bucket," he snapped. He threw another handful of chips at the dealer. "Again."

The Gambler's Fallacy: every loss brings you one round closer to that inevitable win. It's an investment. Knowing that it was a fallacy didn't do shit. Did knowing you had a drinking problem get you sober? No. There's a steep, slippery slope to climb after admitting you have a problem.

Sure, it was doubtful the next hand would hit pay dirt, but it *might*. And might was one step closer to apology money for the old lady; closer to refilling the college fund he'd drained for his six-year-old. 'Maybe' was the prospect of getting out of the roach motel and sleeping on sheets that actually had a threadcount. He didn't hope, really. It was just possible, and that was enough hook to get him biting.

The dealer eyed the chips. "Sir, that's three grand you just threw down. You might want to take it easy."

"And if I wanted advice, I'd mail fucking *Ask Alice*," Jack barked. "Deal the cards, rug-muncher."

"Alice says: *If he calls you a rug-muncher, he may be a latent homosexual*," read Fritz, leafing through an issue of *Cosmo*. He clicked his radio and said: "That true, Jorge?"

"*Si*," Jorge said below. "Rug-muncher is homophobe."

"No, she means the guy's still in the closet."

The radio hissed as Jorge thought. "Why homophobe if in closet? Closet is full of shoes."

"Can one of you pricks watch the winch, please?" Perry sighed, pulling the lead on a nylon cord. "That thing overheats, my hands are gonna be mincemeat."

"Just drop it?" Fritz gave Perry an expression he hoped would translate to: *duh?*

"And risk the wrath of Miss Frenchfries?" Perry scoffed. "Sorry, Fritz. I like my job."

"The wench is fine. Look." Fritz waved at the electric spool as it whirred away.

Perry took up the slack, sighing. "Winch, Fritz. *Winch*. With an *I*."

Fritz rubbed the back of his neck. Perry got moody when they were moving heavy cargo. It was tiring. "What's the difference?"

"A wench is archaic for a prostitute or young woman. A winch is that thing hanging off the balcony."

They were six stories up at the Olympus, hauling a grand piano into a suite reserved for Sophie DeFrites, a popular song-writer from Canada. The room already had a piano in it, but Sophie insisted she couldn't play without her own set of ivories—which had turned out to be mammoth. They couldn't fit the singer's piano in the elevator, they'd be damned if they had to move it up six flights of stairs, so they'd picked up a rig to pull the thing in through the balcony. Problem was, the winch was an older model, and the rental guy warned it might overheat if they drove it too fast.

"Meh," Fritz shrugged. "You know, technically, both could pick up a guy."

"Just pay attention. Idiot. Be professional."

"I am being professional, Perr. I'm wearing the hardhat."

"Just watch the speed."

"Besides, if the thing goes flying, it's not like a plastic dome's gonna stop the damage," Fritz said, completely missing the point. He keyed his radio. "Jorge, you wearing your hardhat?"

"*Si*, but if it falls, I'm going back to Tijuana."

"You guys are so tense," Fritz chuckled, leafing through the magazine. "Hey, get this—apparently an ice cube and a feather duster will rock his world…"

The fly zipped along the cool night breeze. It beelined (or, perhaps *flylined*) toward the glowing tower of the Olympus. Below, drifts of people squeeged along the Strip. The fly came in low, among the cataclysmic screech of traffic, dodging a windshield, veering from the grill of a pickup, and soared again when it hit the roundabout.

It swept up the building, following the cord holding a piano twenty feet off the ground, and landed on the top of the spooling winch. It reared back, rubbing its front legs together as if it were about to dive into a bottomless smorgasbord of cow-patty—and if flies could grin, this one did.

"Huh," Fritz said. "Apparently, if you put peanut butter on your nether regions, you can have a dog get you off—doesn't that count as bestiality?"

Perry sighed. "That's the last time I get you a magazine."

The fly jittered along the winch, then found an opening and crawled inside, thinking: *You know what'd be really good right now? A cigarette. If, you know, I were big enough to smoke a cigarette.*

And you think you have it tough.

It's tough luck, is what it is, thought Ferret. In the course of two hours, he'd blown over six grand. So much for redeeming himself with the homestead. No matter—he still had enough cash to grab a chili dog at Pink's before he took a detour up Blazaar to find a hooker.

Perks of the job: he'd pick her up, take her back to his motel and fuck her until he was tired. Then, he'd flash his badge before she could exact payment. Prostitution was still illegal on the Strip, no matter what the tourists thought. Besides, nobody talked while tonguing the balls of the Law. She'd either go to prison and have to dry out, or she could partake in the remains of the coke pusher's stash he still had in his glovebox.

Either way, who gave a fuck? It wasn't like it was his problem. His problem was how he'd pay off the motel for the next two weeks. Extorting them was probably an option, but Ferret's mind was already burnt out on schemes for the night. He needed a blow job. He needed sleep. Needed to forget how much he'd lost inside.

He fished out a cigarette and went to light it, but the breeze put out his lighter three times. He moved over to the alcove off the side of the roundabout, carefully missing the pylons set out on the walkway.

Above, the winch screeched, revving, chortling, and exploding in a plume of smoke. The line gave, slicing through Perry's palms like razor wire. He howled. The piano fell, and Jack Ferret finally lit his smoke.

The piano crushed him like a cherry tomato, landing on a C-major as blood and chunks of flesh spattered the roundabout.

Nobody noticed the fly escape, chuckling in a mini-muppet voice.

Kevin's cigarette fell out of his mouth as a protracted shriek erupted from the crowd nearby. People rushed forward, then doubled-back when they landed on the splattered sleuth. Feed-back squealed through his ears, and he absent-mindedly adjusted his bellhop hat.

"Son," a voice through water.

A hand on his shoulder. The sound crashed back.

"Son? What happened?"

Kevin spun to find a regal-looking man in his sixties and a young blonde hugging his arm. He wagged his head, trying to shake the image of the crushed man from his mind. One moment he'd been lighting a smoke, prompting Kev to do the same; the next? Well... How else could you put it? He was three gallons of chili.

"The uh..." Kevin blinked. "Ah... Well, he got hit by a fucking piano?"

The regal man nodded. The blonde stifled a gasp. "Well... I think we'll get the car now, okay?"

Kev tried to switch into work-mode. "Of course. Sorry."

He grabbed the man's keys and dodged the gory scene on his way to the garage. He found the bronze Mercedes, climbed in, and planted his head against the wheel, the horn blaring through the car park.

It had happened so fast. He didn't know whether to puke or giggle, and he hated the compulsion for the latter. Why? Why laugh? Simple, really. What else could you do? It wasn't mirth, it was shock. He pressed the ignition button on the dash, and discovered his hands were shaking. Kevin took a breath, flung open the door, and ralphed on the concrete until he tasted bile.

He tried to focus on what he knew: driving. He could drive pretty well. Paul had run a stint working as a cabbie, and taught Kev how to drive. He focused on that, wiped his mouth, and peeled back to the lot.

Three seconds later, the couple was gone, and a voice came from behind. "You believe that shit?"

Kev turned and found Jones: thirty-one, bald, and cut out of burnt chestnut. "Well, duh, dude. I saw it happen. Piano just creamed him."

"No, I mean that motherfucker didn't tip. You believe that?"

Kevin rubbed his temples violently. "Motherfucker."

"That's what I'm saying. What time is it?"

Kev sighed, happy to latch onto something normal this evening. "Uh, quarter-to-three."

"Well, ain't this the night of small fuckin' pleasures."

"Yeah, well my shift's done. Have a good one, Jones."

"Hey, fuck you, Kev. I'm here another half-hour."

Kev sighed, waving him off. "Oh sure, man. I get it. Your life's a fuggin' tragedy."

"Tell that to my missus."

Kev shrugged. "I'm about to go get wasted at the Horseshoe. Bring her by, maybe I will."

A half-hour later, Kev was feeling better. He was on his third glass of bourbon, deciding to chase away the night with sour mash. The Horseshoe was packed, all glitz and cheer. Outside, people flocked along Fremont. Kev found himself falling into a semi-pleasant stupor.

He sloshed his drink back and flagged down the bartender.

"Anton? 'Nother round, please."

"Piece of advice, kid," an old guy grumbled, three stools over. "Keep drinking that shit, you'll wind up with a bummed liver before you can say titty twister."

Anton came back with another round and Kevin drained it, eyeing the stranger: an over-boiled hotdog in a gray suit and a tweed fedora. He looked like he'd fallen out of a bad '40s movie.

"Let me enumerate the ways I give a shit," Kev said. "Oh, wait... I think I don't."

"Clever," the old guy said with a grin. "Wanna know the difference between you and me, kid?"

Another round came and Kev smashed it back. "Sure, why not?"

"I can afford to be a prick."

"Uhuh. Well, big-ups."

"Youth always misses the point, don't it?" The guy chuckled. "Young guy like you, probably working part time. You're fullah shit, kid. You got an inheritance or something?"

"I got better," Kev said, producing an AmEx card. "Pay it off as I please."

"Ha! Kid, that ain't real money. That's just a piece of plastic bullshit."

"I'll use that one the next time they call asking." Kev grinned. "I'm game if you're about to share a money tree."

The old guy wagged a craggy finger. "Nothing's free, sonny-boy. You want money, you gotta earn it."

Kev sighed. *What a buzzkill.* "Well, what if you don't have time to earn it?"

"Then you gotta be connected—have people earn it for ya. Has it occurred to you to rob a bank?"

Kev tried to get a figure on the guy, but all he did was grin. "You're serious?"

"Not entirely. It's an option is all."

"Robin Hood, type thing?"

"Something as. Making money's all about who ya know, kid."

Outside, an ambulance's siren wailed, Kevin spun to watch the bleating lights scoot down the promenade, thinking of the guy killed by piano. "Yeah, what if I only know losers?"

But when he turned, the guy was gone. The glass was gone. There wasn't any money on the bar—it was as if the old guy had never been there. Kevin wagged his head, blinking, wondering if the combination of shock and booze had caused a hallucination. There was a smell like roses on the air.

On the table in front of him was a napkin, the words KENT & WORTHINGTON, TOMORROW NIGHT scrawled across.

"What the…?"

A hand clapped his shoulder. He turned and found Jones, next to his peeved-seeming girlfriend.

"You owe me a drink, motherfucker," Jones said.

"Fine, but you're covering my shift tomorrow."

"Sure man," Jones said. "So why don't you tell Maxine what you were saying earlier?"

CHAPTER 9
A WOK TO REMEMBER

James Pym Fukuzawa had bitten the head off a scorpion in Thailand. He'd broken an MMA fighter's pinky on a dare. He'd mopped the floor with every pimp, pusher, and bouncer who'd ever looked at him sideways. Once, he'd even crushed a man's skull with a fourteen-inch stir-fry pan—which was how he earned his nickname.

There was only one thing that sullied his reputation as a brass-balled, pan-welding badass—a secret Brie Cassiday hung over him any time she needed a favor: birds. Ever since he'd seen the Hitchcock film as a toddler, he'd been tormented with a constant fear of dive-bombings. It was so bad he couldn't even eat chicken without having an anxiety attack. Brie had found him out when she brought a bucket of the Colonel's crispy-fried to a job for a snack, and Jimmy fainted.

Jimmy liked Brie: she was smart and capable and was always nice to him. But this morning, he kind of wished she'd never been born.

He'd spent the night snorting lines off the stage of the Slipped Nip Strip Club in the Financial District. It was his usual haunt—a place where he could do blow and eat bottomless shrimp without interruption. This was mostly because one night, he'd snapped a businessman's arm in three places for trying to pet a dancer named Penny, and the owner, Jerry, had said: "Jimbo, you're grade-A. Feel free to have all the blow and shrimp you want."

Brie's first text had interrupted a shoulder rub from Penny. The following messages ruined both his sixth line and his twelfth shrimp cocktail. Now, he was here, with only a half-hour nap in the interim. His head ached. His suit itched, and he'd be furious if it weren't for the fact that he was about to brain a guy with a wok.

He grabbed an elevator and got the room number from his phone. He produced his wok (a Taylor & Ng 14" carbon-steel nonstick with tempered handle) from his jacket and set off to find the room. It might have been the lack of sleep or the coke hangover, but the hotel seemed labyrinthine. After a good twenty minutes, he found room 1804.

He went to kick the door in, when a rhythmic thumping sound syncopated by a woman's grunts came through the paneling.

"What the?" This was definitely not part of the plan. Should he knock? Was he sure he had the right room? How would he feel if he happened upon Brie bonking the guy she was planning to rob? Well, that part would mean seeing her naked, and while he wasn't big on potentially seeing another guy's dong, the rest of that notion was fine with him.

He went to knock, when the door exploded inward. Brie had her back to him, brandishing a stiletto like a caveman's club. "You sonofabitch!"

"Brie?"

But she wasn't looking at him. "You're not even French!"—she looked at the thing in her hand—"*Ugh.* You're fucking kidding me. This isn't real, either?"

"*Desolé,*" said a voice hidden behind the door to the bathroom.

Brie screeched. Before Jimmy could grab her, the door slammed shut, and the rhythmic thumping resumed.

"Cut the shit, fake-French-boy. You're not fooling anybody."

"But *chère,* I can explain…"

"Don't even—" Brie fumed. "You know you almost had me going."

"I thought I did have you—how you say?—*going* last night. I am confused."

"Oh, you mother—" *Thump. Thump. Thump.*

"But, *minou,* I must insist—"

"What"—*Whack*—"Did I"—*Whack, Whack*—"Just say?" *Whack, whack, whack.* "Gimme the bag."

Then, a scuffling sound, and that was it. Jimmy raised the wok, braced his shoulder, and the door flung open. Brie spilled out with a large black duffel on her shoulder.

"Sorry," she said. "Let's go."

Jimmy held the wok out as if to say: *But I came here to hit a guy?* "But what—"

"No time for questions, Jimmy. Let's move." Brie started hobbling toward the elevator on only the one heel. Jimmy fell in beside her.

"…Is that a—"

"Yes," Brie snapped.

"Tell me that's not a goatee," said Jimmy Wok.

"It's a *fake* goatee, doofus."

Brie punched the button for ground level and the elevator started moving. She had the duffel in one hand, and the fake goatee clenched in the other, looking like a squirrel she'd just beaten to death.

"You mean…"

"Yes, Jimmy. I stole a guy's goatee. Get over it."

"Well, you don't need to be mean about it." The big man pouted.

Brie felt a twinge of remorse. She'd stolen him from sleeping-in for nothing, and now she'd yelled at him and called him a doofus. She wasn't mad at Jimmy. It was just, well… this morning had not been going her way.

"I'm sorry. I'll buy you a coffee."

"It's just… isn't that kinda cruel? I'm sure he was attached to it."

"Not enough," Brie sighed.

The night had gone well—perfectly, in fact. But this morning, while the Frenchman slept and Brie rooted through his closet looking for cash, his phone blipped. Out of curiosity, she'd gone over and looked, and she found the name Ruby Cobb on his notifications.

From here, it came together: the guy beside her wasn't Miguel LaSoirée; wasn't an industrialist from Monaco; wasn't even fucking French—it was Josh Harlan. Ruby *had* set her up. And by the time she'd figured it out the douche-nozzle was awake, grinning, and still talking in that lame-ass fake French. She should have known better, but she was desperate, and desperation has a way of failing to help you think critically.

So, when it all came down, she'd resorted to violence. There are few stronger forms of persuasion than a swift yank to the facial hair—so it had surprised her somewhat when it came off his face as easily as a strip of Velcro.

"I don't get it," Jimmy said. "I thought he was just some French guy?"

Brie liked Jimmy a lot. He was useful, but his capacity for catching the obvious was on-par with a jellyfish. "It was an act, J. He's a friend of Ruby's. She set the whole thing up and played it off like he was just some scuzzwad at the bar. I should've known better."

Jimmy put a consoling hand on her shoulder. He motioned to the duffel. "Not a total loss?"

"Right." Brie tore open the zipper, reached inside, then threw the bag against the wall as if it were full of spiders. "No," she said. "No, no, no."

"Uh… Is that?"

Brie hung her head. The bag was full of bills, but they were completely the wrong color: pink, yellow, and blue. She took a deep breath to keep herself from exploding.

"It's Monopoly money."

On top was a fancy-looking business card. It read:

Nice scam. We should work together.

—JH

Jimmy sighed, staring at the ceiling. "So, who am I going back up there to hit?"

At the Noble Bean Cafe, Josh Harlan sat across the table from Billie Black, sunglasses covering a welt blossoming on his face in a shape remarkably similar to a frying pan.

"What happened to your face?"

Harlan shrugged. "I had an interesting night."

"So it worked?" Billie had been biting her nails all night, worrying the fake goatee and nose she'd given to make him look more French hadn't been enough.

"Well, the glue needs some tinkering, but yeah. Like a charm."

A twinge of pride, then a twinge of regret. "I can't believe you *lost* it."

"What do you want from me? Put out an APB on runaway facial hair?"

"If you knew how expensive that stuff was, then yeah. That'd be a start."

"If we pull this off, I'll pay you back," Harlan said. "You've got my word."

"And if we don't?"

"Have you had the scones here? They're unbelievable. Seriously, it's like the chef puts crack in them."

"Harlan…" She shot him a glare that, when roughly translated, said: *Change the subject again and I will shove a prosthetic segue up your ass.*

"We're fine, Billie. Really. I'm kind of a professional."

Billie still had reservations with transitioning from effects-specialist to thief. Sure, she'd worked enough films to know the angles—and Harlan did have a good plan. But, there's a pretty big difference between pretending and actually doing. Now that the lines were blurred—even though they were just in a cafe eating crack-laced scones—her stomach was twisting with worry.

At any millisecond, the feds would march in and cuff them. Then it would be crappy meals, nauseating outfits, and probably twenty-five years of being somebody's bitch in prison. Billie wasn't ready for that.

At first, she'd agreed to do just the one disguise: give Harlan a new face, maybe an ascot or cravat, and never learn why the grifter needed it. Plausible deniability. She wasn't sure what it was, but she'd worked enough buddy-cop movies back in LA to know it was good to have.

But, when he'd offered more work, and told her the take was just under eight-million—a sum she wouldn't make in six years at the shop—with the bills, a choking inventory, and the douche bag landlord harrying her—well... How do you pass that up?

Hence, the worrying.

"What about cops?" she said.

Harlan grinned. "Actually, that reminds me."

Billie's world started to pinwheel. Of course! He was undercover, or maybe a freedom-hungry CI looking for a scapegoat—he could be *anyone*.

"Shit," she said. "This is a setup, isn't it?"

"Huh?" Harlan's brow stitched, confusion supreme.

"I knew it. I knew it was too good. That guy over there"—she motioned to a guy in a fedora—"he's your handler, isn't he?"

Harlan waved her down. "That guy's just a hipster, and nobody's handling me. I mean, not technically."

"Enough." She raked her hands through her hair. "Just slap the cuffs on me and get it over with."

Harlan drained his coffee and smiled. "Billie, nobody's setting you up. I'm just working with a cop."

"Oh, sure!" Billie was almost shouting. "You're doing that thing where you secretly work with the cops until you get your take, then you send me and the rest of us to prison."

"Uh, that's only super boring?"

"It is?"

"Yeah. Way below my pay grade. Really, Billie. The agent's harmless."

"*Agent?*" she repeated. "As in, FBI?"

"Yup. So no worries."

Billie wagged her head. Her heart threatened to jump out of her chest like the creature in *Alien*. "That's actually kind of a lot of worries?"

"He wants something only I can get. He's a teddy bear. Totally non-threatening. Besides, what with the *Most Wanted* and whatnot, when's the last time the FBI's actually caught a guy?"

"Still, consider me *not* trusting you."

"Billie, he's a tool. You've got nothing to worry over."

"Maybe it's just an act?" Well, people did that, didn't they? Billie began to worry that she'd seen too many movies.

"Maybe," Josh said with a grin. "You wanna meet him?"

Paul Cassiday felt like he was becoming the deadbeat dad in bad TV crime serial. *Brie Cassiday was just a normal girl,* the raspy narrator would say. *Until tragedy landed her and her brother under the wing of a nefarious cardsharp. She descended into a life of crime: An expert cat burglar, she robs unsuspecting tourists—a predator; whipsmart, cold-blooded, ruthless... And all she wanted was to become a veterinarian.*

Every month, when the time to pay his debts came around, guilt circled him like a carrion bird. So, while he drove from Boulder to the Strip, he tried to figure out where it all went wrong.

He'd been a legend: taxi driver by day, cardsharp by night. He'd drive all day, scamming passengers, taking the long way to the casinos (a ritual among cabbies). When the sun went down, he'd head to the blackjack tables and count until the shoes went dry. The money was steady, but it was more than that.

It was outrunning casino managers, slipping away from the game minutes before the security goons descended. The allure of the outlaw: trouble always nipping at your heels. His name spread around the Strip. He became a myth. You can't not be a little proud of that.

And it was smooth sailing, until '89, when everything changed. First, his sister Josie and her husband crashed their Volkswagen off the side of the Hoover Dam. The kids—seven-year old Brie and newborn Kevin—fell into his custody. Then, he fell into the custody of Gavin Whelan, the Bellagio's then-manager.

It was a night like any other. The shoe was cold, so he'd been betting light. A hand grabbed him by the shoulder—not rough, but stern enough to let him know he was fucked. Paul took a sip of his drink and found Whelan standing behind him.

"Let's take a walk," he said.

They took him to a room that looked exactly like the place you'd expect to be taken if you got caught cheating in Vegas. Windowless cinderblock. A bare bulb. They tossed him on a metal chair and a behemoth covered in scar tissue commenced beating the complete shit out of him.

"You got a lot of nerve, Paul. Running your game here," Whelan said.

Between punches, Paul managed a smirk. "Thanks, Gav."

"Where are the kids?"

"You know, I was gonna tell you. But then you started hitting me and now I'm feeling all forgetful and woozy."

"Maybe we can help you remember." Gavin motioned to a guy in the corner, who wheeled over a caddy with a ball-peen hammer on top.

They smashed each of the knuckles on his left hand, saying, "You will not cheat in this city again," over and over, as if conjuring the wrath of the luck gods for meddling with the system. Paul's vision began to strobe.

"Alright boys," Whelan said. "I think we've made our point."

They dragged him out the back exit to a town car. Whelan straightened the gambler's lapels. "One more time."

Paul sighed, his hand throbbing under the icepack they'd given him. "Gavin, there's nothing you can do to me that'll make me tell you."

Gavin eyed him, patiently. "Well, Paul, I'm not in the business of killing children. So here's my offer: Five grand, every month. But one day, when they're grown up, I'll come looking. You give them to me, you keep on living. That's the deal."

Of course, Paul never cracked. He figured given enough time, Whelan would move on, maybe even forget. But every month, going on twenty-two years now, she'd appear. Sometimes a svelte brunette, others a waify blonde—but always a woman, and always offering the same choice: the money, or the names.

He pulled into the parking lot of Rocco's Tacos to grab lunch for Brie and him before they looted the storage locker, thinking of his conversation with Jezebel:

"Just give it up, stud. Gavin might not even kill them right away. Don'tcha wanna settle this thingie once and for all?"

"Let's do this," he said. "You ever come this close to my family again, I will put a big bullet in that pretty little head of yours."

She chuckled, stuck out her tongue. "Sweetie, I'd love to see you try."

Just thinking about it made his arthritic knuckles throb. *Yup*, he thought. *Definitely a spicy chorizo kinda day.*

CHAPTER 10
FINDING MR. WEASEL

Agent Max Reyes rubbed a nicotine patch on his arm in a suite at the Tropicana. The shades were pulled. He'd felt a pressure headache coming on yesterday, and now it was threatening to go full-blown migraine.

In hindsight, Max realized he hated everything about this job. He hated that his superiors wouldn't issue a warrant. He hated that the suspect seemed like a stand-up citizen. He hated Harlan. He hated Vegas. His body's reaction to all this hate was a migraine and cigarette cravings—and he hated that, too.

The upshot was, the Tropicana was the first hotel he'd encountered where the coffee maker made actual coffee. But, this didn't stop his habit of taking a sip and spitting it back into the cup, and that… Well, you know.

He sat on the bed, watching a red blip move across the city on his laptop. The blip represented a GPS tracker embedded in Harlan's wrist. Max knew he was having one pulled over on him, but what baffled him was that after two days, Harlan hadn't even left the city.

Max sighed, running his fingers through his graying hair. He decided to dump the coffee, shower, and shave.

He was halfway across his chin when the doorknob twisted.

Max bounded across the suite, grabbed his Beretta M9 from the nightstand, and whipped around just in time for the door to open, and his towel to fall to the floor.

Josh Harlan came in with an attractive frizzy-haired woman. "Indecent exposure," he said. "You're under arrest."

Reyes tossed the gun on the bed and grabbed his towel. "Where the fuck have you been?"

"Uh, not staying here." Harlan walked around the room, wearing a sort of disappointed grimace—the kind rich women gave Men's Warehouse fashion (Reyes had recently been divorced, and for some reason the look reminded him of his ex-wife.) "I've got a suite at the Venetian. Pack your things."

"Two days. You expect me to move into a room you probably stole? After disappearing for two days?" Reyes resisted the urge to just shoot him and write it off as a *he pulled first* thing. "I'm taking you back to prison."

"Reyes, dear, I know it's a big step for you, trusting a criminal mastermind and all—"

"Questionable on the mastermind." He could take him out to the desert. Nobody would ever know.

"Whatever. You want my help, you need to let me work, Max."

Reyes massaged his temples. Yes, this was definitely a migraine. "Sipping margaritas and getting a tan is not work, Harlan."

"I put a crew together in two days. How is that not work?"

Reyes wagged his head. "Crew?"

"Yes, Max. For the thing with the casino? I've got my sleight of hand guy, my burglar's on the ropes, and my wonderful disguise specialist, here. This is Billie, by the way."

Reyes fixed his towel and extended a hand. "Hey."

Billie recoiled as if Max were coated in dog spooge, when actually, it was just shaving cream. "I want you to know, I have complete plausible deniability."

"Uhuh… Well, welcome aboard." Then to Josh, "You still need a driver."

"I've got a couple prospects. It's time for Mister Weasel."

Max groaned. "It's so much paperwork…"

"Who's Mister Weasel?" Billie said.

"I'm telling you," Josh said. "We can't skimp on the tech whiz. Make your call, we'll be at the bar."

Cigarette, Cigarette, Cigarette! Max's mind shrieked. "It's two in the afternoon!"

"And we're thirsty," Josh said. "Come on, Agent. Quit being such a Maxy Pad. We'll see you there."

Billie snorted and the two headed downstairs. The door clicked shut.

Max slumped on the bed, his head throbbing mercilessly. "How do I get myself into this shit?"

The '67 Chevy Nova pulled up in front of Brie's apartment and sputtered. It was pumpkin orange, turbo-charged, in desperate need of a wash—and significantly over-described, considering it was just a car.

Brie was in hangover gear: cutoff jeans, a baggy Nirvana tee, and her hair pulled back in a ponytail. She had her Fendi backpack, and sunglasses to shield her headache. She trotted down the steps and climbed into the Chevy.

"Morning," she said.

Paul dangled a bag of Rocco's in front of her. "Breakfast?"

Brie fought back a wave of nausea. Paul grinned. They peeled off up MLK onto East Craig. A mile past Nellis, they stopped and ate. Then, they pulled in front of a squat horseshoe-shaped adobe structure with arrays of teal doors.

Brie didn't remember her parents. She only remembered Paul, and how he'd talk fondly about her mom the few times she'd seen him drunk. Beyond that, they were cyphers. So this was big for her. Her burrito cut the hangover, and in a smash-cut they were at her parent's unit, Paul fiddling with the lock.

"It's jammed," he grumbled. "I haven't been here for a while."

Brie shrugged, whipped off her backpack, produced a micro-screwdriver and a hammer—and in ten seconds, she'd popped the door off its hinges. They peered inside.

"Well, crap," said Brie.

"I know, it's a little crowded."

Foster Father, master of understatement: the place was jammed full of lame memorabilia, racks of art, hundreds of books—including a set of leather-bound journals that she shoved into her Fendi when Paul's back was turned—a bunch of heinous furniture, and an antique roulette wheel at the back.

"And it stinks," Brie said. "What is that—mothballs and... dried lizard?"

"No, that's the chimichangas." Paul shrugged. "I farted."

"Nice." Brie sighed, appraising the stuff at rapid-fire. "...So, roulette wheel?"

"Yup," Paul said, rolling up his sleeves.

They started hauling junk out of the way. About halfway through, Brie stopped, wiping her brow. "Paul, we need to talk."

"I know."

"I got conned last night." Well, there it was. She'd expected to throw down something a little more elegant, but now it was out, and it was too late to make it pretty.

"I figured. You know, the hangover and whatnot."

Brie took his arm, feeling like a giant saccharine bullshitter. "I'm sorry. I did my best."

"I know, kid," Paul wrapped an arm around her and sighed. "Okay, my turn."

"Huh?"

"Brie, I'm really sorry. But I haven't been telling you everything."

"You don't need to put this on you, Paul. I fucked up. I lost my sense of judgement and—"

"No, Brie…"

"—I'll talk to Ruby. I'll take out a loan, or something."

"No. Never order a plate you can't—"

"Maybe I can steal Trump's combover. That's gotta be worth a lot… That was a joke. I don't think I could get it from him. But still—"

"Brie—"

"Maybe if he was asleep. I mean, I *did* steal a guy's goatee today—"

"Brie!" Paul's voice echoed down the hallway. Brie stared at her feet, then started moving shit out of the way to get to the wheel.

"It's about the debt," Paul said.

"I know, Paul."

"No, you don't." Paul threw a stack of paintings across the hallway. "I'm paying off a guy to protect you and Kevin."

"…Huh?"

"Look. I might not make it out of this," Paul said. "If that's the case, there's things you need to know. You and Kevin are—"

"No, Paul. Not an option."

"Dammit, Brie. Let me finish."

"No." Brie was rattled. She'd never seen him this angry, but she wasn't about to show it. "You can't just give up. You can't just give in like that. You didn't teach us to be that way—and like hell if you get to turn back on that."

Paul bowed his head. "Listen, I've been paying off a guy named Gavin Whelan to keep you and Kevin off his radar."

"You mean it's not a gambling debt?" Brie couldn't believe it, so she shoved more junk out of the way and they hit the roulette wheel.

"Whelan's been leaning on me since you were kids. I never told him your names. He's—"

"So, I'll just meet him and take it over?"

"No, Brie. That's dangerous."

"So what?" Who cared? If it could get Paul out of debt, she could handle the rest. "We're gonna sell this, and I'm gonna talk to him."

"No. You have no idea who you're messing with."

"I don't care, Paul. I can take care of me and Kev—why does he even want to know who we are to begin with?"

"It's complicated," Paul said. "Look, the guy has ways of killing you that you'll never see coming. Brie, I'm telling you because you need to know… For when I'm not here."

Brie wheeled around. "I'm not hearing this."

Paul grabbed her shoulders. "Yes you are. You have to hear me on this, kiddo. Stay away from him. Leave the country if you have to."

"Oh hey, we've reached the wheel of destiny. So, I guess this conversation is over?"

"Brie…"

"Paul, we're gonna settle this," Brie said, placing a hand on his cheek. "I'm not losing Kevin, and I'm *not* losing you. Also, I know a gal."

Before Paul could argue, Brie produced her phone and hit the speed-dial.

"Ruby," she said. "Guess who owes me huge?"

In the middle of an empty Thai restaurant, Ruby Cobb sat across a table from the leaders of the *Los Cobras Autoeroticas*—the Southwest's leading ring of cocaine distributors. All of them thought the name translated to "The Sexy Car Driving Cobras" and had killed most of the people who'd tried to correct them. They were a little twitchy.

A Glock, a Walther PPK, and two Uzis lay on the table between them, each of the members thumbing their safety as one plays with a bar coaster.

Their names were the Blade, the Hammer, and the Flame—but Ruby thought of them as Grumpy, Fidgety, and Frowny; the Peruvian Marching Dwarves. (Well, she wasn't above questionable nicknames.)

"You need to slow your effin' roll, pumpkin."

"You set me up with Harlan and don't even give me the warning, even after I specifically express my non-interest? *You've* got explaining to do," Brie said.

"You lost me," Ruby said. "I thought you were shacking up with the French dude?"

She scrawled some numbers on a check and passed it to the Cobras.

"The French dude was a fake dude. It was Harlan. I saw your name on his phone literally this morning."

"Well obviously I'm in touch with him," Ruby said. The Cobras shared pleased expressions over the check. "Did you read what I wrote him? 'Cause I'm fairly certain it had nothing to do with you."

"Whatever. The fact remains, he wouldn't even know to fuck with me if you hadn't mentioned my skill set. You owe me, bitch."

"Oh, fine," Ruby sighed. Brie could take things so personally. It was charming, really. "One second, 'kay?" Then to the Cobras: "Will that be all, gentlemen?"

With that, they packed up their heat and scuttled out of the restaurant. Ruby waited until she heard their Escalade screech off before she continued.

"What do you need?"

"Five grand for a vintage roulette wheel. And by tomorrow."

Ruby did the math in her head. "I can do that. What's in it for me?"

"...I'll be your best friend forever?"

"And?"

"I'll buy you coffee for a month?"

Ruby grinned. "I'll call you back."

The second she was off the line, her mind went to work, scrolling a rolodex of fences, logistics, and how she could extort them into paying full price before even seeing the product. She slipped out of the restaurant, and by the time she'd passed the MGM, she had her answer: she needed some muscle, and a pawnshop owner to terrify.

Up ahead, the volcano in front of the Mirage erupted, sending a spew of fake flame into the air. The sun glimmered across the edges of the Pyramid: it was going to be a long kinda day.

Tommy "Mister Weasel" Carlyle was one of those rare convicts who left prison looking better than he'd entered it. In the three years since Josh had seen him, he'd put on about twenty pounds of muscle, shaved off all his hair, and caught a tan.

"So lemme get this straight," said Billie Black, ogling the hacker through the tinted glass of the town car. "That strapping hunk is a nerd?"

"Genius." Josh grinned, throwing the door open. "He's a genius."

Tommy climbed in.

He'd earned his nickname being the sneakiest console cowboy to ever hit the web. At fifteen, he'd hacked NASA. Fired from Google, Facebook, Apple, and a dozen other tech firms, he went freelance in 2005. By twenty-two, he'd breeched the Pentagon, doing them a solid and fixing their firewall on the way out—but not before he'd swiped files on Project Pegasus, Area 51, and most other hot topic conspiracies. After releasing them on YouTube, the feds nabbed him, mid-wank to pirated copy of the new *Hobbit*.

For his achievements, Tommy was sentenced to fourteen months without technology. Apparently, he'd spent them pumping iron. After that, Tommy had served his time teaching HTML as part of a rehabilitation program he'd spearheaded. And despite his sabbatical, Mister Weasel lived on in infamy—mostly in Reddit and 4chan mythology.

"Josh Harlan," he said with a grin. "Long time, no see."

Josh slapped the muscular hacker's hand. "It's good to see you, buddy. Welcome back to freedom."

Tommy gave Billie a hungry sort of once-over. "And who might this attractive slender woman be?"

"Tom, this is Billie Black, disguise whiz," he said. "Try not to drool."

Tommy had been in prison a while. He took Billie's hand, and was a little surprised to see her blushing (he still forgot he'd become a beefcake.) "A master of disguise, huh? I'm totally holding your hand too long, aren't I? I've been in prison a while." To Harlan: "So, you've got a job cooking?"

Josh grinned, pleased that Tommy hadn't lost their shorthand. "And then some. We've even got an agent."

Reyes twisted in the driver's seat. "And the first chance I get, you're both back in prison."

Tommy gave him a *fuck you* glare, then came back to Josh with an expression that said: ...*Huh?*

Josh shrugged. "He grows on you."

"Right," Tommy said. "So the job?"

"Secret files from the newest casino to grace the Vegas skyline." Josh pulled a bottle of Ketel One from a bucket of ice and poured tumblers. He handed one to Billie, then to Tommy, then shoved one into the agent's grip.

"Swell," said Tommy. He raised his glass—the first booze he'd had since the time a guy named Sascha had given him some prison brew and he'd wound up on the floor of the woman's shower room wearing a bra and panties.

"Cheers," Harlan said. "I've got a bug in the mark's office, but we have a lot of legwork to do. We need a detailed layout. Also a staff inventory, some digging on infrastructure... Oh, and I've already been threatened that he'll kill me if I show my face again."

"Gee, I wonder why," Reyes tossed over his shoulder.

"I can help with that," Billie said.

Josh grinned. "What d'you say, Mister Weasel?"

Tommy drained his glass. "Just so I'm clear. You want to go case a joint whose owner has already threatened to punch your ticket and you broke me out of jail just *presuming* I'd help you?"

"Yeah," Josh said.

"Pretty much," added Billie.

"That's what he keeps telling me," sighed Reyes.

Tommy gave Harlan a lopsided grin. "Let's go for a drive."

Two hours later, still in disguise as retirees, Josh and Tommy climbed back in the town car.

"So no problem with the makeup this time?" said Billie.

Tommy started tearing off the prosthetics. "We've got other problems."

Josh nodded, peeling off his latex wrinkles. "How bad?"

"Bad," Tommy said. "Impenetrable security system, an Omniview 7800... It doesn't even exist on the market. Aside from that, about thirty ex-spies on the payroll. More than that if they're off shift."

Josh nodded. "So... Crap."

Tommy shrugged. "Pretty much."

Harlan poured another round of drinks. "So that means you're gonna need..."

"Seems like."

And here, Josh slammed a new drink in Reyes's hand. "And the other thing?"

"That part's easy."

Tommy watched as Josh worked it all out in three seconds.

"Okay," he said. "Let's pick up the magician."

CHAPTER 11
FEAR, LOATHING, AND WHATNOT

The magician lay in a tangle of sheets at the Temple of the Mistress Shangrila, staring at the curtained ceiling. In fact, the whole room was shrouded in curtains: it was like a womb of drapery. The bed was moist. The smell of sex heavy on the air. His forehead glistened with sweat.

He'd been running a stint of couch-surfing around the bordellos that ring the Nevada basin. It was a fine gambit: approach the madam, pretend to be some down-on-his luck sod who'd just fallen off the boat. A little sweet talk and he'd have a room, whatever women he could charm properly, and even a shower when needed. In exchange, he cooked, cleaned, drove the escorts, ran dry cleaning—whatever it took. All part of the act.

The point was to embed himself. Once the ladies trusted you and you could move freely from room to room, all you needed was to find the valuables, swipe them, find a fence, and Bob's your uncle.* Onward to the next before anybody noticed what was missing, and there you are.

"What are you thinking about?" said Yolanda, the voluptuous pink-haired woman currently curled up on his chest.

"I'm thinking about a man," Quinn said. *Not stealing your madam's crystal dildo for twelve grand, if that's what you're implying,* he thought. *That would be wankery,* he added. *And, well... True.*

Yolanda stroked his chest. "Should I be offended, or proud of your bravery?"

Quinn engaged her in a tickle fusillade that ended with some tongue-heavy kissing. When they came up for air: "Not like that, you pontz. He offered eight-million dollars."

"And you're sure it's not like that?" Yolanda deadpanned. She planted a kiss on his nipple, squeezed his todger, and rolled off him. She found his top hat on the floor and slipped it on. "What do you think?"

"I think it's brilliant, love." Quinn grinned as she straddled him. "But see what's inside. It is a magic hat, after all."

She pulled off the hat, and just before she reached in, she paused. "There's not a bunny in here, is there?"

He shrugged. "Only one way to find out, love."

Yolanda took a breath and reached in. She came back with a handful of colorful scarves. "Mmmm!" she said. "Kinky."

Before Quinn could argue—and really, he wasn't planning to—she threw his arms against the headboard and tied his hands.

"That's really kind of tight, love." In fact, he was fairly certain he'd lost feeling in his fingers.

Yolanda put a finger to his lips. She leaned in, nibbled his earlobe. "Relax, darlin'. You're the magician, but I'm the professional."

---

* Fun fact: Quinn's uncle's name actually *was* Bob.

With that, she ripped his boxers off, and the door exploded inward.

They met by the pedophilic statue guy. Ruby carried one of those metal briefcases you usually saw in spy novels. The sun was setting, the Strip coming to life in streams of people. Brie walked up to her, half-expecting Ruby to pass the briefcase and keep walking, like in those spy novels, and said, "Whuddup, bitch?" like not in those spy novels.

"You totally need to stop calling me that," said Ruby.

"I'll work on it," Brie said, nodding to the suitcase. "So, what's in the case? If I open it will it glow and break the narrative and whatnot?"

Ruby shrugged. "If money does that to you, yeah."

"You really didn't know it was him, huh?"

"Honestly, B. I think he had like a fake nose or something."

"And a fake duffel full of fake money full of why I'm standing here," Brie said. She'd decided it wasn't Ruby's fault—not entirely —but a little blame game never hurt. "So much for first impressions," she added. "Like, who pulls a moneybag switch, right off the bat?"

"Actually, I think it was a totally different nose," Ruby said. "His nose is more…"—and here, she made a scrunchy face, which on Ruby was just adorable. And also accurate.

Brie sighed. "Rubes, he's a jerk."

The criminal liaison waved her arms in surrender. "Hey, not disagreeing"—she held up the briefcase—"See? I come bearing cash."

Brie wagged her head in admiration. The little one worked so fast, and was so friggin' cute. She wouldn't last six days, hating her. "I forgive. How did you even get it this quickly?"

Ruby grinned. "I am small, but I have ways."

They reached the edge of the large roundabout of the Olympus. Brie eyed it, thinking: *Every time, no matter how prepared for this I am, I get all pukey feeling when I see it.*

"Way to be cryptic. What'd you do, actually?"

"Sold it to a pawn shop guy, then robbed him and made another six grand. I kept three. Surcharge."

"You payed a guy to rob him?" Brie said. "Wow. Okay. You really are a criminal."

"What?" Ruby shrugged. *"Ways."*

"You're so cute and scary," Brie chuckled. "Remind me to get you to give me lessons."

"Kinda think you've got it covered." Ruby eyed the casino, a hint of worry. "You're sure?"

Brie nodded. "Paul's been in the trenches long enough. It's my turn."

"Okay, then," Ruby said. "Just FYI, I'm taking a spot on Harlan's team."

Brie hugged her. "I'll bake you a cake when you're in prison. The nail file will be in the center, and don't eat it—it'll be made of lead."

Ruby chuckled. "I thought you should know!"

"So did I! Bitch."

"Stop that." They reached the entrance, and Ruby paused. "You're sure you don't wanna join? I'll watch your back."

"Hmm. Lemme think." Brie sighed, just to let Ruby think of all her reasons against it. "You know? Maybe… Oh wait, *nope.*"

"Harlan and I talked, B. He says he could use you."

"Oh, sure. He could use us both. Ride our butts straight to prison." A pause. "I'm gonna rephrase that last part."

"Yeah, good call."

Brie turned back to the casino with a steadying breath. "Okay. On with it, then. Time to meet the Wizard. Wanna walk me?"

Ruby hung back, regret on her expression. "Would. But kinda can't."

Right, she was about to rob the place. Not exactly a great plan to walk in. Brie nodded. "Thanks for helping."

"Good luck, pumpkin," Ruby said.

The first words from Harlan's mouth when he entered the Mistress Shangrila's were: "Fun."

"Not bad," Billie added.

"Agreed," said Tommy.

"I need a vacation," sighed Reyes.

It was an old Victorian: a wide pine porch, cream-colored paneling and jade shingles. Inside, the pine motif continued, framing a wide atrium filled with velvet divans, Oriental carpeting, and about a dozen half-naked courtesans, who all looked up to see who'd let the sunlight in.

Reyes crossed his arms, failing desperately to keep his ogle off a topless brunette on the loveseat to his left. "Can I—uh... Can I wait in the car?"

Harlan slapped his back. "Where is your sense of adventure? It's Vegas, Agent Dickwad. Loosen up."

"Don't call me that." Reyes grimaced. "Don't... Say that... In here—great, now they're all looking at me. Thanks."

"You're paranoid," Josh said, then he winked at the brunette. "Hi. He's new. Can you take care of him?"

"No—" Reyes said.

"Sure," said the brunette. Before the agent could argue, she took him by the hand. "Come on. Let's see if we can't relax you."

Even as she dragged him away, Max shot the grifter a stern finger. "I know you're up to shit, Harlan. I know you're working me, and, given enough time, I'll get you—"

"Wow, so tense!" said Brunette, locking him between her thighs in front of the loveseat. "We need to work that out. It's bad for your *ch'i*. I'm Sophie, by the way."

"Hustle," Josh said, skirting his cohorts up the stairs. He couldn't help giggling a little.

Looking around, he had to admit it: Josh liked what Quinn did with his downtime. Maybe, on another job, he'd do something similar.

They reached the top of the stairs, and Harlan led them down the hall.

"Sunglasses," he said when they reached the room. They all put on their shades, and Harlan kicked the door open—splinters of wood flying in every direction.

"Bloody hell!" cried the magician.

Josh squinted, then ripped off his sunglasses. *"Yolanda?"*

Whelan's office was a pageant of affluence—too rich to know to be humble, Brie thought. She walked in and eyed the grody painting on her left; the dumb trinket shelf to her right. Funny, how the rich always filled their spaces with embarrassing notions of superiority—even if it was a super-cool action figure that cost twenty-grand, which in this case, it wasn't. The digs told you everything about the owner—and this guy was a fucking cliché.

"It's good to meet you, Brie," he said. "Drink?"

"No thanks," Brie said. "I've seen *Mad Men*. I say yes and I walk out of here wasted, sold on some stupid thing."

Gavin chuckled. "Just a curtesy. What brings you?"

The guy has ways of killing you you'll never see coming. This guy? He was like an M.D. in boring. He was milquetoast. "You know that guy Paul, the one you've been harassing?"

"Sure," Whelan said. He sat. "We have an arrangement."

"Well, I'm his representative," she said, feeling like she was on fire. She slammed the briefcase on the desk and slid it over. "This is everything he owes."

Whelan unlatched the case and eyed the bills. "Thank you."

"There's more. I know you've been pushing him for some names. Thought I'd like to give them to you."

Whlean closed the case and put it behind his desk. "Oh?"

"Uhuh. See, my last name's Cassiday, too. I mean, not originally, but that's what you're after, right?"

The tycoon gave her a once-over, grinning. "It is."

"Great. So now that we know each other, Gavin, I'm gonna make you a deal."

"I'm all ears."

"You know who *I* am, but I'm guessing you'll still need to know who my brother is. I won't tell you that, but if you transfer the debt over to me—if you take the big guy out of your aperture, I'll never miss a payment."

"Enticing offer," Whelan said.

"It's not an offer." Brie grinned. "It's your best play. So, how 'bout that answer?"

"Bloody hell!" howled the King of Cups. "You might've knocked."

"Cover your junk," said Josh. "We're getting out of here."

Yolanda popped off Quinn's scepter and turned. "Josh?"

"Oh, bollocks, you know each other?"

"You were thinking about this guy?" she said. "I guess I can't blame you."

"Nice to see you, Yolanda. Please take your hands off my sleight of hand guy."

"Oh, Joshie Bear. Always working, that's your problem."

"You should meet my FBI friend. He'd give you a field day."

Yolanda stood and wrapped herself in a silk kimono. "Think you've got that backwards, doll."

"If I recall, you like it that way, too." Josh bounced his brow.

Yolanda shrugged. "True."

Quinn sighed, wrapping the sheet around his waist. "I'm sorry, how the bloody hell do you two know each other?"

Josh smirked. "Long story."

"Not that long," Yolanda corrected.

"I was on the clock," Harlan said, looking around the room. "Is this like a drape factory or something?"

"Seriously, how *do* you know each other?" said Billie Black.

"She's a thief," Josh said.

Yolanda frowned.

"A thief?" said Quinn.

Josh nodded. "Pretty good one, too. Usually hired by the big agencies to find clients of the thieving variety. Steals from them before they get away."

"Technically, it's reimbursing stolen goods," Yolanda said. "And hi, Tommy."

"Terribly poetic," Josh said. Then to Quinn: "It's time to do the thing."

"I'll need about ten minutes," the magician said. "To, well… to finish some…*things*?"

"You've got me for the hour?" said Yolanda.

"You're a thief."

"Oh, sure. Now he's a puritan."

"Hi, Yolanda," Tommy said, snapping out of a daze (the escort's kimono was still hanging open.)

Josh wheeled around. "Dude, where have you been for the past five lines?"

"I was in prison for a long time." Tommy shrugged, trying to cover the blush in his cheeks. "Sorry."

Josh hung his head. "Downstairs in five, Quinn."

"Roger that," said the magician.

"Pun!" Billie said. "Pun! ...Did no one else catch that?"

Josh led them back down the stairs.

"So, Yolanda, huh?" Tommy said.

Josh slumped on a futon. "Not talking about it."

"Come on," said Billie. "I'm sure it's a good story."

It was. "One I'll never tell," Josh sighed. "Where's the agent?"

"I don't know what happened," Reyes slurred, rising from behind the futon. His hair was rumpled, his collar unbuttoned, an almost drunken glaze over his eyes. "But whoever set it up... Let me say... *Thank you.*"

"We lost him."

"Seriously," Reyes continued. "I thought it would be all raunchy and illegal and degrading. I was wrong. I see that, now."

"It's legal out here," said Tommy.

"Well... good!" Reyes climbed over the back of the futon and flopped beside Josh. "I mean, she *really* worked the tension out of me. I was *so* tense, you know?"

"Uhuh," said Harlan.

"She had oils and everything. I almost forgot what a beautiful woman's hands can—"

"Oh, *ick*," Billie said. "Throw on the PG-13, Penthouse Forum."

Reyes furrowed his brow. "Massage isn't PG-13?"

"Oh, then never mind. What's the going rate on those?" And here, Tommy shot Billie a credulous look. "What? I'm wicked stressed."

Just then, Quinn tumbled down the stairs, still wrapped in a sheet, his magician's hat akimbo.

"Code Harlot!" shouted Yolanda, appearing at the top of the

stairs, a .38 Special trained on the magician. Josh grabbed him as another dozen pistols cocked around the place, and a single shot exploded through the top of Quinn's hat.

When the ringing settled, Josh said, "I'm sorry, isn't the whole place a code harlot? I mean, technically."

Reyes had his hand on his hip—which might have been useful if he hadn't left his service weapon in the car.

Yolanda chuckled, coming down the stairs. "*Code Harlot* refers to when a thief is caught before he reaches the doors." She winked at Josh. "I invented it."

"Nifty. But, not following."

Yolanda kept the gun on Quinn. "Our magician friend has taken something. The Mistress's crystal dildo."

"I'm confused," Josh said. "If he stole her dildo, then why isn't *she* holding the gun on him?"

"Mistress Shangrila isn't a person, Joshie Bear. She's the spirit that lives in all of us—and she'll cut you fuckers down if you move but an inch before returning her sacred crystal dildo."

"...Sacred?" Tommy said.

"Well, it *is* personal," said Billie.

Josh looked around at the women with guns, sizing up the situation. "Deal. Quinn? Give back the sacred dildo."

The magician elbowed him in the ribs and muttered, "I've already got a fence lined up."

"And those are twelve armed ninja women surrounding us. This isn't an argument. Give them the dildo."

Quinn sighed, bouncing on his heels, adjusting his hat, looking around. Josh already knew what he was thinking.

"You're not going to run. Now—"

"KAZAM!!!" the magician shrieked, producing a handful of black stones from his hat and whipping them against the floor.

In an instant, the atrium filled with smoke. Josh grabbed Reyes's arm to clothesline the other three for the door as a hail of gunfire erupted. The bordello exploded with blisters of crackling wood.

Josh threw open the temple's doors, just in time for a carbon shuriken to *thunk* an inch to his left. They scrambled the twenty yards to the town car. Reyes even managed what must've been a paramount in heroics, butt-sliding over the hood and crashing clumsily on the other side before he scrambled into the driver's seat. Tommy flung open the back door and ushered Billie and Quinn in before following. Josh, hanging back a few paces, did a perfect jackknife into the cab before a rain of gunfire peppered its side.

Reyes threw it in reverse, sending the car in a screeching Y-turn out of the lot. As they pulled away, Josh recovered and started to chuckle, nodding at his co-conspirators. Then he broke into an almost maniacal cackle, and slowly, everybody joined him—even Reyes.

All according to plan. Max's badge safely in his pocket. The dildo already in Yolanda's care. A cubic zirconia in the magician's hat. Nobody hurt. Nothing lost. Perfect. Sure, he'd arranged the whole thing, but knowing the dance's numbers didn't take the fun from it.

When the door closed, Gavin Whelan grinned and headed over to his wet bar to celebrate. He'd agreed to Brie's bargain. *Brie.* If he'd only guessed his favorite cheese, he could have resolved this ages ago. No matter. He knew now—at least the first of the final two names he needed to wipe out the candidates. His work was so close to being finished, he nearly did a two-step of victory with his beverage in hand.

"Well, that changes things some, doesn't it?" said Jezebel, who appeared in his chair, kicking her feet up on the desk.

Whelan poured a second drink and came back. "I don't even think she knows what she is. That's good. We need to keep it that way."

"Splendid," Jezebel grinned, tossing back the scotch. "What next? Please tell me you're gonna make me do something interesting."

CHAPTER 12
HARD CHEESE

A MESSAGE

"Paul, it's B. I've got some good news that'll probably infuriate you and it can't wait. Anyway, I'm in a cab. I should be there in a few minutes. If you're not home, I'm raiding your fridge, so you better be there. I think—well, it's just good news. I'll see you soon, okay? Bye."

The answering machine beeped and the red light started blinking. The woman slipped out the front door into the night.

The apartment was quiet.

Brie shoved a handful of bills in the cabbie's hand and said, "Don't worry about the change."

She bounded out of the cab and took the stairs two at a time. A gentle breeze came from the west, the palms swaying beneath a cloudless sky.

Paul was free: paid up for the month, and never needed to worry again. Sure, he'd be furious, but Brie had gotten used to having that effect over the years. She was his daughter, after all. She existed to make him suffer.

She couldn't help but grin when she reached the door. It felt like those moments on Christmas morning when he'd unwrap a gift—anticipation; felicity. She took a steadying breath and slipped her key into the deadbolt.

"Paul?" She came in, tossing her keys on the table in the main hall. The apartment was L-shaped, with a living room on the left, the kitchen at the back, and the bed and bathroom making up the tail.

The lights were on. A muted Giants game played on the TV.

"Hello?" Brie poked her head into the living room, but the lumpy couch was empty.

She followed the hall toward the kitchen, where she found him on the floor.

"Paul?" He slumped there, against the counter under the sink, one hand on his abdomen, the other to his side; a thick puddle of red surrounding him. "Paul... Pau—Pa..."

There was blood on his shirt. Too much. A four-inch gash in the middle.

"No," Brie said, feeling her insides twist. Her pulse fluttered in her ears. "No, no, no..." She grabbed a rag from the sink and fell to her knees beside him. She heaved his shoulders into her lap and pressed the rag against the wound. Stop the bleeding...

"It's okay." Choppy breaths. "It's—We're just gonna stop the bleeding—and then—"

His head lolled to the right, eyes staring blankly at the ceiling. It was here she realized he wasn't breathing.

"Okay—I... I just..." Phone. Where was the phone? She pulled herself up on the edge of the sink, hands vibrating. She took a step toward the living room when the floor seemed to skew. She went to steady herself on the counter, but lost her footing on the blood-slick floor and went down. Right beside him.

The phone clenched in her hand, but she didn't remember finding it.

"9-1-1, what is your emergency?"

Had she dialed? "It's my dad—he—he stabbed... I mean, he's been stabbed."

"I'm sending a response team. What's the address?"

Everything was backwards. "What?" she said. "Address?"

"Where does he live, Brie?"

"376 Peacock Crescent." It felt like there'd been a whole conversation she wasn't present for.

"Just stay on the line. We're on the way."

" 'Kay." Brie hung up the phone.

She waited. She waited so excruciatingly long that she could physically feel the time pass; a binding in her chest, her breath shallow and raspy. Silence seemed to stuff itself in her ears like cotton balls. Everything took on a dreamlike aspect as she sat, splay-legged on the floor.

Suddenly there were legs in blue cotton moving around in front of her. Men. One of them carried a yellow case and the other crouched in front of Paul.

"Ma'am, was he conscious when you found him?"

"No. Uh. No. I mean. I don't think—"

The second EMT crouched beside his partner and pulled a bunch of tubes and wires from the case. "Needa intubate."

Brie stood, still clutching the phone, watching as they worked.

"Pressure."

"Got it. Pump him."

They produced a mask and plastic catheter they threaded into Paul's mouth. One attached a plastic cylinder to the tube and started squeezing air into him. Brie couldn't stop looking at the stripes on their jackets.

"No pulse," said the other EMT. "Defibrillate?"

His partner sighed, shaking his head. "Man, he's cold. Call it."

"What," Brie said. "Call what—you…"

The man stood and came over to her. "Miss, I'm very sorry. It looks like he bled out before you even arrived. The coroner will be able to tell you more."

"Coroner?" Brie wagged her head. It felt like she was underwater.

"I'll make the call," a voice said, but she couldn't place it. Again, she fixated on the stripes of the man who was speaking to her.

"Is there someone you can call?"

"I—"

A radio chirped.

"O'Maley," said the EMT.

Radio murmurs followed. The men talked to each other, but Brie's gaze fell on Paul, laying there with tubes sticking out of him… She couldn't hear anything.

Flashing lights filled the entrance, where the door hung open.

The coroner zipped Paul's body into a bag while the uni-formed guy talked.

"And no signs of forced-entry?"

"Force, no—no force. I just… He was… He was in the kitchen." Brie watched as they hauled the bag onto a gurney and wheeled out of the room.

"Did he give any indication that this might blah blah blah blah—"

"What?" Brie tried to focus, but everything moved too fast.

"Did he have any enemies?" The guy with the notebook might as well have been a lamppost. She needed to go with Paul —would they revive… Was he—he…

"Bowling," Brie said. "People thought he cheated at bowling, there were some guys who hated that he rolls a perfect strike and… He gave Del Taco a one star review? He… I… I don't—it just—I was…"

Brie felt a hand squeeze her shoulder. She looked up and found the cop wearing a sincere expression. "We can do this another time."

"That would probably be good."

"I know this is difficult," he said. "They're going to autopsy. It could take some time. You can head there whenever you want. Is there someone you can call?"

"My brother," Brie said. "I—my brother. I have to tell him."

Another squeeze. "I'm sorry for your loss. You need to drink something. Get some air. It helps to take a walk."

"Okay," Brie said.

In another instant, the place was empty. She looked at the blood streaking the floor, then wagged her head and went back to the foyer where her purse lay.

She picked it up, started fishing for her phone, and found herself heaving bile onto the carpet before she blinked. She wiped her mouth and took her phone out of her purse. She called Kevin, and got his voicemail.

"Kev, it's your sister. It's—well… Uh, I—I'll call you back, okay?"

When she got outside, everything blurred like drunk-vision. She realized it was because she was crying, and—well, you know.

"Well, that sucked," said Billie Black, slumped on the couch in what Josh had been thinking of as the brainstorm room.

It was an abandoned mall complex, north of the Strip. One of many, it had been built in the boom of the '80s, and when the housing bubble popped, the investors bailed, leaving the prospect of high-end shopping abandoned—a perfect time for a guy with Swedish bank accounts to pick it up for a song. Harlan planned to flip it and sell when the market went up again, but in the meantime, it made excellent headquarters.

"Bloody bungered it, you did," Quinn said. "I could've been killed!"

Tommy massaged his temples. "You're actually the reason we almost *all* got killed."

"That's exactly my point," slurred the magician, topping up his whiskey. "I've pulled that gig, what? Six, eight times with no trouble. Then you lot show up and everything goes cock-up."

Josh sighed. "Guys—"

"He's saying it's your fault," said Billie.

Quinn furrowed his brow. "He is?"

"Yeah," said Tommy.

"Yeah," said Billie.

"Well, then." Quinn shrugged. "I don't recall inviting you all. I think it's me who's been fucked over."

"Uh, excuse me?" Josh said, wagging the crystal dildo in front of them all. "Quinn got his dildo and nobody got fucked over. Except the ninja babes. So can we please move on?"

"No," Billie said. "I signed up to do disguises. Not almost get shot on account of some drunk klepto magician with a bad accent."

"People love my accent!"

"People! People? Hi, leader of the pack, here. We've got bigger fish to fry—as in the Olympus."

"Oh, right," Billie grumbled, standing and pacing the length of the room. "Because we're off to such a great start."

"We've had some setbacks, but—"

"But you're a wanker?" Quinn suggested.

Josh rolled his eyes. "Of the two of us, who cheats at Go Fish?"

"This is a nightmare," Billie said. "I'm going to go to prison with a bunch of idiots."

Just then, a young, freckle-faced kid in bellhop garb entered. "Uh, am I interrupting something?"

"We weren't talking about a burglary if that's what you heard," Josh said. "Tommy? Grab him."

After trying Kev's cell another three times, Brie headed home. She couldn't handle the coroner's office tonight, and the cop had advised she drink something. So, when she found a half bottle of Stoli in her freezer, she thought, *What else should I do?*

And what else *could* she do? It was either go to the hospital and accept the night's events, or run with the moment's clarity and get mind-bogglingly drunk. This was what people did, wasn't it? Drink away the bad news, suffer it through the lens of hangover tomorrow… She knew the reprieve wouldn't last, so she decided to crack the bottle and send herself on a trajectory towards passing out before it could catch up with her.

Cliché, maybe, but if it worked—why not? Numbness greeted her like a soggy blanket.

Everything was different, yet everything was exactly the same. Nothing about her apartment had changed: she still had the records, still had the couch and the comfy bed to flop into later.

Comfort is found in odd places. She threw on a CCR record and slumped on the couch.

She eyed her backpack, sitting on the coffee table, full of the journals she knew would send her spiraling back to crying fits and nausea. Well, fuck it. It was going to happen anyway, wasn't it? She could either drink and read, or drink and worry about Kevin. And—well—she couldn't handle any more worry in her nerve-jangled state.

So she grabbed her backpack and produced the leather-bound volumes. She selected the first one, swigged the vodka, and began to read. Maybe there'd be something in here that could help her piece together what had just happened. Probably not. But, worth a shot, right?

"Let the Midnight Special, shine a light on me," Fogerty sang.

Diary of Josie Siegel: October, 1987

Dave and I met the man today. We were at the Horseshoe and he just sort of appeared like he always does and gave us some dates to look up at the library. Weird, detective novel stuff.

David seems to trust him. But, I dunno—he gives me the willies. Sitting there, drinking booze like water, chain-smoking and whatnot... There's something shifty about him. Like he's got a bigger plan.

We still don't know we'll go through with it. It's crazy, right? Running off and doing the bidding of some weirdo you meet at a bar? Definitely bonkers territory. I told David. He hasn't seemed to listen, yet. Typical.

Friday was date night—you know, lacy underwear and all that— so we went to the Flamingo and got drunk on Mai-Thais. After considerably too many, we started working it out. The plan is this:

I, the conveniently-placed maid, will do some dusting and—when nobody's looking—I'll go into the big guy's office and swipe the diamond. Dave will be waiting out front in the Volks. So alls I have to do is book it and—oh, wait, it's definitely bad luck to explain your plan... Suffice it to say, we've got one.

Anyway, when we met the guy, I try to get more out of him.

I go, "Who is this Whelan cat? How'd he get the diamond to begin with?"

And he gets all fidgety.

So, after an inhuman amount of drinks, he spills. "Apparently way back," he says, "a certain relative of you, David, was partners with that snake-shagging fuckstick. Whelan betrays him, takes the diamond, and pow! All kinds of heinous shit transpires. Also, how about a few million for it? Would that shut you fucks up? I'm drinking here."

So now, Dave's obsessed. I think we might go through with it—I mean, with Brie, and planning to have another... We *do* need the cash. Time'll tell.

PART II
OH, INVERTED WORLD

"If you can't imagine it, think clumsy silence. Think bits and pieces of floating despair. And drowning in a train."
— Markus Zusak, *The Book Thief*

"Rage, rage against the dying of the light."
— Dylan Thomas

CHAPTER 13
THE BIG FAT DUH

Las Vegas, 1947

Benjamin "Bugsy" Siegel swirled ice in his tumbler. They'd closed about an hour ago: all the chairs turned up on tables, the lights low, and the coffers full of cash. For all its glitz and pomp, the Flamingo made a pretty good place to unwind when the doors were locked for the night.

Soon, he'd drive over to Adeline Cassiday's, a swell number: twenty-three, doe-eyed and all leg. But then, just showing up was a little lazy, wasn't it? No, it'd have to be a bottle of champagne, a rose from his garden, and probably a foot rub. For all the mistresses he had around the city—despite the fact he was involved in a long-term arrangement with his old lady in California—it seemed like the mobster could never escape foot rub duty on the way to a good fuck and a night's rest.

No matter. Fates worse and all that.

He slugged his whiskey, and was about to grab a refill when footsteps came from behind.

"Ya know, if you're trying to sneak up on me, you're doing a crap job of it."

"Why would I try to sneak up on you?" Gavin Whelan said.

Ben grinned and twisted to greet his business partner. "Thought you might be a woman."

"I get that a lot."

"Have a drink, Gav?" Bugsy motioned to the bottle on the bar.

Whelan waved him off and took the stool beside. "I can't stay."

"I know the feeling," Ben nodded. "I don't exactly have a date, but I'm thinking of changing my mind about that. What's up?"

Gavin sighed, planting his elbows on the bar. "Ben, you and I've been working together, what, a year now?"

"Damn fine year at that." Ben refilled his glass. *Here we go*. For the past three months, the kid had been badgering him to upgrade his share in the casino. Ben had dodged it as long as he could, but now…

"I want to know when we're going to revisit our arrangement."

Like the fucking clockwork. Bugsy sighed, shaking a cigarette out of his pack and sending a great cloud of smoke in the air when he lit it. "We've talked about this, Gav-oh. You've got your fifteen and you've been doing a crack job and all—"

"I've paid my dues," Gavin argued. "Attendance is up. We're booking all the big-timers. And you know I know what kind of profits we're turning."

Bugsy wagged his head. "Time's not right, kid. It ain't about success; it's about trust. Trust takes time. I promise, you'll get yours. Just not yet."

"Well, then, when? When, Ben?"

And here, the mobster's patience cracked. "When I fuckin' say so. Okay? I'm the guy at the top. I'm the one making the calls. Remember that."

Whelan rubbed his lip. "This isn't a partnership."

"Well, it is what it is."

Gavin sighed, patted the bar, and rose. "You're sure about this?"

"Surer than sure. You ain't ready, kid. Go get some rest."

With that, Ben turned back to the drink: *this-conversation-is-fuckin'-over*-like. He started thinking of Adeline and foot rubs again. Whelan's footsteps drifted away, then stopped a few paces out.

"I wish you'd reconsider."

"And I wish I could have one goddamn drink in my own bar without interruptions," Ben snapped, wheeling around. "Life ain't worth a shit wishin'—well, would you look at that."

Because Whelan had a .45 snub nose revolver—*his* revolver—pointed right at Ben's face. Brass fuckin' balls this guy had. Ben chuckled. "Kid, you know this ain't the first time I've had a gun pointed at me."

"Well, there's a last time for everything, Ben." Gavin pulled the trigger. The .45 slammed against his palm as the shot ripped through the air. The bullet went in through Bugs's eye, then mushroomed out the back of his head, spraying the bar with blood and chunks of bone.

"Huh," Ben said, then his good eye rolled up and he flopped off his stool like a sack of bricks.

Gavin took a breath. His ears were ringing. He didn't know where to go from here—he'd always planned to shoot the mobster, but hadn't thought of what would come next.

"Oh, balls. What the fuck did you do?"

Gavin wheeled around and found a sharp-featured brunette in a lacy dress coming over. She must've heard the sound from the street. She walked right past him and crouched in front of the body.

"Huh, that's different."

"I'm sorry," Whelan said, training the .45 on her. "You weren't supposed to see that—"

"Get that thing out of my face, fuckwad."

"But—"

In an instant, she was in front of him. She ripped the gun out of his hand and tossed it by Ben's body. "You have no idea what you just did, do you?"

"I—ah—I kinda shot my boss?"

"Yeah. Color that The Big Fat Duh." She sighed, raking her hands through her hair. "Somebody probably heard that. We'll need to move him."

"Wh… I mean who are you?"

"I'm your new best friend. What do you think about California?"

Gavin was having trouble following the woman's train of thought. "What are you talking about?"

"Guy's got a mansion in California, right? Let's put him there."

"But that's a three hour drive—"

"Yeah yeah, not what I asked. How about California?"

Too weird. The fact that he'd just killed a guy was enough. But this woman just showing up and babbling nonsense was too much. "What?"

"Forget it. Just come over here. Take my hand."

"How is that supposed—"

"Oh, Jesus. Just get over here and take my hand."

Despite himself, Gavin obeyed.

"There, was that so fucking difficult?" With her free hand, she grabbed Ben's corpse. "I'm Jezebel, by the way. You might wanna clench up. People hate this part."

There was a flash of blue, and the Flamingo was empty.

Brie held Kevin by the shoulder as the State PD debriefed them. In the room next door, the coroner pulled a sheet over Paul's body. It was a quiet morning at the hospital. A few orderlies chatted by a coffee maker. The nurse working the desk organized her files for the day. All details Brie took in because she'd take anything over listening to the officer, who spoke holding his hat at his chest.

Neither Brie or Kev heard it, but the gist was such: Paul had died of a knife wound to the sternum. The blade had nicked his right coronary artery. He'd probably bled out an hour before Brie found him. An investigation would be opened, but given the lack of fingerprints or murder weapon at the scene, it was doubtful they'd have answers any time soon. He gave them some paperwork, which Brie signed on autopilot, and disappeared through the entrance.

"I thought it'd take longer," Kevin said. "Not just 'He's dead. Here's some paperwork.' " He sighed, rubbing his eyes. "Just like that."

Brie didn't know what to say. She'd been feeling this a lot over the past twenty-four hours. No wise sisterly quips. No simple consolation. Just long, stupefied silence.

"You wanna get a coffee?"

Kevin nodded. Then he took her in his arms, and squeezed. They stood like that for a long time as the hospital drifted by around them. When he pulled away, both of their shoulders were wet with the other's tears.

At the cafeteria, they sat across from each other, weak coffee in styrofoam cups, stale doughnuts half-eaten on paper plates.

"I think I know who did it," Brie said. "When we were raiding the storage facility, he told me who he was paying off."

Kev chewed a chunk of doughnut. "Who?"

"Gavin Whelan."

"That's my boss," Kevin said.

"It gets weirder," Brie continued. "He said he was protecting us from him."

"Why?"

"He didn't say."

"It doesn't make sense," Kev said. "If I'm on his payroll, why would he even need Paul to find me?"

Brie winced at the sound of Paul's name. She'd been actively avoiding it. It was easier to talk about him that way. "But we both have Paul's last name, and like a million other people do, too. He was probably looking for us under Mom and Dad's name. We were hidden."

"I still don't get it." Kevin sighed, tossing the scrap of pastry onto the plate. "Why?"

"I found some of mom's journals in the storage locker. There's all kinds of stuff about a guy named Whelan. I think there's some family vendetta Paul was keeping from us."

"'Kay," Kev said. "But why would he kill him? If the only person who could tell him our identities was Paul—"

"Not the only person." Brie took a long breath. "When I found out, I told him."

"What?" Kev nearly knocked over his coffee with the hand gesture. "Why? Brie, why?"

"I thought I could take over the debt and keep you safe. I didn't know it would go this way. All this time, he's been fighting and it seemed so simple. I thought I could fix it, and now he's— and it's…" Tears welled in her eyes. Brie's chest felt like it was about cave in on itself. She couldn't handle it: losing Paul and now Kevin would know. "It's—*I* did this. It's—"

"It's not your fault," Kev said. He reached across and squeezed her arm. "You couldn't have known."

Brie wiped the snot from her nose. "You don't hate me?"

"No more than usual." Kev grinned, because it was his way of saying he loved her. "So, obviously we can't go to the cops. How do we make him pay?"

Jezebel sat at the bar of the Moonshiner Tavern on Fourth Street, guzzling an old fashioned. The goddess was troubled. Ever since she'd slipped the knife into Paul Cassiday's sternum, she'd been moody. She overslept, was rude to her barista at Starbucks, and had an inexplicable craving for Baskin Robbins. She moped. She pouted. And even though she'd hexed a man to fawn over her, repeatedly going, "Hey, you look familiar, can I buy you a drink?" with no recollection of the ten previous times he'd done it, she found no pleasure in the hijinks. She was in a funk. It bothered her.

She sloshed back her drink, flicked her finger in a spiral, and the man in gray linen came over, his tie loosened, hair askew. "Hey, you look familiar. Can I buy you a drink?"

"Old fashioned, extra bourbon, extra bitters, screw the orange."

The barkeep came back with the refill. Linen Guy said, "I'm Richard."

"Do I look like I give a shit?" Jezebel snapped. "You've done your thing. You can go. Come back in five minutes."

"Okay, enjoy your drink." Richard grinned, ambled back to his table, blinked a few times, and forgot.

It was weird. She'd killed dozens of people before—many of whom more innocent and most in far more interesting ways—and still, this one bugged her. She began to worry that spending so much time among mortals had softened her.

"Gee, it's almost—what's the word," a man said from beside her. "Oh, that's right, *human.*"

Jezebel grumbled, swishing the drink before her. "Well, at least I'm not—*what's the word?*—Oh, right. *Dead.*"

A cigarette lit. "Well, whose fault is that?"

"Yours," she sighed. "Idiot."

The ghost chuckled. "Well, at least I'm not going flooey."

"I am *not* going flooey. Go away."

"No." Ben Siegel made a smug grin. "Fun fact of the afterlife, toots. I don't hafta do shit unless I wanna."

Jezebel massaged her temples. "If you were alive, I'd pop your head like a zit, ass-monkey."

"Heh, good thing then, ain't it?"

"At least I don't look like a week-old hotdog," she said. "I do not need this right now, Ben. Fuck off. Go be creepy and shit."

"I'm haunting you. I thought you'd like it."

"I'd like you to go take a shower in hellfire."

"Heh. Well, things go your way, that might be the outcome."

"Not now," she groaned.

"Fine. I can see you're havin' a moment. Prolly 'cause you're a murdering floozy. Just a thought."

That was it. Jezebel coiled up and went to coldcock the specter in the chin, but when she wheeled around, he was gone.

"Hey," Richard said. "You look familiar, can I buy you a drink?"

"Dick!"

"...Yeah?"

After shaking stick for the third time to the memory of Sophie's topless backrub, Max Reyes was beginning to unravel. Here he was, Agent of the Bureau, wanking to the touch of a hooker. He'd been compromised. Between the professional implications and his staunch Catholic upbringing, the agent worried that either his palms would grow hair, or he'd get the call from Quantico dismissing him.

It was simple: he'd been alone too long, lost his bearings, and gone off the deep end. It was bound to happen. He'd just thought he'd had more time.

To celebrate, Max had ordered one of everything on the room-service menu. He sprawled across a bed at the Venetian, and relished at the idea of Harlan footing the bill. The bureau would never know—and at this point, he might as well enjoy himself. Max had been through hell, and he realized he'd never celebrated surviving it. He was always working. He never stopped to pat himself on the back, or—well… other places. He'd earned this. A vacation, or at least, something close to vacation. Also, he might be a bit drunk.

He sipped a fifty-dollar glass of merlot and watched the GPS tracker. It had been frozen on a location west of the Financial District since he'd left Harlan to work out his plan. It was comforting, knowing that despite the fact he was conning him, Harlan wasn't going anywhere. He knew he should be monitoring the grifter, but—well, he was, wasn't he? Maybe not the way he'd been trained to, but this was the best he could manage.

Maybe a bubble bath. A bubble bath would do nicely. It might help him concentrate on what to do next. He could always arrest them later, right? If not, well then, he'd take that long-due vacation. Screw ethics.

Tommy Carlyle considered himself an ethical criminal. He was driven by curiosity, believed he should be allowed to know anything that tickled his interest—and wouldn't let the legal system get in his way. It was a backwards sort of altruism that brought him to most of his antics. People had a right to know stuff, and nobody had a right to hide it from them. For country? For *safety*? He'd pored over dozens of classified files, and had never found a secret the public couldn't handle... Of course, a lot of them would spur calls for re-election, so maybe there was his answer. The point was, he broke the law, but only when doing so seemed worthy.

Harlan was the opposite. He broke the law because it was fun. Still, in the fifteen years they'd worked together, they'd established a trust. At the end of the day, the driving force was the same: they never stole from people who weren't bad news; never hurt anybody who didn't deserve it—in fact, from the hacker's perspective, they'd never done anything that didn't make the world a somewhat better place. Sometimes justice meant breaking the law.

Berlin, 1997. Tommy meets Harlan on a routine safecracking job, where at the last second, Harlan admits it's full of Soviet secrets he's been hired to retrieve. Also, the safe is uncrackable. Josh's endgame was stealing the entire safe—the result being a helicopter chase to a chartered jet in Turkey. A rough, nasty theft, with a lot of explosions and gunfire. It was here Tommy first suspected Josh of having a thing for action-movie endings.

Paris, 2001, where they conned an art thief into thinking the Manet they'd swiped from the Louvre was actually centerpiece to a cult of art worshippers. This one ended with Harlan faking his death at the hands of the cult. The painting was sold to New York's MoMa.

Brazil, 2006. They pretty much pulled an Indiana Jones—swiping a recently discovered Mayan artifact that was rumored to contain the spirit of a war god. The result was an airplane chase out of the country, followed by miffed archeologists, a disgruntled local government, and about two-dozen dart-blowing indigenous people who thought they'd stolen their god.

In all the past endeavors, he'd trusted Josh. Knew he could work them out of a bind if need be. But now, prodding around the digital defenses of the Olympus, knowing what Harlan was planning, Tommy was beginning to doubt.

"It's a crap idea," he said.

Harlan was splayed on the sofa next to him. "Why?"

"You know why. You are moderately very responsible for the death of her foster dad. You're suggesting using her vulnerable state to get what you want? It's a bad fucking idea, Josh." Tommy sighed, typing. "Moreover, it's just plain wrong. And did I mention it's bad?"

"It's not like that, buddy."

"Well, what *is* it like?" Tommy said. "Also? We need to get someone inside. I can't do shit from here."

"That's exactly my plan," Josh said. "We need her."

Tommy took a long breath. "And how do you, of all people, plan to make that happen?"

Josh shrugged. "I'm gonna give her a break."

"You know," Jezebel said. "I'm a little curious. How does Oz the Great and Powerful lose a couple of kids just because they changed their last names?"

Whelan sighed, checking his impatience. "Have you forgotten the twelve investigators we hired? Every time they got close, they'd call in saying that they'd fallen in love and quit the business."

"Yeah," Jezebel sighed, wistfully. "Detectives are such suckers for a good cliché."

Gavin sipped his whiskey. He knew the goddess was behind the disappearances. She'd never admit it, and he couldn't prove it, but he'd spent enough years in her company to know when he was being toyed with.

"You know, I am capable of telling the difference between a coincidence and a pattern."

"Well, pumpkin, if you'd stop hiring boozehounds with a hard-on for Marlowe, someone might get the job done."

"My resources aren't the problem," he said. "Maybe I should be blaming you. Maybe you're keeping them from me."

"*Moi?*" the goddess chuckled. "Gavin, you're wicked twisted. Just because I'm all-powerful doesn't make me all-knowing."

"So you say," Whelan sighed, pouring another drink. "But that secret seems like something you could uncover just by snapping your fingers."

"Woah, hey. A moment, please. I'm the god of luck. Not the Capital G." She finished her drink and motioned for a refill. "I'm not even sure that dude's still kicking. Besides, it's not like you're totally powerless."

It was true. In addition to binding the goddess's will, the diamond did grant him a certain license. You don't live for over a century—most of which in the company of a smarmy deity—without learning a few tricks. Time let him see the big picture. What happened before no longer mattered. He had the two final candidates in his scope. Now, it was a question of how to move next.

He could kill them, certainly. Once they were buried, he could relax; never fret over losing the diamond again. But the other thing so many years alive had done was strip him of feeling. It had been ages since he'd felt anything. Passion. Excitement. Uncertainty. In the final leg of catching his destiny, it all came crashing back. Being this close gave him a feeling he'd first mistaken for indigestion: anticipation. Perhaps they could live a while longer.

Besides, the one thing he hadn't found in all his years was the goddess's ability to see into the odds of things: the future—or, rather, *futures*.

"I'd still like to tap your foresight," he said, bringing Jezebel her refill.

"Well, precious, you whomped the hornet's nest," she said, taking a sip. "No matter how you swing it, they'll come at you with all they've got. And they're *totally* gonna join Harlan's little caper crew."

Gavin couldn't stifle the grin. He'd let Harlan live on the instinct that he'd become useful. Now it seemed all but kismet. Of course! The grifter was obviously plotting a strike against him for putting him in jail. Now that he'd killed the Cassidays' patriarch—a fact they'd no doubt figured—it was perfect: Whelan had turned himself into a common enemy. They'd attack together, and then he'd have them all where he needed to wipe the slate clean. Gavin wondered if he didn't inherit a bit of the goddess's foresight, not even realizing how he'd set himself up for this.

He raised his glass, then noticed his hand was wrinkled and veiny with the sheen of wax paper. His vision strobed. Gavin took a deep breath, calmed himself, and he was back to normal. The visions of his true age had been more frequent since he'd killed the last candidate. After Paul, they'd come almost daily. He blinked.

"Are you thinking over there?" Jezebel said, kicking her feet up on the table. "Or just strokin' out? No biggie. Just curious."

"You'll need to get close to them," Gavin said.

"Already done, pumpkin. Glad you're keeping up."

CHAPTER 14
REQUIEM

By the fifth grade, Brie was already running her first scam. Not a big one, but a scam any full-grown burglar would crack a smile over. Brie knew she was too smart for school. School was dumb. The teachers were more dumb. Her classmates were very dumb. And the peanut butter and banana sandwich Paul brown-bagged for her every morning was dumbest of all.

"It's good for you, honey," he'd say. "It'll make you grow up strong, and before you know it you'll miss how easy school is."

"But it tastes like bum," she'd reply.

Clearly, Paul didn't know what it was like. Still, since she respected the big man's wishes, she agreed to go to school with the dumb work and the dumb teachers and the dumb kids. But no way would she suffer the unnecessary dumbness of a PB&B sandwich.

And thus, a scheme was born.

"Wanna trade?" she said in the cafeteria.

"I dunno," said Matthew Fletcher, a ruddy-looking kid with a sand-colored bowl cut, eyeing Brie's drooping paper bag with suspicion. "What is it?"

"Peanut butter and banana."

"Eww. No thanks. That's gross."

"It *is* gross," Brie said, brandishing the bag like the Holy Grail. "That's why it's awesome."

Matthew shrugged, unconvinced. "What's it like?"

"It's like boogers."

"I don't know…" the Fletcher kid said, already thinking: *boogers are pretty awesome*.

"It makes you smarter," Brie said. "My dad told me."

"He's not your dad."

"I know. I just call him that. My real dad's dead."

Matthew shifted awkwardly. "Sorry."

"But he was really smart, too," Brie continued, sensing the hook. "And *he* ate PB&B all the time. My new dad says he built spaceships."

And here, she leaned back. Brie had learned pretty quick that second only to boogers, spaceships were the pinnacle of awesome for boys (and let's face it, those kids are onto something.)

"No way!"

"Yup."

"Like… the ones that go to the moon and stuff?"

"Yup."

"Okay. Deal." The Fletcher kid stuffed his hand into his jeans, scrambling.

Five minutes later, Brie was in line, ordering a grilled-cheese and chocolate milk, when a big, hairy adult hand landed on her shoulder. It belonged to Principal Weinstein: a towering, chunky penguin of a man.

"And how are we today, young lady?"

Brie shrugged his hand off. "Fine."

"Mister Fletcher tells me you traded a peanut butter and banana sandwich for three bucks. Is this true?"

"No," she said, twirling her pigtails. Normally, this was kryptonite for adults. "He tried to sell *me* his sandwich. I told him no. PB&B is nasty."

"Indeed," the Principal mused. "You know, taking money from other kids is wrong, Brie."

"I know."

"And if you ask me, three bucks for a peanut butter sandwich is pretty steep."

"I was gonna sell it to him for five!" *Oh... Crap.* Maybe not everybody at school was dumb.

Twenty minutes later, Brie sat in the office while the Penguin Man talked to Paul. She kicked at the carpet, enjoying the buzzing sound it made. Across the room, the secretary looked up from her paperwork and smiled.

"You want a lollipop?"

"Not really," Brie said. "I was gonna get a grilled cheese. Now my life is over."

"Oh, Brie. It's not that bad. The principal is just going to tell your dad what you did, then he'll take you home for the day..."

"And *then* my life is over," Brie suggested.

The secretary's face tightened. "Brie, your foster dad. He doesn't... You know... *Hit* you, does he?"

"No." Brie kicked the carpet again. "I was just being dramatic."

The woman looked surprised. She went to say something, when the principal's door flung open and Paul came out. In the background, Brie could see the Penguin Man holding his nose for some reason. Paul nodded at the secretary and came over. "Let's go."

In the parking lot, he put his arm around her shoulder. "So, I hear you're a master thief now."

"Principal Weinstein is a jerk."

"Yup," Paul said. "That's why I punched him in the face. So have you figured out the lesson, little amigo?"

"Yeah…" She pouted. "Don't steal."

Paul opened the door to the Buick and smiled as she climbed in.

"No, kiddo. The lesson is *don't get caught.*"

It was a cool November morning when Paul was buried in Woodlawn Cemetery. Brie and Kevin stood between Ruby Cobb and Jimmy Wok, across the coffin from a handful of cabbies, another handful of patrons of the bar Paul tended in Boulder, and a few hungry-looking men who'd said that Paul taught them everything they knew about counting shoe.

Ruby held Brie at the wake.

"I'm so glad you're here," Brie said.

Ruby's gaze was hidden by a lace veil. "Of course I am, doll."

Jimmy kissed her cheek. "Been to a lot of these. This one? I fuckin' hate it."

Brie chuckled and took the big man in a bear hug. "Thanks, Jimmy. Nice suit. Borrowed?"

"Stolen," said the forlorn Wok.

The priest talked about the sanctity of life. He talked about the ascension of the spirit. Then, he sang an Irish dirge. Brie held Kevin's hand as they watched the casket slip into the ground. She felt a tear roll down her cheek. Everyone stared at the ground while gray clouds rolled overhead.

Then came the condolences.

"I'm sorry for your loss."

"Sorry for your loss."

"I'm sorry."

"So sorry."

"Fucker always called me on being too drunk," said a wiry man in glasses. He grinned. "Good judgement."

"He taught me how to scam the tourists," a man in black corduroy mumbled.

Then a woman in an ankle-length charcoal chemise approached. She rested a hand on Brie's shoulder. "He let me blow him for cab fair in the '80s. Good guy."

After the crowd petered out, Brie, Kev, Ruby and Jimmy all stood around the grave, none of them talking. They just watched as it came to an end.

About a lifetime after that, when the backhoe came in, they headed for the gates of Woodlawn.

"I've got a lead," Ruby said.

"Gavin Whelan," Brie said. "Yeah."

"Turns out he's the guy Harlan's after."

"Fuck that guy," observed Jimmy.

Brie kissed his cheek. "It's a lot more than that, too. From what I read."

"Mom's journal?" Kev said.

Brie nodded.

"Well then," Ruby said. "What better way to get back than—"

"I'm in."

"That was fast," Kev said.

Ruby nodded. "I'll do some talking."

Jimmy Wok wasn't so convinced. "Woah, wait. Brie, I know shit's fucked up. But didn't I hit that guy like a day ago?"

"You did," she said with a shrug. To Ruby: "Do what you need."

Rubes gave her another hug, then headed for a town car, producing her phone. It didn't matter any more. The way she'd pull it off was a nonentity. What mattered was vengeance. If she found that with Harlan? Good. She'd kill him afterwards.

To Kevin, "So, beer? Copious amounts?"

Kevin frowned. "Uh, I'm kinda their ride."

Brie wagged her head. "Bro, just because I'm doing something doesn't mean—"

"They need a driver," Kev said. "I'm not gonna do *nothing*, Brie. I'm sorry. It's just… I'd love to go for beers. I'd love nothing more. But I can't. Work to do, and whatnot."

Brie nodded, hoping she was hiding any sadness that might give her away. "I get it. I'll see you soon, broheim."

Kevin clenched his lip, then climbed into the town car after Ruby Cobb. They drove off.

He'd taken her payout, her best friend, and now her brother— he'd taken everyone from her. Yes, this was it. Brie was going to kill Josh Harlan. How didn't matter. Sooner would be better.

So they met on the overpass to New York, New York. Harlan was watching the cars pass along Las Vegas Blvd., wearing a blazer, one of those floppy driver hats, and a Zeppelin T-shirt. As Brie approached, he turned and flashed a grin.

"Can I have my goatee back?"

"Nope."

"Okay, but you should know it was borrowed and expensive."

If it weren't for the chain link dome covering the footbridge, Brie would have chucked him into oncoming traffic right there.

"Don't care," she said. "So a little Ruby told me you're working a job on Gavin Whelan."

"Per-maybe-haps. Why?"

Yup, she totally should've opened with socking him. Now he was milking it. Fucker. "I want in."

"You were in the moment you stole my Monopoly money." Another grin. "And speaking of which—"

"Nope." Oh, great. Now she was seething. Every tendon in

her body screamed *Hit him! Hit him! Hit him!* "That stunt got somebody killed, you know."

"Sorry." He shrugged, without a trace of sincerity. "But it also got your attention, didn't it?"

Brie raked her hands through her hair. "You're insane."

"Eccentric," Josh corrected. "Lot of people make that mistake."

"And missing the point. If it weren't for you, he'd still be alive."

"Uh, yeah. If I recall—and I am little fuzzy after getting beaten with a shoe—you *stole* it. I didn't ask you to take it, and there's no way I could know what the stakes were. Look, I could bullshit you. I could say *sorry* 'til the cows come home, but there's no angle where I change your mind. Either way, here you are, looking to join my band of bandits."

"Thieves," Brie said.

"Huh?"

"It's band of *thieves*, moron."

Harlan stared off into the night, thinking. "Damn. You're right. Honestly, Brie, I gave you the duffel hoping you'd join, and here you are." He shrugged. "That was my only intent."

Brie sighed. Clearly, this was as close an apology as she'd get from this sociopathic douche. "You are a sociopathic douche."

Josh nodded. "Again, my reputation does the preceding thing."

"So I hope we're clear," she continued. "The reason I'm coming aboard isn't you. Gavin Whelan killed my father. I want twenty minutes in a room with him to find out why. You get me that, I'll help you."

Harlan chewed his lip, thinking, then said, "Done. Now do you want to hear my plan? Or should I see a go-go dancer named Miss Galaxy and call it a night?"

Brie rolled her eyes. "Where to?"

The grifter waved toward the entrance to New York, New York.

"What are we gonna do in there?" She sighed. Not even five minutes and she was already exhausted by him. This was every bit as bad as she'd expected.

"See a go-go dancer named Miss Galaxy," Harlan said. "And I'll tell you the plan. You don't get woozy, do you?"

It turned out Miss Galaxy was not only a fiercely territorial stage presence for a gal in her undies; she was also well-connected, and had managed to procure the item Harlan asked for. Brie watched as the dancer produced a small black case from somewhere no such thing should be kept, and Harlan put it in his jacket.

He returned with a grin. "This way."

They threaded through the miniature knockoff of NYC's Meatpacking District. Brie frowned. "Nu-uh. You just took a package from a stripper's package, and I am *not* going to a hotel room with you. I know how that ends."

Harlan laughed. "It came from behind her. She's a go-go dancer, not a stripper. And we're not going to a hotel room." They reached a row of elevators. "We're going to the roof."

And so, the first encounter Brie had with Josh in earnest was a roller coaster—literally. They've got one of those on the roof of the casino.

There is a weird kind of anonymity a roller coaster provides: It's populated, but everyone's too preoccupied with whirling around the roof of a casino to eavesdrop. It runs a fixed amount of time, has minimal surveillance for lack of a way to descramble the audio, and it's conveniently out of earshot for certain writer-types who might scribble down the plan.

When they climbed off the ride, Brie said, "Let's get a drink."

"*D'accord,*" Josh said in his improbable accent. Now that she was sober, Brie couldn't believe she'd fallen for it.

"You really need to work on that."

He took her to the martini bar at Aria, where they had fresh truffles with their drinks. Brie wasn't so much taken with Josh's tastes as she was with the taste of fresh truffles. (Which are awesome, by the way.) She barely listened while he gabbed about some FBI guy he was conning, and stealing a dildo from a whorehouse with his magician buddy.

From what she did gather, it sounded like she'd just signed up with a bunch of fucktards who were bound to get caught—after all, they *had* taken Kevin. She was glad to know her end of the job was safecracking, and after another round they'd figured out how to get her her time with Whelan.

Then, they had another round, went bowling at Circus Circus and ate *Pink's* chili dogs. After that, Harlan took her on a tour through her city that was a surprisingly fresh riff on an old tune.

He'd clearly been to Vegas many times, but the way Josh showed it, the Neon City came off re-imagined. He led her through casinos, playing slot machines for fun rather than profit. He walked her down the Strip, where they slurped huge cups of slush-flavored vodka. He told her stories of crimes-past. They made fun of buskers, dodged clappers handing out call-girl cards, and played a game of drunken pickpocket with the droves of tourists moving around them.

Somewhere in it all, Brie lost herself. She rediscovered laughter. She rekindled excitement, and despite her bummed-out day, she was having fun. For a moment, she forgot her reasons for being here. No responsibilities. No baggage. Just movement.

Then, in front of the Bellagio's fountains, it crawled up her spine like a twelve-inch scorpion. Brie stood next to Josh Harlan, completely and utterly horrified: she'd enjoyed herself.

And he'd made her feel this way. He'd conned her into feeling better. The truly scary part was, she'd sort of known the whole time, and she'd let it happen. In fact, part of her had wanted—no—*needed* it.

Okay, Brie thought. *So he's definitely evil...*

CHAPTER 15
GROUNDWORK

Quinn Donovan was slumped on the couch in the brainstorm room, magician's hat pulled over his eyes, snoring like a phlegmy air-conditioner. He dreamed of hookers (a regular occurrence) and was just getting to the fun bit when he was awoken by a stern elbow to the ribs delivered by Billie Black.

"What?" he snorted. "What?"

"So that's the plan," said Josh Harlan, standing next to a projector displaying schematics of the casino on the wall. The rest of the gang sat in a half-horseshoe on the couches. "Questions?"

"Nope," they said in chorus.

Well, clearly Quinn had some catching up to do. "Just the one," he said. "What was the sodding plan?"

To his left, Ruby Cobb raised an impatient eyebrow. "Seriously? He just finished explaining."

"Well, I missed that," Quinn sighed, adjusting his hat. "Bloody passed-out, wasn't I?"

Brie Cassiday, next to Kevin on the opposite couch, stood,

running her hands through her hair. "Can we get back to the point, please?"

"Well, I think knowing what I'm meant to do is a bloody point."

The redhead shot him a death glare, which Quinn considered a compliment. Ever since she'd turned up, the thief had been running a short fuse. Quinn rather enjoyed testing it. Sure, Brie probably wanted to run his bollocks through a blender, but she was quite lovely when angry.

Harlan sighed, tossing the remote for the projector on the coffee table. "You seriously KO'd for the big explain?"

"It's pretty integral," Tommy added, crossing his arms.

"Well, *excuse* me," Quinn huffed. "When I went out you lot were talking about *Pokémon*. Thought I had time is all."

Tommy pointed furiously. "Charmander is *not* irrelevant!"

"Yes," Brie groaned. "He is."

Tommy looked at Harlan, holding his arms out, bewildered. "I can't work with these people."

"I actually agree with Tommy," Kevin said. "Charmander is adorable"—then, thinking he might benefit from a dose of machismo—"and *badass*."

Brie gave him a rueful stare. "You're lucky I love you."

Ruby rubbed her eyes, head sinking into the couch. "I hope they have death in prison."

"Uh, folks?" Harlan said. "Can we try on some optimism? I just told you my plan and haven't had a single compliment. A lesser man would be self-conscious."

Quinn felt like he'd been hit with a bag of cinderblocks. "Oh, I need a drink."

"Haven't you had enough?" Brie glared.

"Gal's got a point," Ruby agreed.

"I—well—probably, but—"

"People love my plans," Harlan said, slumping on the couch. "Tommy? Back me up."

The beefy hacker tilted his head. "Slideshows and everything."

"So will somebody give me the sodding Cliff's Notes?"

"Slideshows aren't going to get us into the impenetrable safe," Brie said.

"I actually found them helpful," said Kevin.

"I knew working with you was a bad idea."

"Excuuse me?" Quinn sighed. These gits were bloody hopeless.

"Maybe we can find another safecracker," Harlan said to Tommy.

"Oh, so now I'm the problem?" Brie snapped.

"Sure, Josh." Tommy said, rolling his eyes. " 'Cause that's suddenly an option. Didn't you specifically say—"

"CAN EVERYBODY SHUT THE FUCK UP FOR THIRTY SECONDS, PLEASE?" Billie stood, hands balled into fists.

Wildly, everyone did.

She took a breath, then to Quinn: "The Cliff's Notes: we're gonna infiltrate a casino with an improbable security system that already knows half of our faces. Hack a system that can't be hacked. Break into an elevator that won't move without an eyeball..."

"And we can't fake an eyeball," Tommy added.

"...We can't fake an eyeball. Then you steal an impossibly huge diamond from an impossibly weird location. Meanwhile, Brie cracks an impenetrable safe."

"It's not actually impenetrable," Brie corrected.

Billie waved her off. "Don't break my focus. So we pull another improbable feat and not only rob the place, but walk out the door and drive off into the sunset in yet another impossible scheme."

"Improbable," Harlan said.

Billie wagged her head. "What?"

"He's right," Ruby said.

"It's improbable," Brie said. "But totally within the realm of possibility."

Bille sighed, slumping her shoulders. "Thanks, grammar hammer."

Quinn rubbed the back of his neck, letting the information whirlwind sink in. "So, what you're saying is, we'll very probably get caught?"

Harlan grinned. "Exactly."

"Right," the magician said. *Bugger it.* "Crack on, then."

It started with a delivery of three-hundred pounds of sheet metal, two mechanic's workstations with professional arrays of tools, an acetylene torch, fifty feet of sculptor's styrofoam, a small kiln, a roller board, and a bottle of Glenfiddich to taunt Quinn with. Then, everybody went to work.

Snippets beneath the neon bigtop of Circus Circus: drifts of mullets, a middle-aged woman pushing a baby stroller full of chihuahuas, families snapping pictures of the mullets. A trapeze act featuring werewolves in clown outfits in the main amphitheater. A handful of apparently unattended preteens gleefully brutalizing a whack-a-mole stand. It was… Well, it was a circus.

Billie Black sat at a NASCAR-themed bar, nursing a gin and tonic with a curly straw. A man in a bowler hat and a hot-pink cutoff hoodie emerged from the throng of weirdos, carrying an oversized suitcase. He sat next to her and ordered a screwdriver. His name was Vermeet.

Billie passed him a cash-filled envelope under the bar.

"No problems?"

Vermeet nodded. "Four pounds powdered latex. Two of rubber cement and all the brushes, knives and scissors you need, my dear."

"The silicone and the fake hair?"

"Should be in tomorrow or the next. I gotta say, Billie, this is a big order for you. Whatcha cooking?"

"It's a thing," she said, slurping her drink. "A secret thing... I mean, a set—It's a secret set thingie."

"I see," he said, which he didn't.

"It's not for crime, if that's what you're implying." Then, feeling like she'd just confessed to murder, Billie stood. "I gotta go."

Vermeet shrugged. "Toodleoo."

Back at the abandoned mall, Tommy sat in the makeshift kitchen they'd erected in the shell of what would have become a Starbucks. The guts were all there: the stools, bar and counter already installed. The brewing stations had never arrived, so a drip coffee machine sat in their place, somewhat dwarfed by the bar.

He hunched over his MacBook, humming Vivaldi's *Spring* while he weilded a torrented copy of Photoshop. The coffee-maker bubbled and groaned ominously, and—not for the first time—he longed for a green-aproned twentysomething failed by the corporate education system to make him an espresso.

He was creating fake IDs that Brie, Billie and Kevin would use. Billie had given him some rough sketches of her plans by way of disguises, and he was editing their headshots to match. His fingers moved across the keyboard with nimble fluidity, fast and elegant. When he finished the pictures, he'd upload them to the proper databases to tie off their aliases. But for now, he coasted.

The coffee maker sputtered and beeped. He went over, poured himself a cup, sipped, and sighed wistfully.

"Again, the Photoshop whiz is under-compensated," he said, to no one in particular. "Typical."

Tell me about it, bubbled the coffee maker.

The main foyer of the mall was all high ceilings and dusty concrete. A fountain sat in the middle of a wide arc that branched off into the building's hallways. Twin escalators, tarped-over when the investors had bailed, led up to the second story, which opened up in a wide gallery overlooking the fountain. A magnetic winch was fixed to the domed ceiling, whirring fervently as Brie Cassiday descended the two stories on a nylon cord, going, "Woooooooooh!!!!!"

On the ground level, Kevin sat cross-legged against the fountain, leafing through an armored vehicle manual, sighing. "Oh yeah. You've got this. All the pros go 'Woooooh!!!!' "

Brie landed on the floor, catching her breath, feeling the flush in her cheeks. "Oh, it's fun. You remember fun, right? I hear it's… well, *fun*. You wanna try?"

Kev eyed the nylon harness, thinking: *that's gotta deliver the world's biggest wedgie.* "I think I'll stick to driving."

Brie adjusted the harness, thinking: *If it weren't for thongs, this would be the world's biggest wedgie.*

" 'Kay. Suit yourself."

She pressed a button on the thumb-mounted controller, and the winch pulled her back up, dangling from the ceiling like a spider.

"I'm just glad I get to do the thing Paul taught me," Kev said. "I think he'd be proud of that."

Another whoosh. Brie was back on the ground. "Are you saying my part would bore him?"

"No, I don't mean that. It's just..."—he sighed—"Everything he's ever taught us—I think he'd be proud, wherever he is."

Brie unlatched the harness from the great carabiner and adjusted the straps. Okay, maybe it *was* worse than thongs. She stared out the frosted glass running the front of the building, feeling the sinking feeling in her gut that she'd been adjusting to for the past three days. Grief is like gravity: you may not notice it, but it's always there. And when you least expect, it tugs.

"What if he's nowhere?"

"Huh?" Kev tossed the manual away, rubbing his brow.

Brie went over and flopped on the floor beside him. "I've been thinking about it a lot. What if... What if he's just—you know—*gone*?"

Kevin shook his head. "I don't accept that. He's dead, but that doesn't mean he's gone. You don't just stop because life does. I don't know if it's an afterlife or whatever... But I just know. Wherever he is—however he's there—I just know. Like I can feel it. And I'm sure he'd love how we're avenging him."

Brie tried to look him in the eye, but Kevin stared off at a point on the floor intently, nodding; the hint of a grin. She took a long breath. She liked what she heard, wanted to believe, but from what she knew—how she felt—she couldn't. To Brie, a hole had been ripped in the world: the place Paul had filled. Now it was empty, and he was gone—just gone. She didn't get it. How could her brother maintain this kind of optimism? They hadn't been raised spiritually, so...

"How can you know that?" she said, staring at the ceiling.

"Because I have to." Kevin shrugged, eyeing the winch above. "So how does it work?"

Elsewhere, Ruby Cobb sat on the derelict counter of what could have been a jewelry store, watching as a big-ass counterfeit diamond crashed to the floor next to a wood podium.

"Bollocks!" Quinn Donovan howled, frustration strumming angry chords on his psyche.

Ruby chuckled. "I think more *sleight* and less *hand* next time."

"I can't bloody concentrate." The magician massaged his wrist, fuming as he circled the podium. A bead of sweat trickled over his temple.

"Don't you do this for a living?"

Quinn nodded. "Usually there's a healthy dose of whiskey involved. How long?"

Ruby looked at her watch. "Two hours. You seriously can't handle a movie without drinking?"

"What would the fun in that be?" He grinned, weakly. "Two hours, that's long enough, innit? Let's celebrate with a—"

"You make the switch clean, once? I'll let you have a shot."

"I'd do better with the short first and the bottle after, love."

Ruby sighed. What, did people normally find this guy's accent charming or something? How dare he call her *love*? He didn't even know her—not even her last name… In fact, it was a miracle he even knew what he was doing at all.

"If Whelan smells booze on you, you won't even make it past the lobby. You need to be sober. Now—"

"Have none of you people heard of breathmints?" Quinn grumbled. "Look, it's not like it's showtime or anything. *One* drink, puppet. I'm bloody dying here."

"Call me *puppet* again, and you truly will be," Ruby said through clenched teeth.

"I just don't think it's a good idea," said Billie Black.

"Every act of genius starts off with a bad idea," said Harlan.

The Fremont TruckLot: an arcade of chunky tire, gleaming bumper and high-powered diesel, where miles beneath the topsoil long-dead sauropods mourned the guzzling of their liquified kin. Josh and Billie walked, browsing.

"I don't get why you couldn't find a magician who already got his white chip in AA," Billie said. "I know a guy. It's not too late to enroll him."

"He's Irish," Harlan said, as if that explained it all—which in his mind, it did. "We can get him sober for two hours. Besides, breathmints'll probably cover it."

"Fine, but that still leaves the rest of the team."

"What about them?"

"Well, they kinda hate each other. And definitely you."

"Pre-show jitters," Josh said. Every team he'd assembled always went through a period of hating or not trusting each other—usually focusing their issues on him. Eventually it would break. It always did. "You know, this isn't my first rodeo. Trust me. By the end of this, everybody will be best friends. Let's do the thing."

As if on cue, an enormous man in a white linen suit came over. "Well, now. What do we have here?" he said with a syrupy drawl. "A couple? Lookin' for an affordable Caravan, perhaps?"

"Nope," Harlan said, feeling a chill run up his spine. He was a con artist, and for conmen, there are few things as terrifying as the car salesman. It was like looking in a fun-house mirror at your craft: a painter seeing the world through finger-paint. "Billie? Tell him."

The salesman grinned. "A matriarch, now? Well, bless my jumbly jowls. I ain't seen one of those in—"

"We need two F800s," Billie said, with a look as if she'd just stepped barefoot in cat-sick.

"My, those are powerful beasts. I happen to have two, just this way. Y'all follow me, now. I'm Lionel, by the by."

As they followed the great gabardine man across the lot, Billie whispered, "Is this guy for real?"

Harlan wore a grim expression. "Just don't ask any questions and we might get through this with our ears attached."

In front of the two behemoth trucks—which looked kind of like the front of a semi-truck attached to a sixteen-foot flatbed—Lionel beamed. "The finest of the fleet. Big enough to haul a dead horse across state, if you're needing that sorta thing…"

"We'll take them," Harlan snapped.

"Might I interest you in the four year insurance plan? We've got a special runnin' for twenty-thousand. It's a steal—"

Harlan stuffed a wad of bills in the man's meaty paw. "Take that, come back with the keys, and please, whatever you do, just stop talking."

Lionel made a look as if to say: *how dare you assault my unflappable Southern Charm?* Then he eyed the stack of cash and brightened. "Back in a jiffy, y'all."

When Lionel waddled away to whatever hell he came from after giving them the keys, Josh and Billie were panting.

"That was fucked-up," she said. "That was super fucked-up."

Josh squeezed her shoulder, steadying. "I know."

"I feel like there are ants under my skin."

"Speaking of, I've got a pit stop to make," Harlan said, then dangled the keys as if they were crack treats for effects specialists. "Race you home?"

Sundown. Max Reyes sat in a rental Prius, parked across the street from the abandoned mall, rubbing a fresh nicotine patch on his arm. By day three of watching the frozen blip on the GPS tracker, Max began feeling like he was being taunted, so here he was.

Why he was drawing it out was beyond him. It wasn't like he

wasn't supposed to know what the thieves were up to. But years of law enforcement had made him wary of entering buildings. Not that he needed it, but Max felt naked without a warrant or at least probable cause—the only training he could fall back on was *knock-and-announce*.

So there was his plan: just roll in, knock, and announce. "Hey guys, what's up?" Like he was supposed to be there. Like part of the team. Besides, he actually *was* part of the team. It wasn't like he was going to bust them or anything. Just checking in.

He climbed out of the Prius and headed for the entrance, when a beautiful, sharp-featured woman in blue pinstripe intercepted.

"What are you doing here?"

Without thinking, Max fell back on cop-speak. "I'm asking the questions here." Before the words even left his mouth, he could feel them wither on the air. The woman gave him a chagrined expression.

"Olivia Figg-Newton," she said, flashing a badge. "Interpol."

"Max Reyes," he said, going for his own badge and coming back with a room service menu. "FBI... I usually have a badge."

Figg-Newton didn't miss a beat. "You know who's in that building?"

Max nodded. "One of them is my CI."

"Like fuck he is," she snapped. "Two of them are on my watch list, and I've been given a tip that they're planning a big job on one of the casinos."

"Wait, wait." Reyes went to wave her down. "I can explain—"

"For all I know mister FBI guy without a badge, you're one of them."

"I'll radio my super," he said. "Two seconds."

He went back to the Prius for his CB, when he felt a sharp crack in the back of his neck. The street flickered, and he was out.

"Figg-Newton? Seriously?" said Jezebel, slipping the nightstick back into her purse. "Amateur."

She sighed, fished the keys out of the agent's pocket, then dumped him in the trunk and peeled away.

CHAPTER 16
TITS-UP

Beverly Hills, 1947

Virginia Hill's mansion was all white with country blue trimming. A wide porch hugged the front of it, manicured lawn rolled down to the street.

The sun still hadn't risen, and all the lights inside the place were out. Gavin followed Jezebel up the walkway to the front door, the body of Ben Siegel slung over her shoulder like a dead pig.

Gavin was still adjusting to the fact that a moment ago, he'd been in the middle of the Flamingo, standing next to the woman by the corpse. Then, the sensation of digesting bad seafood, and now, here. All in a flash of blue. It was as real as when he'd pulled the trigger on Bugsy. Real, but still so much impossible to accept. So he followed. Jezebel adjusted her grip on the dead man and threw open the door.

"Come on," she said.

Gavin couldn't shake it. "How did we—"

"Magic. Come."

He followed her into the moonlit foyer. She took a right down the hallway and went through a set of french doors into the study. Inside was a wall of expensive-looking books; a large maple writing desk in front of bay windows overlooking the porch. Next to the desk was a couch and a leather chair with tattered corners—clearly the kind of thing Ben did a lot of sitting in when he got to visit.

Jezebel was apparently thinking the same thing. She dumped the corpse in the chair. She adjusted him, then took a step back—the painter adjusting perspective.

"What d'you think?" she said, putting her hands on her hips. "Does it work for you?"

"Honestly, I'm still working on how we got here," Gavin said. He was too jangled to judge the staging of a body—hell, he hadn't even fully accepted shooting the guy.

As if she could hear him thinking, Jezebel nodded. "There's some stuff I should probably teach you."

"Me?"

"Sure. You're the new keeper of the diamond. Might as well know what she's capable of before you take her out for a spin."

"But... Ben said you needed the words to have the diamond?"

"Exactly, pumpkin," Jezebel said, brushing her hair from her face. "Just say, 'When the goddess rolls, her dice are loaded.' "

"When the goddess rolls, her dice are loaded?" Whelan wagged his head. He'd been expecting some ancient incantation—Aramaic or Latin or something... "That's it? What is that?"

She shrugged. "It's an old Greek thing."

Somehow, the conversation had brought Gavin back to an objective state. He looked at the body and started thinking. It looked good—well, *dead*, but well-placed. There was just the one thing: "What happened to the bullet?"

"You should know. It fucking killed him, didn't it?"

Whelan tipped his head toward the body. "Not what I meant."

"Ah, right." She bit her lip and began wandering the room, as if looking for a set of lost keys. She circled around behind Bugsy, eyes narrowing. A grin spread across her face. "How about…"

She snapped, and the window exploded, spraying glass all over the living room as Ben's body writhed in the chair. Bullet holes appeared in his sternum, his head, and strafing the bookshelf behind.

"That better, pumpkin?"

Gavin had jumped a good four-feet in the air. He squeaked, "…Uhuh?"

"Swell. Time to go." She chuckled, grabbing his hand and yanking him back through the foyer.

When they reached the lawn, the shock began dissipating.

"So… You can do magic?" Whelan said.

"Sweetie, it's easy. Let me show you."

Another flash of blue, and they were gone.

Steve Halverson was next to Phil Gibbons in the Perch. They were running data from the past three nights, finding the best way to exploit clientele for the upcoming grand opening. So far, they'd learned pumping a hint of thorazine with about three micrograms of nitrous oxide into the air seemed to get people in the best mood for spending—especially with the tiny amount of Ecstasy syphoned into the bars. A perfect cocktail.

"So, like… does he wear a crown?" said Steve.

"No, no," Gibbons said, slugging the rest of his coffee (which also had a hint of X in it). "His title is self-appointed. Kid just turned twenty-one. His dad bought him an island, so he declared himself prince. The locals haven't even met him."

"Gee, and I thought my childhood was rough." Steve grinned. "When's he in?"

"Friday. The room's already set up with towers of booze and a ball pit."

"Gentlemen," said Gavin Whelan, appearing behind them.

Steve tried to conceal the shudder running up his spine. No matter how many times the boss did the magic appearing thing, well, it just freaked Steve out.

"Hey boss," said Gibbons. "We were just talking about our upcoming guest."

The tycoon nodded. "Everything in order?"

"Seems like," said Steve. "You want a copy of the itinerary?"

Whelan paced the curve of the Perch, watching the video feed of the casino running on the opposite wall. "I'm here on different business."

"More villainous antics?" said Gibbons.

Steve glared at him: *Dude, shut up.*

Whelan looked confused. "Villainous?"

"Yeah," said Phil. "Like more evil-plan type stuff?"

"I don't think evil is—" Whelan sighed. "It's... *necessary.*" And here, he gave a look of genuine concern, as if the villainy of killing three people in the past week while plotting another two murders had never occurred to him. "How are the fields holding on the slots?"

"Like a peach." Halverson hammered some keys on his console and brought up a big green status-bar. "We keep running like this, by opening night, we should be able to get you another ten, maybe twenty years without anybody feeling like they missed it."

The tycoon nodded, examining his hand while he balled it up and loosened it repeatedly. Steve noticed the shock of gray hair strafing Whelan's crown had spread. He looked... well, older.

"It's not enough. The effects of dispensing with the candidates are getting worse. I'm sure you've noticed." Here, Whelan motioned to his salt-and-pepper.

Steve and Phil shared a problem-solving gaze. "We could crank up the juice? Get you another ten or so per night?"

"More," Whelan said, his voice almost a whisper. "I need much more than that."

"You're talking about big dump?"

Whelan slumped his shoulders. "You still haven't changed the name?"

Phil shrugged. "We've been busy."

"I'll make some calls," said Steve. "And for what it's worth, boss... I think it looks distinguished."

"You're gonna be okay, Kev." Billie was under one of the Ford F800s, welding a nine-foot roll cage to the flatbed, and for a second, it appeared as if the truck were talking and smoking.

Kevin was perched on a stool, like Rodin's *Thinker*, offset slightly by the giant plaster dome around his head. His nose was full of the smell of stale coffee-breath, beer, and plaster—which smelled kind of like feet.

They were in the makeshift garage set up in the receiving area of the mall. A mechanic's paradise: a wall-to-wall array of tools, a corner-section workbench where a six-pack sweated. The rest of the shop was given to the two behemoth trucks, and enough sheet metal to roof a small village. It was cool, dark, and oily. Exactly the bare-bulb sort of setup you'd expect from a special effects master's lair.

About an hour ago, Billie applied plaster to Kevin's face to form the bust she'd work off to make his disguise. She'd given him a beer, let him drink, then wrapped the plaster and stuck a straw in his mouth to breath through. She worked on the trucks while they waited.

Hands pressed against the crown of his head. "Hold still. You're gonna be fine."

A crackling sensation, and air sucked in as the plaster lifted off his face. He rubbed his eyes, taking great gulps of fresh air. Billie stood before him, holding two nearly perfect halves of the mould.

"It smells like balls in there."

"Well, duh, goofball," she chuckled. "It's plaster, not a facial. Gimme a hand."

Kevin got off the stool and Billie handed him a pair of tongs. She guided him over to a small kiln and popped open the lid. A corona of heat came off the opening. Kevin deposited the shell into the kiln, moving like a lab worker handling plutonium. Billie slammed the lid, set a timer, and cracked two beers.

"You know, I wasn't just talking about the plaster when I said you'll be okay."

"I know." Kev gulped his beer. "I also know you're making me help you to keep my mind off shit."

"Never said I wasn't," Billie said. "I lost my dad, too. I know how it feels. How it hurts."

Kev nodded, picking at the label on his bottle. "Was it sudden?"

She smiled softly and shook her head. "No. It wasn't. But I'll tell you this: go easy. It doesn't ever really get better, I won't bullshit you. But you do learn how to deal with it."

Kev drained the rest of his beer with a sigh. "I keep having all these flashes. Weird moments we had together. Like him teaching me to fish. This time I shot him in the nuts with a paintball gun. A whole bunch of brunches. It's like they won't stop coming, and every time feels like *I'm* the one getting nutted by the paintball."

Billie put a hand on his shoulder. "Eventually, those flashes will be the best part of your day. It's how we remember folks."

"I guess it just doesn't seem like enough," Kevin said. Odd, he'd been keeping strong for his sister, and now, talking to a woman he barely knew, everything just came out like hangover puke. "Like, a whole person just becomes snippets, and then that'll fade away. It's… Well, it sucks."

"I know, sweetheart." She squeezed his arm. "Why don't you tell me about him?"

Kev took a breath and tried to figure out how to begin the story of Paul Cassiday. That's when howling came from somewhere in the guts of the building.

Across town at the Venetian, Jezebel pulled the agent's Prius into the roundabout. She gave the keys to a bellhop and hauled the unconscious Reyes out of the trunk. Strangely, this didn't throw the bellhop at all. He bounced a quizzical brow as Jezebel draped Reyes over her shoulder.

"Too many drinks," she said, patting his butt. "Bad idea, taking your husband to a strip club in Vegas. Tell your friends."

She swept through the casino to the elevators and fished Max's room key out of his pocket. She climbed on and hit the button for his floor. Then, she made a pit stop on the way to his room to grab a carton of cigarettes from a vending machine. She strolled down the hall, the comatose agent bouncing against her hip.

They reached the room. She swiped the key and slipped inside.

Without even looking around, Jezebel hauled Reyes into the bedroom, tossed him on the bed, and straddled him. She found his handcuffs sitting atop his luggage and latched him to the bedpost, nibbling his ear as she did it. He didn't stir.

Then she grabbed him by the belt buckle and tore off his pants. She ripped open his shirt and removed his shoes and socks. Once he lay, naked and spread-eagle on the bed, she opened the pack of cigarettes and lit one.

She went out to the minibar in the living room and poured

herself three fingers of Bushmills. Then, she popped her head back into the bedroom.

"Hey Maxy, everybody likes a smoke after. Here." She tossed the pack on the bed, grinning at the label which read: SURGEON'S WARNING: CIGARETTES CAUSE EXCRUCIATING DEATH.

Then, she went back to the living room, took the bottle of Bushmills, had another drag of her cigarette and tossed it onto the low-pile shag carpet by the couches. It smoldered as she slipped out of the suite, hanging the DO NOT DISTURB sign on the doorknob.

Inside, thick black smoke churned out of the carpet as the polyester shriveled. An orange tongue of flame licked the air, inspiring about another dozen, and the suite went up in flames.

He didn't stir.

"AAAAAAHHHAHAHAHA!!!" howled Quinn Donovan, whirling around the main alcove of the abandoned mall. "I knew it. I bloody knew. You lot doubted me and here we ruddy are. I did it!"

Brie, Josh, Kevin and Billie converged from opposite hallways.

"Did what?" said Harlan.

Quinn brandished the fake diamond, a wild grin splitting his face. "Knicked without so much as a wobble, thank-you-fucking-much."

"That's the commotion?" Billie sighed. "It sounded like you were fisting a blender."

"Where's Ruby?" Brie said.

Quinn swished a half-drunk bottle of Glenfiddich toward the door. "The bird took off. Said she was getting some air or something. But we're missing the point here, you ponces. I did it!"

Then, another howl as Quinn commenced a staggering pirouette around the room like a toddler on a tilt-a-whirl.

Harlan snagged the bottle. "You're drunk?"

"Correct!" Quinn nodded, which put his balance off, so he put his hand on the wall to compensate. "I say we all have another belt. Celebrate."

"You were supposed to do it sober," Brie said through gritted teeth, her left eye twitching slightly with rage.

"Well, none of you lot told me that, did you?"

"Yes," Brie said. "We did."

"You did?"

"At least several times," added Josh.

"Well…" The magician swayed, brow stitched in deep rumination. "Bollocks, then. Who wants a belt?"

Brie pinched the bridge of her nose. To Harlan: "This is hopeless. I told you, leave him alone for one second and he's wasted."

"Hey, I'm a bit on the piss, but—"

"How is this my fault?" Harlan chuckled. "Your friend is the one who left him unattended."

"Ruby wouldn't have left if this idiot hadn't been working her last nerve," Brie said, waving admonishingly at Quinn. "This is on you, Harlan. You promised."

"And I plan to make good on that, okay?" Harlan eyed the ceiling, the source of all calm in arguments. "It's not opening night. We'll be fine."

"Breathmints?" Quinn suggested.

"Shut up," Brie, Tommy, and Billie chanted in unison.

"You keep saying that," Brie sighed. "But everything about this job keeps coming up disaster."

"Maybe we all need something to eat," Kevin suggested. "Stress and hunger never go well together—"

"I don't think burgers are going to help sober up the Great Boozini," Brie snapped.

"Nice," Billie chuckled.

"You don't need to get snippy with me. I'm trying to help."

"I lasted bloody two hours!" Quinn sighed. "You sods don't seem to get it. It's my *process*. I can't concentrate without a sip or two."

"Which begs the question," Brie said, marking her point in the air with a finger. "Why, Josh? Of all the sleight of hand guys in town, you pick the walking tequila worm."

"I rather like that."

"Shut up!" they chorused.

"Of the two of us," Harlan said to Brie. "Who is A) the thief who couldn't pull off a simple bait and switch, and B) not in charge?"

Brie nearly ripped her hair out in frustration. "And what *do* you do, Harlan? You don't crack the safe. Don't hack the system or build the escape vehicles and disguises. So... What?"

"Benefactor. Planner. Master thief."

"I don't see any of the benefit you're giving."

"You're tunnel-visioned, Cassiday. Just because you can't see something because you're hellbent on revenge doesn't mean it's not there."

Brie gave him the coldest of glares. "I should drop you for that."

"Go ahead," Harlan said, holding out his arms. "I'm right here. Drop me. Prove me right."

Quinn sniffed, a frown stitched on his brow. "Do you lot smell something?"

"Something what?" Brie snapped.

"Something burning?"

Billie's face went pale. "Shit. The mould..."

Before Kevin could even nod, a snapping sound, then a

whooshing sound, and water poured from the overhead sprinklers like a flash storm.

"Aha!" Quinn pointed to the ceiling, grinning. "See? Not my fault."

"Uuuuughhhh!!!" Brie screeched, grabbing the magician by the collar and riding him to the ground.

Billie sprinted back to the garage.

"Who turned the fucking sprinklers on?" Kev said.

"They were never off," Harlan sighed, the sprinklers slicking his hair over his face.

"And again," Quinn said. "Not my fault."

Brie reeled back to coldcock the drunk magician, when the sprinklers went out, and Tommy Carlyle appeared in the entrance to the brainstorm room.

"So," he said, holding a soggy MacBook. "Who here knows what water does to computers?"

"Tell me you had a backup," Josh said.

"Did," Tommy said, raising the other hand to reveal a dripping backup drive.

Billie came back with the charred remains of Kevin's facial mould. "Well, at least I'm not the only one back to square one."

Brie eyed the two experts, seeing the failed job before her. "I'm gonna fucking kill him, now."

"Not my fault!!!" cried Quinn.

"Tommy?" Josh said, motioning to Brie as she made to choke-out the magician.

Tommy pulled her off. "Enough. Now, who's got a laptop?"

And here, Brie slugged him. The sound was like a batter swinging a home run.

"Ow," Tommy said, holding his nose. Streamers of blood ran down his face. "Same question."

CHAPTER 17
TWO SIDES TO EVERY GAMBLE

Kevin Cassiday knew most of the fun ways to take the edge off. Rent overdue? Bong blitzes until pay week. Dumping by a some-times-girlfriend? Bottle of Jack would always do. Fight with friends? Some E and a night on the town would find you new ones. But when it was Brie who made him angry—when he wanted to punt babies with frustration, and pretty much any time he couldn't afford the other three vices—he drove. Driving always brought him back to a level playing field. Not to mention, the other assholes might deny it, but he was starving.

So he found himself behind the wheel of his souped-up Silver-ado, paying a drive-thru clerk at Five Guys for a bagful of burgers. He'd discovered that for a driver, the planning phase of a heist rendered him useless. He didn't have anything to rehearse; a persona to memorize; or a—well, he still wasn't sure what Billie was building. All he had to do was drive, and until then, there was a whole mountain of nothing for him to slog over. Thus, the burger run. Sure, nobody actually admitted they wanted it. But

Kev knew that once everybody had eaten, they'd be able to figure out what the next move was.

He tossed the burgers in the passenger's seat and pulled out towards Tropicana, moving to upshift into bat-out-of-hell mode, when a woman appeared in front of him. Kev hit the brakes and the Silverado lurched as she strutted over to the driver's side, red-painted lips curling into a smirk while he rolled down the window.

"Nice truck."

"Yeah. You were about to get real friendly with it. Walking out in traffic: bad. Make a note."

"Uhuh," she said, craning her neck to hear the engine. "And making an entirely different purr than the body tells me. You do that yourself?"

She was sharp-featured, painfully pretty, and she winked. Kevin fought back a wave of nervous excitement, opting to play it chill. "You can do that by ear, huh? Cool."

"Good with a wrench," she said, still heeding the engine. "Studly."

The scent of jasmine and citrus caught his nose. Kev steeled himself, affecting the wise-cracking driver persona he'd been crafting. "Well, aren't you just the well of mystery. What exactly did you plan on happening when you walked in front of me?"

She batted her eyelashes, grinned. "This?"

"And uh… Er… What if I didn't stop? I mean, it's dangerous."

The woman chuckled, brushing a swoop of raven hair around her neck. "I saw you waiting for your order. All pent up and annoyed-like. You're a driver, right?"

Be cool. For god's sake, she's so babely, be cool, man! "…So?"

Well, maybe the cool austere needed work.

"So *duh* you're gonna stop in time." She chuckled, playing with her hair and making a big scene about the low cut of her top as she sighed. When she caught Kevin looking, she grinned. "I'm Jezebel."

"I, uh—Kevin. I'm a driver?"

Okay, let's be fair. He was only twenty-three.

"So, mister driver," she said, stroking the shape of his open window, biting her lip. "Give a girl a ride?"

Kev cleared his throat. "Where you headed?"

"My hotel," she said. "Give me one of those burgers, I might even show you the room—what'dya say, stud?"

Kev popped the lock on the passenger's side and she climbed in. Despite himself, Kevin couldn't take his eyes off her cleavage. "I uh..." Again he cleared his throat. His voice came out hoarse. "I like your top."

"I know you do," she said, grabbing his hand and forcing him to upshift. "Wait 'til you get it off of me."

The engine revved—however you choose to read it.

About the same time, across town at the abandoned mall, Brie Cassiday was sitting on the roof, dangling her heels over the edge. She leafed through her mother's journal, the palms below swaying in the evening breeze. She'd come up here to dry off and cool down, and presently was regretting the irony in that last part. The desert got frigid after sundown. She was angry, but still she shivered against the nighttime air.

Footsteps behind. Brie turned to find Harlan coming through the entryway, a bottle and two tumblers in his hands.

"Hungry?"

Brie closed the journal and stared off over the twinkling neon night. "If you're asking me to dinner, the answer's no," she said. "But I'll take a drink."

Harlan sat beside her, placing the tumblers on the edge of the roof. "Well, your brother's off getting everybody burgers, so I think I meant the drink." He popped the cork and poured them each a few fingers. "Oh, and I told him to get you nothing. Figured you weren't hungry."

"So what did you mean when you asked *Hungry?*"

Harlan grinned and handed her a glass. "Scotch is a meal, right?"

"Maybe for you," Brie said. "Last I checked, a meal means nourishment."

He shrugged. "Food feeds the body; scotch feeds the soul."

"Cute." She chuckled, taking a sip. "Didn't know you wrote for *Hallmark* in your spare time."

"Myeah. Heard it from a guy in Spain once. Seemed vaguely appropriate."

Brie sighed. "What do you want?"

"I wanted some air. I brought the second tumbler in case I dropped the first." Then, off Brie's expression: "Oh. Am I intruding? I can find another place to drink if you're dead-set on moping or something."

"Don't be glib about that. Be glib about anything and everything but that." She shook her head. "God, I hate you."

"I get it," Harlan said. "I understand—and, for what it's worth? I *am* sorry, Brie."

She rolled her eyes. "Like you're even capable."

Josh gave her a forced grin. "I was seven, when my folks bit it."

Brie could see him leading her. "Sorry." Perfunctory. She'd heard it enough to have it memorized.

Josh sipped his drink. "I'm a third-generation con. I saw it coming then, even though I didn't know what I was looking at. Simple beat-bag. Ma and Pa s'posed to split the profits, but they both got greedy. One brought home the take, they go to divvy, and wham— they're off." A long sigh. "I watched them gun each other down over three, maybe four-thousand bucks. They stuck me in an orphanage, and a Lemony Snicket novel later, here I am. The point is, I know what you're feeling, Brie. I'm not trying to play it. I'm not going to use it to my advantage. You'd do whatever it takes to make things right, and I'll help you as much as I can. I mean that. And I'm sorry. Whatever part I played in it, I'm sorry, okay?"

Brie stared at the ground, tilting the whiskey in her glass. "You see, that? That's the part of the story you lead with."

Josh shrugged. "I don't give that shit away for free. I just wanted you to know, what you're working for? I get it. I want to help. And I promise I'll get you as close as I can so long as I'm not locked up in a storage locker getting the shit beaten out of me."

Brie chuckled. "Valiant."

"Whatever," Josh said. "Refill?"

"Sure. Wanna hear my exit strategy? Mister speechify?"

Harlan chuckled, refilling her glass. "I'd love to."

Meanwhile at the Olympus, fifty-three MIT grad students squirreled out of a Greyhound. They were all early-twenties, casually dressed, and tittering at the prospects of the casino before them. A suited chaperon brought them to a quartered-off section, cutting a velvet rope as they went. They were here to pull slots and study permutations of probability, and while the waitress came around with comped drinks, as they brandished notebooks and clicky pens and sat at their three private rows of slots, a bigger plan was unfolding.

One-by-one, a bit like a firing squad, they settled in and started pulling the levers, tolls jangling above them with the flashing exuberance that leads many to their end.

Below, Steve Halverson and Pete Gibbons stood at the console, watching a big red status bar climb toward the 100% mark.

Following a hydra of cables that vaguely resembled a Rastafarian's dreadlocks was Gavin Whelan, strapped into a machine that was essentially a giant aluminum hoop—his hands and feet fitted into clamps in the position of da Vinci's *Virtruvian Man*.

"How are the levels?" he called over the hum from the machine.

"Holding," said Steve, tapping his keyboard.

"Seventy-eight percent and counting," said Gibbons, his eye on the big red bar. "Another half hour and we'll be at ten years."

Whelan shook his head. "It's not enough."

"Okay, so we let it ride another thirty minutes—"

"No," the tycoon said. "I mean what we're pulling, it won't be enough. I can feel it. We need to take more. Prep for full extraction."

Steve and Phil shared a nervous expression.

"That could fry the whole power grid."

"And with opening night two days away…"

"It's not just that, Boss. We crank the juice like that, we won't be able to regulate."

"One spike and… Well—"

"You might explode a little."

Gavin went to wave them off, but was stopped by the stainless steel clasp around his wrist. "I understand the risks. We'll have to try our luck."

Halverson raised an eyebrow. "You really think having her in tow means—"

"I've seen it work," Whelan snapped. "Do it."

Gibbons wiped his brow. "Gavin, you're sure…?"

The tycoon nodded, his chest heaving. "I've had enough warning. I need to be sharp for what's coming. Get it done."

"He seem fidgety to you?" Phil said under his breath.

"Honestly?" Steve whispered. "He's kinda freaking me out." To the boss: "Okay, Gav. Cranking it to eleven."

He grabbed the big red lever on the console, then looked at Gibbons, shrugged, and threw it upward.

Back at the Virtruvian machine, a whine sang through the metal: brassy, squealing, a bit like a dog whistle. Whelan panted as the sound morphed into a wavering note, playing both high and low through a tremolo—a single guitar note of foreboding.

The lights strobed as the sound deepened, as if the machine were sucking noise out of the air around them. Everything —even Phil's coffee—vibrated. The metal holdings around the tycoon's wrists and ankles began glowing a pale blue. The light built in clusters, percolating before leaping down Whelan's limbs.

Then began a whooping noise; a slow slush of electric cacophony as the power built. Further... Further... Whelan started writhing against his shackles.

The sound rushed out, and at once the room was filled with a deafening kind of silence. Then, it sucked back with a vicious whirl, and the lights exploded.

A great cloud of electric blue came from Whelan's clasps. Halverson and Gibbons rose from behind the console as the light collected in a cloud around the tycoon's torso, whirling and frothing like a featureless monster.

Before anyone could speak, the light rushed in a column towards Gavin's gaping mouth, and leapt down his throat. His arms, his legs, even his ears began to glow.

White-hot light exploded from his chest as Whelan screamed in either agony or pure ecstasy. Neither man at the console could tell you.

All was quiet above. Well, as quiet as you ever get in a casino: Machines blipped and whirred. Gamblers cheered. Glasses clinked. People moved, trying so hard to pay attention to everything that they missed the small stuff. Such as over at the sectioned-off rows of slot machines for the MIT students, where it really was quiet. One astute guest almost turned to her friends to ask: "Hey, do you see that blue light coming out of the screens of the slot machines and apparently eating people?" but *No,* she thought. *I think I'll keep that to myself.*

They hunched, C-shaped over the slots, notebooks and pens long pushed to the wayside. Bruises around their eyes, skin like tracing paper. Features very nearly mummified, as if a century ago, they'd sat down and forgotten the reason they'd come.

Down the row a bit, a lone slot machine tittered for a twenty-cent win. In front of it was a woman of about seventy or eighty, her outfit mismatched, her gray hair frizzled. She pulled a token out of her pile with a weak grin, and plopped it into the machine. Then, slowly, creakily, she grabbed the lever and pulled. She smacked her gums, watching the slots roll in front of her.

Bloop-Bloop-Bloo-Bloo-Bloo-Bloop! Another win. Five in a row now. The machine was a dud—there was no other way, statistically, she could ever pull this much on progressive slots. But, no matter. She was winning. What else mattered when you hit a streak? So, she kept on playing, a grin spreading over her tremendously wrinkled face.

Her name was Beth Hutchins, three months away from graduating with honors; a cheerleader—and pretty kickass at algebra, too. Back home she was chased by quarterbacks and classmates, all blonde hair and big eyes with a decent figure.

None of that mattered, though. She'd forgotten her past, every moment leading up to now. Now, all that mattered was the token, the pull, and the rolling spools of fortune. Her skin was like a raisin and her hair was like straw—it'd be nice if her looks had gone later, but oh well. At least she could still disprove mathematics. And she was winning—so what else mattered?

She dropped another token in the machine and pulled. The slots did their spin, and landed on a row of apples. Another win. *Screw you, probability!*

Beth cheered. She was winning, and she was *still* only twenty-one. Life wasn't all bad.

"So that's the plan," Brie said while Josh poured her another drink.

"I like it," he said. "It works. But what if the room they put you in doesn't have a vent?"

She nodded, glad she wasn't the only one who'd thought of that. "Remember that guy who hit you in the face with a wok?"

"Sure, why?"

Brie grinned. "Exactly."

Josh thought about it. " 'Kay. Good plan."

Brie's phone buzzed in her pocket. She fished it out. Blocked number.

"Hello?"

"Well hey there, pumpkin," said a woman's voice. "How's bereavement treating you?"

Brie felt her insides clamp down. "Who is this?"

"Oh, just your plot twist calling. Wondering how you feel about your brother. I've got your brother here, by the way."

"Bullshit," Brie said. Kev should be back with burgers by now, right?

"Is it?" said the woman. "Say 'hi,' Kevin."

"Hi, Kevin," said Kevin. He sounded like he might be drugged.

"So, I guess you and I have a conversation needs having. Would that be right, sweetpea?"

"You've got about three seconds to tell me what you want before I find you and turn you into something people pour gravy over," Brie said.

Harlan blinked, drinking, an obvious *What the shit is going on?* expression.

"Good threat," the woman chuckled. "Here's mine: you've got about twenty minutes to hightail it over to Venetian before your brother becomes a memory wrote in pink mist. Toodles."

The line disconnected.

Before she even had to tell him, Josh said, "I've got a plan."

CHAPTER 18
COMPLICATIONS

Nevada, 1989

David Siegel stood on the gas pedal of his '86 Volkswagen. The engine roared. Rain beat down on the hood. It was midnight, and his wife Josie twisted in the passenger's seat.

"Come on, Dave. Floor it. They're gaining on us."

"Hate to break it to you, dear," he said, steady on the wheel. "But I'm afraid this *is* floored."

With the rain, the road was like black glass. Behind, two Buicks closed in on the bumper.

They were headed for Arizona, and about a quarter-mile from the Hoover Dam, decided they were being followed. Dave had faked a couple of lefts to shake them, but they were on the Volks like sharks trailing the scent of blood.

Dave downshifted, pulling onto the dam.

"We'll catch the highway on the other side," he said, shaking his head. "All this over a diamond. Remind me to kill that Bugs guy if we ever come back to this state."

"I'll remind you if we make actually it out of the state."

"That's the spirit, honey. We're gonna have to address your negativity once we're on vacation."

"Well, I hope you like orange jumpsuits," she said, looking in the side mirror.

"I don't think they'll be jailing us if they catch up."

"Oh, well at least there's that," she said. "More stepping on it, please."

"Still stepping. Boy, if I could just get them to veer off course…"

Dave twisted to suss out the situation. He could fake braking and hope the first car would swerve into number two? It was possible, but Dave wasn't a stunt driver. With roads like this, it could end with a seven-hundred foot drop to oblivion, and, well —after stealing a priceless diamond, that end had significantly less sun and tropical beverages than he was hoping for. He turned back, looking for a rocket button, a warp-speed drive—anything to make them go faster.

What he found was a deer, black as pitch, filling the headlights. Dave mashed the brake pedal, instinctively pulling to the left. Toward the drop off the dam.

The Volks jackknifed the guardrail, bounding up, and teetered. The undercarriage raked against the truss. Metal screeched and buckled. Then, the hood dipped, and the Volks slid over the side of the dam in a spray of sparks.

The deer bowed, shuddered, and shifted into the form of a woman. She shook her hair out over her shoulders and strutted, naked, over to the edge. A moment later, there was a sound like crushing a giant soda can, and a tiny fireball erupted from the base of the dam.

"Step one," she said as the Buicks pulled up beside her.

A flash of blue, and she was at the base of the dam, stealing a fisherman's rowboat tied to the bank. She paddled over to the steaming mound of Volkswagen. The water was shallow here, but she hadn't thought to grab a pair of rubber boots, and really, really didn't want to step in that gunk barefoot.

The diamond was in a leather satchel stuffed in the back seat. She took an oar and prodded, ignoring the corpses up front—Josie mashed against the dash and David skewered by the steering column. She hooked the strap over the oar and fished it through the window.

"Step two."

Then it slipped, splashing into the water.

"Dammit." She sighed, tossing the oar to the side, and stood.

She jumped in, waded over to the wreck, and snatched the satchel from the water. Then, she climbed back into the boat and headed for shore.

When she got there, he was waiting. Gavin Whelan, in a pressed gray suit with a bloodred tie; his hair greased back, as was the style. He straightened his cufflinks as she crawled out of the boat.

"There's a dress in back," he said, motioning to one of the Buicks.

"There fucking better be," she said, handing him the satchel. "And a towel? That water was nasty."

She strode past him and a goon handed her a towel. She dried off, ignoring the chill of the September night.

"I'll make it up to you."

"I know you will." She climbed into the car and slammed the door. The driver scooted around front and started the engine.

Whelan squeezed the satchel, stifling a grin. That had been close. If either David or Josie had known the words, he'd be finished. It was exhilarating.

The window rolled down.

"And a bath balm," Jezebel said as they peeled off. "I feel disgusting."

Brie, Josh, and Jimmy Wok strode under the fake sky of the Venetian. Along the fake-cobbled streets were shops, restaurants, beer kiosks, and even gondola rides down the imitation Venice channel. They slipped past the spectacle and hit the elevators.

They climbed on. Brie slipped a duffel bag off her shoulder. Josh looked up at the big man and grinned.

"No hard feelings, *Ratatouille*. You've got a killer swing."

Jimmy gave him a tired expression, then commenced staring at the light-up numbers above the door.

"You sure this is gonna work?" said Brie.

"It worked on you, didn't it?"

Here, Jimmy growled menacingly, which of course only provoked more grinning from Harlan.

"Barely," Brie said. "If she catches on…"

"People see what they want to see, not what's in front of them. Seriously, now you're doubting the plan?"

Before either Brie could answer or Jimmy could hit him, the elevator dinged.

"Showtime." He pulled a Walther P99 out of the bag and handed it to Brie, then a Ruger LPC, which he handed to Jimmy, but the Wok waved him off.

"I'm good," he said, brandishing his Taylor & Ng.

Brie took the pistol and gave it an uncertain twirl. "What happened to big guns?"

"Best Billie could do on short notice. Ready?"

Brie and Jimmy shrugged.

Harlan nodded. "Okay. Let's threaten some bad guys."

The room Jezebel had texted Brie was the first on the left.

When they arrived, Josh motioned for them to stop.

"He better've gotten the burgers."

"Did we make a decision on what we do if she's got a gun?" Brie said.

Josh tilted his head to Jimmy. "He hits her in the head."

Jimmy shrugged. "Works."

"Go," Brie said. She was here to kick ass, fake firearms or not. If she had to choke the bitch out with her bare hands, she was game.

Josh reeled back and kicked the door off its hinges. They moved into the room, falling into a *Three Musketeers* 'V' with guns ready.

"Hey guys!" Kev slurred from the bed. His cheeks were flushed, covered with lipstick kisses. He smelled of liquor, B.O.— and what Brie was trying furiously to deny was sex—wearing only his boxers.

Brie said, "Are you drunk?"

"I'd say he's more than that," said Harlan, panning around the room.

"The fuck kinda kidnapping is this?" said Jimmy. "They take you, hold you hostage, and what—get you drunk and bone you while they wait?"

Kevin shrugged, giggling. "They're really okay people."

Brie gave him the withering look she'd mastered changing his diapers. It made him cower and search the floor for his jeans, all without a word.

"You're an idiot," she said.

"True," Josh said. "But let's face it. This could be worse."

"Handsome's got a point," a voice came from the bathroom. The door swung open as everybody wheeled around. Jezebel came out wrapped in a towel, and pulled a knife on Harlan, who was closest to the door.

Josh spun, knocking the knife away and grabbed her by the waist. Her towel fell to the floor.

"Kinky," she said. "I like," she added, rubbing her bare bottom against him. "Wanna snuggle?"

"Your snuggle buddy's already on your neck, Hepburn." Josh motioned to the pistol he jammed into the nape of her neck. "But what are you doing after? I could move some stuff around."

"Hey!" Kev said.

Jezebel grinned, brushing away Harlan's gun as if it were a pizza flyer. "Sorry, doll. We had a connection, but I'm not ready for a long-term thing."

She strolled over to the bed, straddled Kev, and kissed him back onto the bed.

"You're fucking kidding me," said Brie.

"We have a connection!" Kev said.

"And you two didn't see her coming," said Harlan.

"You got here about a half-hour late for that," Jezebel chuckled, nipping Kevin's ear. "I mean, oh no! Please don't shoot."

Brie walked over and cocked the pistol, her mind a white slate of rage. She pressed the muzzle of the gun against Jezebel's forehead. "Touch my brother again, it'll be you who ends in pink mist."

"Well, I mean, a few more times…?" said Kev. Then, off Brie's *I will so totally kill you* expression, "What? It was nice."

Jezebel shrugged. "I have a way."

Brie ripped her drunken brother off the bed. "Put on a shirt. We're leaving."

Kevin dressed and they backed out of the room.

"Call me!" said Jezebel. That's when Jimmy whacked her in the head with his wok and she hit the floor.

They walked down the hall. After a few paces, Brie slapped Kevin in the back of the head.

"Ouch! What the shit?"

"You realize you just shagged the bad guy, right?"

"No," Kevin said. "I mean, I'm pretty sure she wasn't a guy. Not that it would bother me if she'd been before or anything, but..." Off their expressions: "Oh, fuck off. What? Seriously, what?"

"She was probably gonna kill you," said Brie.

"She did have that vibe," added Harlan. "Trust me, kid. I'm kind of an expert."

Brie shot him a murderous glare.

"See? Proof. Right there. Look at your sister. That's the look."

"Eeewww," said Kev.

"Eeeewww," said Brie.

"Well, not like that," Josh said. "The point is, we saved your ass."

"Idiot," added Brie.

"Well, in that case, thanks guys," Kevin said, wrapping his arm around Jimmy, pointing without a subject. "You guys are awesome. That whole thing was awesome. Oh, by the way, I got burgers..."

"You left them back in the room."

"Oh..." Kevin frowned. "So can we go back?"

"Look, the point is, tiny fire-breathing dinosaur, stacked up against a doofus not-so-ninja turtle and an overgrown iguana with a flower on his back—practical shit aside, he's clearly the ace choice," said Tommy, flicking keys on the laptop he'd borrowed from Billie.

"Sure," she said, working the finishing touches on the wig she planned to use for her part of the heist. "But he's a fire-type, right? So put him against a Squirtle—who is way cuter, by the way—and he's toast... Or, I guess, soggy toast?"

"Nu-uh," said Tommy, still typing. "Un-ninja turtle Squirtle's still toast if you know how to work a Charmander. That's the whole point. He's got the starter disadvantage, but, you hang in there, he evolves into a dragon—who doesn't want a dragon?"

Billie gave the hacker a once-over. "You wanna get a drink after this?"

Before Tommy could answer, Harlan, Brie, and Jimmy Wok came into the brainstorm room, a wasted-looking Kevin stumbling behind.

"Motherfucker's got a point!" Kev slurred. "Flying, fire-breathing, cute as shit motherfucker. Your water-cannon loser's a smoldering heap of shit. And he's not as cute."

"Woah," Billie said, frowning at the drunk driver. "He's way more endearing sober."

"You shoulda seen him a half-hour ago," said Brie.

"Hey, where's the food?" said Tommy.

"Maybe the not-so-ninja turtle had it?" Billie suggested.

Tommy gave her a look, trying but failing to be patient. "I liked *you* better a minute ago."

"Hey, you got a new computer," Josh said.

"Borrowed," said Tommy. He was still thinking how ridiculous it was that people thought a dragon with a flaming tail was useless against some asshole turtle who eventually evolved into having a pair of water cannons—like that shit made any sense! "And welcome back, kidnapped and the saviors."

"I'm drunk," Kev said. "But I still totally agree. Charmander's the best starter choice. The rest are just stupid looking."

"Coming from you, that's rich," said Brie.

"Oh, pfft." Kev waved her off and flopped on the couch next to Tommy. "You don't even know what we're talking about. Stick to your safecracking and shit."

"Uh… Hello? Who just saved you?"

"From what? Getting laid? Wow, you are *such* a sister."

"I hate to break up this heartwarming feat of family bonding," Tommy said. "But we've got problems. Which do you want first, bad news or worse news?"

"Let's start with worse," said Josh, slumping on the adjacent sofa.

"'Kay," Tommy said. "Well, I managed to recover all the shit we lost when Captain Boozehound set off the fire alarm…"

"Not my fault!" Quinn groaned from behind the sofa.

"That's not technically bad news," Josh said.

Tommy raised a finger, marking his point. "Here's the part where everything sucks: Olympus is apparently hosting a prince of some micro-island off the Dead Sea."

"So?" Josh, Brie, Jimmy and Kevin all said together.

"So," Billie said. "They're moving the grand opening."

Josh hung his head, just to hide the fact he was thinking. "When?"

"Friday," Tommy said. "As in this Friday. As in a week early."

Josh's eyes darted back and forth, doing the math. "That's perfect."

"No," Tommy said.

"It's really not," added Billie.

"You're talking about a day and a half from now," Brie said. "Josh, they're right. That's impossible."

"Maybe."

"No, definitely."

Josh wasn't listening. "There's no way we can miss an opportunity like this."

"Opportunity?" Tommy said. "Dude, I've got three days of hacking to do, Brie's still working out the kinks on the winch system, and Billie's got like…" He looked to Billie, who gave him a *thank-you* smile.

"Even at full-tilt, I'm three days behind."

Josh nodded. "Do what you need to."

"What we need to?" Brie said. "Josh, we can't make three days from nothing. We need a plan B."

"This is plan *A* to *Z*," Josh said. "Seriously? A prince is headed to the casino we're robbing? Am I the only one seeing this?"

"I think the rest of us are stuck on the whole 'it's impossible' section," said Tommy.

"Tommy, you know what I'm saying," Josh said, wagging his head. "Impossible we can do. Think about it. All the money the prince spends has to go in the safe. That doubles our take, easily. We can't *not* go for it."

Billie sighed, tying her hair off in a windy bun. "The trucks aren't ready."

"Plus we don't know where Ruby went," said Tommy.

"Not to mention Quinn's so drunk we'd need a week to get him sober and trained," added Brie.

"And me!" Kevin said.

Brie rolled her eyes. "He'll be fine by noon tomorrow."

"Truth!"

Harlan shook his head. "No, you guys don't get it. Sure, the odds are against us. But this is our chance. We're talking about another ten-million and you're talking about how we can't do it? Guys, we *have* to."

"Sure," Tommy said. "But… Can't?"

Josh gave him a *Seriously?!* expression. "The bug in Whelan's office?"

"Is the only reason we know about this," sighed the hacker. "Changes nothing."

"No," Josh said. "This whole thing? Changes everything. It makes it all worth doing. We need to move."

"It's impossible," Billie said.

"Fine," Josh said. "Let's do impossible."

"They're ten-shades of screwed, El Hefe," Jezebel said, kicking her feet up on Whelan's desk. "And by the way, you're looking fresh."

Whelan shot the lapels on his blazer. His hair was chestnut brown, combed neatly to the side. His skin was smooth, and his eyes were bright. He looked a trim thirty-five, and was clearly feeling the same, pacing the office with a grin.

"Good," he said. "Excellent. I knew it would go this way."

He headed over to the wet bar and poured drinks. Jezebel eyed him, a little annoyed with his new and chipper demeanor. Sooner or later, he'd mellow and be back to his somewhat tolerable self. But for the meantime, it would take a godlike amount of patience not to snap his neck like a twist cap. It was good she was one.

Gavin came back with the drinks. "Tell me their plan."

"Sit," Jezebel said. "Chill." She took the drink and swigged. "Pop a Ritalin. Jeez, you're like a teenager."

"It's been a while since I felt like this," Gavin said, sitting. "Their plan?"

"I swear, if you pop a stubbie over there, I'm not helping."

"I have resources, remember? The plan."

Jezebel nodded, standing. "Well, it's a little complicated."

"Complex systems are doomed to fail." Whelan grinned, sipping his drink. "How does it go?"

"Well," she said. "It starts like this—"

And here, she grabbed the tycoon by the back of the head and slammed him against the desk. Wood splintered as his face left a dent. In an instant, Jezebel flashed over to the diamond, sitting on a purple cushion in his wall of trinkets. She went to grab, then Whelan recovered, holding out his hand in a clutching fashion.

The goddess froze as if electrified. Pain sang down her limbs as she lifted off the ground.

"You'd think after all these years, you'd know I see that coming," Whelan said, grinning. He squeezed his hand into a fist, and
Jezebel screeched in agony. "So many years. So many times. So
many ways. Still, you think I'm a fool."

"Aaghh," she choked.

"You know," he continued, softly, patiently. "I think I almost
like you better this way. I hate to hurt you, but god, it feels so
excellent to have you shut up for a minute."

Jezebel made a cat-yakking-a-hairball noise, her eyes rolling
back. Whelan opened his hand, and she fell to the floor, gasping.

"Now," he said. "Their plan?"

INTERLUDE
HOW TO ACCOMPLISH
THE IMPOSSIBLE

A little-known fact: Next to nothing is impossible. Actually, nothing *itself* is impossible. Nothing is the absence of all things. But that absence is, itself, a thing, and—well, the logic's so screwy you could uncork a wine bottle with it.

The point is, most of the stuff people say is impossible is not at all impossible. Starting a car that's already started, that's impossible. Traveling to where you are is impossible. Sleeping through Rick Astley's "Never Gonna Give You Up" is impossible (and so is listening to it).

And that's the list. Taking a neon-blue dump? Well... You'd think, but really it's just improbable.

To sum up a wildly unmanageable concept: most things we call impossible are actually just things that require more effort than we're willing to give. And even when it comes to impossible, it's really only the Rick Astley that nobody will try if they're given a few slices of pizza.

And thus, with the delivery of three extra-large everything-on-them pizzas and one Hawaiian, a sleepless night did fall upon the band of thieves.

BILLIE

Billie inhaled six slices and pulled on her welding mask. She crimped sheet metal, tagged welds and fastened bolts in an almost rhythmic sequence. She shot rivets into steel, assembled five prosthetic disguises, and had Kevin help her finish attaching the nine-foot box to the back of the first F800. She lined the box with diamond-plated aluminum. She finished the accents on four wigs. Then, she tried out the industrial strength adhesive she'd been working on, attaching Quinn's crystal dildo to Kevin's jeans while he napped.

She finished the contours on the heavy iron door and bolted it to the back of the box on the truck. Then, produced a roll of vinyl lettering, a professional grade spray-painter and coated her creation in dull gray. She switched to a can of cobalt blue, and waiting for the first coat to dry, she kicked Kevin's foot, which was sticking out of the newly built cab, quite unconscious.

He snorted to life, then immediately flopped back on the floor of the cab with a gong sound, slapping a hand to his forehead. "Ugh."

Billie grinned. "Wanna beer?"

Kev popped out of the truck, a little green-looking. "How can you say that? How can you possibly beer at a time like this?"

"Stand back and look," she said. "And don't puke. I just did like twelve hours of work in five."

He rubbed the back of his neck and came over to where she was standing.

"Woah," he said, disbelief washing his face.

"Uhuh."

"That's like…"

"Perfect?"

"Yeah. Wow." Kev nodded, approvingly. "Hey, Billie?"

"Yup?"

"Why do I have a dildo glued to my jeans?"

TOMMY

Mister Weasel slammed back three five-hour energy drinks, fingers hovering over the keys of Billie's laptop, the remains of his waterlogged backup drive attached with a USB cable. He flicked open that console window no normal person knows how to operate, typed… And let's face it. He did some stuff that we only know is important because it looked that way.

A "time elapsed" bar appeared in a pop-up, and he leaned back with a grin as it unfurled.

"Good thing I went to college," he said, munching his fourth slice of combination. "I mean, not officially… But those beer spills were pretty real."

Tell us more, bubbled the coffee-maker. *Really, we're enthralled.*

QUINN

After two slices of Hawaiian (something he'd never tried before, but rather liked) and eight cups of coffee, Quinn Donovan still had a headache that felt like a bulldozer driving an icepick through his temple. He tried napping, but the closest he got was a weird sort of semi-dream about a diamond-crusted disciple of the Mistress Shangrila ramming a railroad pike through his forehead.

So, the hangover blooming, he went back to the jewel store and placed the diamond on the wood podium. The gem skipped in his vision—left, right, then left again, right, right, right.

"Stop sodding moving," he said.

He took a steadying breath, and remarkably, his vision cleared. He closed his eyes, tried to tap into his vaporous memory of swiping the stone, then moved. Bugger it, the bird wasn't here, right? If he bugged it up—which he surely would—nobody would notice.

He opened his eyes, about a foot away from the podium. In his hand was the stone, and back on the podium was its replacement.

Quinn's expression broadened. "Ha!"

The podium didn't so much as wobble.

"Ha! Ha! HAAAAAAHAHAHAHA!!!"

A slow clap came from behind. He wheeled around so fast he nearly lost his balance. Ruby Cobb sat on the derelict counter, a grin on her face.

"Well done."

Quinn's expression exploded with sheer glee. "I'm not even bloody knackered and I did it! I did it!"

He reached out for a hug, but Ruby pulled back and he flopped onto the floor.

"Nope," she said.

Quinn recovered, rubbing his nose. "A ruddy hangover. If I'd known that—Oh, love, give us a kiss."

He leapt to his feet, and again Ruby dodged him. "You're not great with *no*, are you?"

Quinn grinned. "Not part of the lexicon. But... What? Shall we celebrate? And where did you come from?"

"The real world," she said. "And also? No."

BRIE, JOSH, & JIMMY

"Yes," Brie said. "We do this, we do it my way."

She, Jimmy and Josh had all had a couple slices each and were nursing coffees in the kitchen.

"What, we're just supposed to trust the pan-wielding giant?" Josh said. Then to Jimmy: "No offense."

"To what?" said Jimmy.

"I told you what I need," Brie said, eyeing Harlan with a tired resentment she felt like she'd been saving. "You're asking us to do the impossible. Well, this is how."

"But the problem is—"

"What's my take?" said Jimmy.

The conman pinched his brow. "Exactly."

"Jim, you can have half of mine."

"I don't feel right about that."

"No," Josh said. "It's good. Let's do that." He shrugged. "I'm not exactly on a budget, but I'm running out of resources here."

Jimmy wagged his head. "Bullshit."

"I'm sorry, I don't remember inviting you."

"It's fine," Brie said, giving them both a *be cool* gesture. "Jim, I gotcha."

"But?" said Jimmy.

"Great," said Harlan.

"So," Brie said, ignoring the ridiculous dick-wagging happening before her. God, these guys were so competitive. The take didn't even matter to her. Neither of them seemed to remember why she was here, and both were asserting themselves in ways it would be much easier to navigate without. "Let's just pretend I'm not me. I mean forget what you know about me. Let's talk plan."

"I'm good with bashing a dozen goons' heads for free," Jimmy said.

Harlan gave him an expression that said, *So what the fuck was the point of all that?* "What the fuck was the point of all that, then?"

Jimmy shrugged. "I just like annoying you."

"Man after my own heart," Brie said.

"Look," Harlan said. "Once you're down there, it's up to *Yuke Abe* here to keep you safe."

"Not a problem," said Jimmy. "And good reference."

"This is gonna be a long day." Josh pushed back in his chair, stared at the ceiling, and sighed, draining his coffee. "Okay, I think we're just about ready. Run it by me, one more time."

"So," Brie said. "I do the thing, then…"

KEVIN

Kevin ate three slices of Hawaiian and passed out on the couch in the brainstorm room. He'd had a long day.

PART III
IN ACTION

"Other thieves stole everything that was not nailed down, but
this thief stole the nails as well."
— Terry Pratchett, *Sourcery*

"Stealth. Nerve. Speed. More important that any of those
things, however, was one final requirement. Luck."
— Markus Zusak, *The Book Thief*

CHAPTER 19
FRIDAY

Max Reyes awoke shivering. He was soaking wet, handcuffed to the bedpost, his nose filled with the smell of burnt polyester. He was also buck-ass nude. A pack of Marlboros sat on his chest. Something metallic poked his groin, and a throw pillow covered his equipment. He struggled, and the bed squished.

Well, here was a strange situation. A moment ago, he'd been leaning into his Prius for the radio while an attractive Interpol agent grilled him for ID. Now, with no recollection of journey, he was back in his suite at the Venetian, freezing in the air conditioning. A normal guy—or an agent of softer resolve—might have questions… But not Max.

Because when it came to getting hit in the head, he was an expert. Here, there was no mistaking it. The side of his head throbbed, coaxing a flashback to the sound of a telescopic baton extending, then a white-out blow to his melon, and now, pain.

He grimaced, propping himself up on his elbows, and scanned the room.

"Santa-fucking-Maria."

The door to the bedroom was scorched, hanging off the frame at a funny angle. The hallway outside was also charred. The whole place twisted with a *Fear and Loathing* level of destruction.

Well, that explained it. Fire. Someone had set his room ablaze and the sprinklers went off. And of course, nobody had entered. He'd bet money there was a DO NOT DISTURB sign on his door. In Vegas, if you paid for an executive suite, you could do whatever you wanted—and you could handle your own god-damned fires. The sprinklers would handle the danger, and you'd wind up with a bill the length of your arm as a memento.

But bigger questions troubled the agent: *Why am I handcuffed? Why am I naked? And how in blue-perfect fuck do I get out of this?*

As if on cue, a knock at the door. "Room service."

"In here?" Well, this would be awkward.

She wore a French maid's outfit. The top of fishnets and a hint of garters beneath the hem of her skirt, her blouse half-buttoned to reveal a considerable amount of cleavage—all tied off with four-inch pumps and a feather duster. Hell, toss on a raunchy jazz riff and you'd have a porno—not that Max watched porn.

"Oh my!" she gasped.

"What kind of a maid wears heels to work?"

"Who says I'm a maid?" She thumbed the end of the feather duster. "This thing is all kinds of useful."

Part of Reyes's mind (the part not thinking about what she meant by that) thought, *How much weirder could this get?* And of course, the answer was, *Much.*

Because it was Sophie, chief magic hands of the Mistress Shangrila, standing at his bedside. "Well, this is a first. Usually the handcuffs happen after I show up."

"I, uh—well normally I'd buy dinner and apologize for my existence before this."

Sophie chuckled, then crawled onto the bed and straddled him, brushing away the pillow and making a surprised gasp when the metal thing on his unit poked her.

"Sorry," Max said. "Sorry. Sorry. I kinda got knocked out and…"

Here, she reached between her legs and grabbed his junk along with whatever was on it with a playful tug. Max's mind went nuclear. Her warmth on him. Her thighs on his hips. The skin contact… In an instant he felt a climbing erection—and as usual, arguing would do nothing.

Sophie bit her tongue, amused. She came back with the key to his handcuffs.

"I've got a proposition."

"Didn't we just go through six of them?" Max said as she nibbled his ear.

"You and I have unfinished business, Agent."

Okay, forget everything. Clearly, Max was still passed out and hallucinating.

"…Uhuh?"

She pulled back, stopping when their noses met. Her lips an inch from his, she whispered, "But that's not the proposition."

Max was stuck on the part where her hand was wrapped around his tackle. "…Uhuh?"

"Officially, I'm here on behalf of the Mistress Shangrila. It appears you and we have a thief to catch."

"Harlan," Max said, and here, his erection wilted a little.

Sophie didn't let it for long. Again she tugged. "He has the Mistress's sacred dildo. We want that back, so—"

"I help you find him and we both get what we want?" Reyes suggested. *Oh god, oh god oh god oh god…*

Sophie grinned. "Mutually beneficial."

There was no training nor life experience that Max could fall back on. She was touching him in ways he'd only imagined before, and well…

"Deal," he said. "But you'll need to uncuff me?"

Sophie grinned. "Now, about that unfinished business."

She slid her underwear to the side, and what happened next is just none of your business.

Sundown. In the brainstorm room, Tommy Carlyle set four egg-timers in a row across the coffee table. He steepled his fingers and sat back, thinking, *'Nothing is more vulgar than haste.'* And not even good *'vulgar'*…

"Okay, Brie. Two minutes and it's your cue."

"Why didn't I get an earpiece thingie?" said Ruby Cobb, sitting next to him on the couch.

"No earpieces," Tommy said. "The OmniView would pick up on that like a fart in church."

"I thought you were a genius hacker—you couldn't find a way around that?"

Tommy motioned to the egg-timers. "This isn't a workaround?"

Ruby shrugged. "I guess. So who are you talking to?"

"Myself," said Mister Weasel. "It helps me concentrate."

Timing the whole thing was the only solution. Sure, if he were just trying to impress the criminal liaison, he could probably come up with something grander—but if it worked, who cared how fancy it was?

"Remind me why you're my assistant?"

"Emotional support?"

"That usually involves support."

"I'm here, aren't I? What do you want—a soundtrack or something?"

"Funky jazz, please."

Ruby sighed, then hit the play button on *Zeppelin II*.

"Actually, that's better." Tommy wound up the first egg-timer, and as it began ticking away, he said, "Okay. Step one."

"What was step one?" said Ruby.

"So anyway," a security goon said, patrolling the hallway containing the Olympus's server room. "She says 'It's the violence of your job influencing him.' So I say, 'He was being bullied, it's self-defense. Would you rather he just rolled over at took it?' Then she goes, 'There's other ways to solve conflict.' To which I scoff and, well—"

"Now you're on the couch?" said his partner.

Goon One hung his head. "Pretty much."

"Well, kinda proved her point with that, didn't she?" Goon Two grinned.

They nodded as a woman in business casual passed carrying a black canvas shoulder bag. She smiled, flashing her ID, and continued. The goons panned to check out her figure. Then, she turned and caught them mid-ogle, and they scrambled to look busy doing security stuff elsewhere.

Brie moved over to the door to the server room and gave the digital lock a once-over. She pulled the dry-erase marker wired to a small chipboard (this time with a fresh battery) and shoved the end of the marker into the bottom of the lock. She pressed a button on the chip board. The lock chirped, red light flashing twice. Then, it switched to green and the deadbolt unlatched with a whir.

Brie grinned—Billie's prosthetics tight like a clay mask—and slipped into the room, relieved to be working again. It gave her a break from thinking—a sort of Zen Burglar-flow. She threw the duffel on the ground, unzipped it, then wiggled out of her pencil skirt. She pulled a pair of overalls out of the bag, stepped into them, and zipped up. She tossed her skirt and heels in the duffel and came back with a pair of leather boots.

Once she'd changed, she grabbed the small gunmetal tube out of the bag and strolled into a bay of servers to her right: black monoliths, all flashing arrays of green lights, arranged with the neatness of tombstones in a military graveyard. She checked the number penned into the palm of her hand, found the tower with a matching label, then pulled the spool-up USB cable from the tube and plugged it into the back of the server.

Then, she mussed up her hair and pulled on a hat with *OmniView* embroidered on the front. She wiped the ink off her palm, collected her things, and headed back through the entrance.

Back in the brainstorm room, the first egg-timer dinged. "Whole Lotta Love" opened in a thundering riff, and Tommy did a jazz-hands flourish over the keyboard, face twisted in deep preparation—a sprinter awaiting takeoff or, well, *Zoolander*.

Ruby wound up the three remaining egg-timers, setting them back on the table as Tommy descended upon the keys, sounding like a crew of cockroaches doing tango: *Click-Cli-Cl-Cl-Click click click...* When he got up to speed, he was almost in sync with the egg-timers.

Tommy sent a feed of the OmniView's display—the one Olympus staff used—to the projector. The screen lit up with a grid of camera angles; vectors narrowing in on the big betters on the floor, biometric readings, a scrollable manifest of guests, and six world clocks in the top left. Ruby leaned back, crossing her legs.

"I thought we couldn't hack them?"

"No," Tommy said, fingers still flying across the keyboard. "We can't hack *it*. This is just a mirror of what security sees. We can't do anything to it without a red flag."

"But doesn't the system know you're mirroring it or whatever? I thought it was impossible."

"It can only see if we try to get past it. It can't see that we're seeing it." Tommy sighed, trying to find the right analogy to explain this in layman's terms. "You know that phrase, you can't see the back of your eye?"

"Yes. No. Kind of."

"Well," he said with a shrug. "It's like that."

"That's like the worst analogy ever."

"Shh, I'm concentrating here!"

"And, I'm trying to understand stuff. You're not very helpful."

"Uhuh," Tommy said. "Well, not very helpful has two minutes to find and hack the safe's elevator, so shush."

"But if you can't hack the eye—"

"It's not the eye!" Tommy snapped. "It is like an entirely different body part that you can't see... It's like your nose."

"But if you're mirroring then you can—"

"Not applicable to this analogy," he grumbled, all the while rooting through layers of code to find the system that ran the elevator. He typed, then typed, then typed some more; losing himself in what Ruby thought looked like the Matrix.

"Well how many analogies are there? I'm sure even the audience at home is confused by now."

"Can you just let me work? This is going to take forever—done."

Ruby sighed. "Can you speak plainly for two minutes?"

"Actually, now we've got five," Tommy said, grinning while a prompt appeared on the OmniView: a big red box, flashing ALERT! ELEVATOR FAILURE IMMINENT.

Josh Harlan stood across the street from the Olympus, wearing a chambray shirt, black jeans, a black Stetson, and a Bono-esque pair of rose-tinted sunglasses, eyeing the great concrete tower with a grin when his watch beeped. He chewed a stick of Big Red, and cut across the street (which, by the way, is a felony in Vegas). He slapped the bellhop's shoulder.

"Think heavily on your future affairs, pardner."

"Uh… Okay?" said the bellhop, whose name tag read: JONES.

Harlan chuckled, stuck a hundred-dollar bill in the bellhop's hand, and said, "Anyhow, I gotta see a barkeep about a drink. You keep hold of your britches, now, Jones."

Southern drawl like syrup. He'd lifted it from the car salesman. Before Jones could respond, Harlan was through the doors and basking in the air conditioning. He sucked back a big drag of cigarette-strewn oxygen, grinning at everyone moving around the lobby, then descended the steps into the casino, headed for the disc-shaped bar in the middle. Along the way, he noted all the big players at the tables.

He sidled up and grabbed a stool, rapping his knuckles on the bar. He spun a three-sixty while the barkeep came over.

"Three fingers of Bookers, two ice cubes, and a tip if you're snippy."

The man in the apron nodded, poured, and slid the glass down the bar. Harlan caught it, sipped and said, "Ah, good sling."

Then, he slid the man another hundred. "Now, amigo. Here's what I need. I'll take the bottle. I need some ice. I need a private room. And I need a gal in a skimpy outfit to keep me company."

"What am I, Zeus?" said the barkeep.

Harlan slid another five bills across the bar. "Y'are now. Will there be anything further needed?"

The bartender gave his stack of cash an appraising glimpse. "I'll make a call."

"You do that," Harlan said, turning back to the action transpiring in the casino, sipping his drink.

And speaking of drinks, Quinn Donovan came into the casino, shaky for having not had one in an hour. Considering everything he was about to do, he felt like someone should've given him the St. Crispin's Day Speech. *We few,* he thought, *we buggered few...*

Well, he was paraphrasing.

The elevator brought him up the side of the casino. Quinn felt like there were ants crawling under his skin. He was wearing a tweed suit, a fake beard, a pair of horn-rimmed glasses and an annoying bloody tie. His shirt clung to the bullets of sweat on his back. What was it with people? Who wore suits? Sods, that's who. The odd vest and top hat—that he was fine with. But a full suit was bloody uncomfortable. Impractical. Stiff. And he had ruddy ants in his skin.

The elevator dinged. Quinn took a steadying breath, cleared his mind, and stepped off. He came into the reception area for Whelan's office with a grin.

"Alright, love," he said as the secretary looked up from her iPad. "Here to see the big man."

She gave him an incredulous eyebrow, swiping. "You are?"

"Harry Langtree," he said. "I'm a representative of SpyTech."

Without looking up, she tapped a few times, checking his credentials. Then, reading, she brightened and turned to him with a sort of professionally-thrusted enthusiasm. "Mister Langtree. This is a surprise."

"Well, surprises are my specialty." He grinned, laying on charm as thick as he knew how, failing completely to remember that he was in disguise as a bearded nerd. The secretary gave him a beleaguered expression, a sort of *Do you have any idea how many times a day gross dudes flirt with me?* look, and Quinn cleared his throat awkwardly.

"I mean you're not on the books," she said.

"Ah, well that would be." Quinn adjusted his tie, looking around the reception area for an object he could steer the conversation toward. Probably a bad call, considering the place was styled in minimalist motif. "I'm in town on a conference and thought I'd pop in, see how the system's doing. It's very white in here…"

The secretary flipped through a schedule on her tablet. "Oh, he's actually got an opening in ten minutes."

"Lovely. I suppose we'll have to amuse ourselves in the meantime," Quinn said. Despite his performance, he was actually quite used to pretending to be someone else. He did it every night he worked Fremont, then again any time he knocked off a bordello. The problem was, he didn't know how not to be crass.

The secretary rolled her eyes. "Mister Langtree, I'm actually quite busy at the moment, but feel free to have a seat."

She motioned toward the bank of couches across the room.

Then, the blipping sound of a Facebook messenger notification came from her computer. In fact, the entire window was still open at her desk. Quinn raised an eyebrow: *Busy, are we?*

She smiled curtly. "Magazine?"

CHAPTER 20
SOUTHERN CONSORTS

Josh Harlan stood at the craps table next to an attractive brunette named Vicky, twisting his fake mustache and chewing a cigarillo. Vicky dangled the bottle of bourbon in one hand, and a pair of tumblers in the other. Harlan eyed the table, smoked, then mashed the cigar in an ashtray with a grin.

"Alright amigos." He slapped a wad of bills on the table and nodded at the croupier. "Color me up, hoss. Now who wants to roll some dice?"

He flashed a grin while the model/waitress/escort poured a pair of drinks. He turned to her, took his glass and said, "Why thank you, sugar."

"Trust me, hun. I'm spice."

Here, Josh tossed off a joyous chuckle and grabbed Vicky by the small of her back. They swapped a tongue-heavy kiss, and he came back, considering. "You know what? You're right, darlin'." Then to the table: "Well, alright. Let's burn some Benjamins."

The dealer pushed over his chips. Harlan wagged his head. "I don't touch 'em, hoss. Call me superstitious. Let's lay down—what do you think, m'dear?"

Vicky shrugged. "I'd be impressed with two million."

"Well let's make it an even three and get you properly twitterpated."

"Three million in," called the croupier.

"Anybody care to match me?" Harlan said to the crowd. "Or shall I throw some bones and resume passing severe tongue to Vicky here?"

Vicky grinned a Miss America grin, then grabbed him by his shirt collar. "This shit is *so* costing you extra," she whispered.

Josh chuckled, patting her bottom and palming an extra thousand bucks into her hand when she went to stop him. "That oughta cover it, don't you figure?" Back to the crowd: "Ladies, gentlemen, and however else you fancy identifying! Is there nobody here wanting to take on a three-mil wager?"

"I believe I can match that," a Parisian accent oozed out of the crowd like a fine camembert. A slim man in a neat suit, with a wavy bristle of hair and a severe nose came forth and put his hand on the table. A pair of attractive blondes flanked him, and each dropped a stack of purple discs on the table. "I'm in. Let's roll some dice."

The croupier handed each of them a pair of dice, and the men and their escorts headed to the end of the table.

"Sevens," said the Frenchman.

"Snake eyes," said Josh. And here, he held the dice out to Vicky. "Would you, darlin'?"

Reluctantly, patiently, she leaned in and blew on the dice.

Meanwhile, the Frenchman's escorts had not only blown on his dice, but poured him a drink, straightened his suit jacket, pawed him significantly, and generally made a nearly gag-worthy spectacle. Josh almost felt a little out-suaved, and to that, he had to give props.

They threw their dice. An unseen kettle drum syncopated the bounce of their rolls. The dice skittered toward the end of the table, the drumbeat rallying up, intensifying, then as the dice slowed: *dum...dum-du-du-du-du...dum.* Also unseen, a gong sang to the end of the roll.

Harlan's dice came up six and three, the Frenchman's five and seven.

Josh shrugged. "I never got a handle on this one."

The Frenchman chuckled. "They call it craps for a reason, *mon ami.* Because it is a crap game. I am Vincent. Vincent LaFleur."

"Josh Randall," Harlan said, shaking Vincent's hand. "Poker's more my thing."

"Odds, wit, and confidence." Vincent nodded. "A better one, indeed. *Mes chéries? Allons-y.*"

Josh swigged his drink and motioned to Vicky that it was time to go. "See you 'round, Monsieur LaFleur."

"And you, *Monsieur* Randall."

Three minutes later, Josh and Vicky were having a drink with a Big Oil guy named Scooter Maverick: mid-fifties salt and pepper with a mustache you could hang a Western anthem on. They sat by the horse racing screens in the video gambling alcove, both having just lost an eighth-million on a horse named Scarlett Fever—the idea being that the horse ran as fast as the disease spread.

But losing's part of gambling. You didn't stew in losses and whine; you stacked forward, until you'd broken the goddamn bank and hiked home in your skivvies—or such was Scooter Maverick's opinion.

It was nigh impossible for him to make a dent in his checkbook. Sure, he'd blown expense accounts, but oil was gold. It was better than gold. Well, it at least had better expense accounts. Maverick Fuels had a virtual monopoly over the southwest sales of petrol, and since Scooter was the owner, he didn't actually know what losing felt like, even though he just had. And despite his greenback cushion, the thing that was really Scoot solace was the leggy brunette whom he appeared quite taken with, Vicky, who appeared to be taken right back.

"Owning the stuff that runs the world is not worth half a night with you," Scooter said. To Harlan: "You sir, are a lucky man."

"Ya-huh," Josh said. "Kinda got the horseshoe. Ever play poker?"

"Don't sell yourself short, stud," Vicky said, ignoring the conman. "I dig a man with some seasoning. Plus I really like your mustache."

Scooter chuckled, waving her off. "Hush now. I'm an old man, my dear. Powerful, sure as Shinola, but old. Too old."

Under the table, Vicky's hand found Harlan's junk and squeezed. He almost yelped, but held it back pretending to stifle a sneeze.

"Well, age is experience?" The hand loosened, then rubbed once, twice…

"Enough of your wiles." Scooter chuckled. To Harlan: "What were you saying about poker?"

Harlan just grinned.

Six minutes after that, Josh and Vicky were at the baccarat table. Josh was frowning, unhappy with how all the felts at the Olympus were purple instead of the traditional green. It made everything that happened feel like some kind of weird dream—and that was annoying as shit.

Across, a man in his early thirties, clean-cut suit and slicked-back hair, wore an intense expression while he shoved a mound of chips forward.

His name was Leo Stillwater, a bigwig stockbroker and recreational pilot in from New York, celebrating the fiscal new year after his firm had plummeted in the last quarter. The IRS had begun investigating him, and his girlfriend of six years had just caught him cheating on her with his secretary.

"It is *always* the fucking secretaries that get you," he said, shaking his head.

In the last three hands, Leo had told his story about a dozen times. Each with no recollection of the previous telling. Also, he was riding a small mountain's worth of coke. He sweated, tugging at his shirt collar.

"Hey, you guys wanna get naked?"

The dealer brought up their cards. Leo scowled at them. "What just happened?"

"We lost," Josh said.

Leo looked nervously at Vicky—who nodded—then slapped the bar. "Well then *what* is the motherfucking *point* of this game? Huh?" Then, a breath. He blinked. "Hey, you guys wanna get naked?"

"We've actually gotta run," Josh said.

"People to see," Vicky added, nodding furiously.

"Oh," Leo nodded. "Okay. But what about that poker game you were talking about?"

Josh looked at Vicky, who gave him a *Don't even fucking think about it* expression, then shrugged. "You need at least a couple hands of millions you're willing to lose."

"I know." Leo snorted. "But what about the poker game?"

Five minutes later, they walked away from a bizarre game of dominos that Josh had only lost because people refused to tell him the rules, and in a little way, that bothered him. Vicky trotted up behind and pinched his butt.

"Now *him*, I'd get naked with."

Him's name was Howie Reed, the fourth of Harlan's targets, a filthy-rich, thirty-four-year-old playboy weapons manufacturer who had a thing for high-ball scotch and week-long adventures in decadence. He owned Reed Industries. Josh hated him from the moment they'd met.

"Yeah, well him I reckon I can do without."

"Oh come on. The guy's worth gazillions. He's been on the cover of *Forbes* and *Time*. Very high-profile."

"Yeah, but I don't like him."

They went through a hallway lined with vending machines and a row of bathrooms, heading toward the third of the Olympus's colossal gambling chambers.

"I'm actually starting to enjoy this," Vicky said, grabbing Harlan by the collar. She shoved him up against the wall, pinning him with one thigh as her skirt rode up. "Let's get the last one and find a room."

Harlan chuckled. "Would that I could, but I'm on the clock."

"And I'm not?" A coquettish brow-raise.

Josh gave her a once-over, nearly breaking character for an instant. It wasn't like he hadn't enjoyed indulgence on the job before. Hell, half the fun of being a criminal was not having a rulebook to follow. But there was a lot riding on this one. Sure, part of him wanted to find a broom closet and shag the bejeezus out of her, but what he was doing was time-sensitive.

"What are you doing after?"

Vicky grinned, pushing off him. "Let's go find our prince."

They found him at the blackjack table, surrounded by a crunch of linebacker-sized men with olive skin. He wore a bright blue Hawaiian shirt, cargo shorts, and a fuzzy bomber-hat. His skin was dark, his features pointed, a neat goatee flecked with premature gray. Prince Caspar Akhtar-Bukhari sucked back the seventh gin and tonic of his existence—and he appeared quite pleased with the effects.

Harlan and Vicky threaded through the crowd, and Josh signaled the dealer to cut him in, then nodded to the prince, who'd been giving him a curious gaze. The dealer gave a slight bow, then dispensed a row of cards to the players.

"Flip 'em."

They did. Josh came up twenty-five. The dealer had fourteen. Caspar pulled a blackjack.

"Yes! I won. I fucking won. I fucking love this game!"

Josh tipped his Stetson with a grin. "How do you feel about poker?"

The prince whirled around, nearly toppling off his stool. He slammed the table. "Who? Me? You want to play some fucking cards? I'll play some fucking cards. I don't know what you mean about this poking thing, but I'll play."

At the end of twenty minutes, Josh and Vicky headed back toward the main room of the casino, taking a hall that contained a cafe, a Vietnamese restaurant, a surf-and-turf buffet, and—conveniently for Vicky—a row of restrooms.

"So that's everybody?"

Harlan nodded. "We'll need to get them in that private room in a New York jiffy."

"No problem," she said. And here, she grabbed Josh by the

belt buckle and dragged him into the restroom, which was empty. She slammed him against the door and locked it. "We have a little time, don't we?"

"You're not arresting me, are you?"

She kissed him. "In a manner of speaking. I never did mention how you'd be paying for my services. I *am* spice, remember?"

Her dress fell to the floor.

"So, that's step one?" said Ruby Cobb. "The rest of us work, and Harlan just... What, dicks around for half an hour? Has fun?"

"Sure," Tommy said, eyeing the egg-timers. "It could look like that. But it's actually pretty complicated."

" 'Splain, please?"

"Well, he has to con five bigshots into a poker game, somehow convince them to put their money in the safe, and he's got to do it all in the next ten minutes before the elevator goes. If he doesn't, then we lose the twenty-million bonus."

"And he plans to do that all while having fun?"

Tommy shrugged. "If he can manage to enjoy himself while he works, then he's kind of earned it, hasn't he?"

Ruby slumped back on the couch. "Fine. What next?"

CHAPTER 21
LOVING AN ELEVATOR

"Mister Langtree. This is a surprise. Please, come in." Whelan led Quinn through the French doors into his office. Quinn looked around, and found the diamond right where Harlan had told him it would be: on the tycoon's wall of trinkets, sitting on a purple pillow display, gleaming like the eye of a god.

"Please, call me Harry," Quinn said.

Whelan grinned, moving over to the wet bar under what Quinn considered to be the worst sodding painting he'd ever laid eyes upon.

"Drink?"

"I'd love one."

Whelan came back with tumblers filled with scotch and motioned for the magician to sit.

Quinn took a chair, stuffing his nose in the glass, taking in the peaty aroma. It wasn't thirst about to be quenched, it was the sight of land after years at sea; sunlight after a decade in solitary; the warmth of spring after a long winter. He swigged, letting the spice roll over his pallet, and swallowed. It was bloody marvelous.

"So, what brings you to Vegas, Mr. Langtree?" The tycoon set his glass on the table and steepled his fingers.

Now that Quinn had enjoyed his drink, he noticed Whelan. He looked, well… younger than he'd appeared in all the photos Harlan had back at the abandoned mall. Quinn hadn't really studied them further than to note the tycoon as just another rich wanker. But there had been wrinkles in the photos. He was certain of it.

"In town for a conference over at the Caesar's Palace," he said. "I figured while I was here, I'd pop in, see how our system was treating you."

"It's doing an excellent job. What conference?"

"What's that?"

Gavin smiled. "I'm a business owner, Harry. When people don't choose my establishments for their conferences, I like to make a note. Send a fruit basket."

"Right," Quinn said. Bollocks! He hadn't expected having to forge an identity, a motivation, and a legitimate sounding conference name on top of it. Hell, he had enough trouble remembering the name of the company he was supposed to work for. "It's an advanced software workshop. All the programmers are in from Silicon Valley, San Francisco, the like. Basically a bunch of us nerds getting together to shoot the bull."

"I see," said Whelan, and if there were suspicion in that remark, Quinn couldn't detect it.

What was the policy when it came to lying a bunch? Follow it up with… A joke? An observation? Oh, right—you finished with a smidge of truth.

"But, if I'm being honest, Mr. Whelan—"

"Oh, call me Gavin."

"—Gavin. If I'm being honest, I'm not really here for the conference. I'm here for the birds. The whole concept of a lady with a tan is rather fetching. Sunshine. Breasts. Good combination."

The tycoon chuckled. "Well, we have good stock of both, Harry."

"So I've noticed. I've been enjoying. Can I ask you something, Gavin?"

Whelan nodded.

"What is the story with that painting?" Quinn said, taking another sip of his drink, regarding the fuck-ugly artwork to the left.

"Prometheus. He stole fire from the gods. This was his punishment."

"I see," Quinn said, nodding slowly. "Bloody awful, innit?"

Gavin laughed. "It reminds me to never get too confident. An Aesop for what happens if you take too much."

Quinn set his empty tumbler on Whelan's desk and said, "You know, I can't help noticing... You've got a lot of valuables out in the open here. With that bugger of a safe in your basement, don't you think it's a little risky just having them out?"

Whelan nodded, accepting Quinn's point. "Some things are sentimental, Harry. You like to have them around you. Sure, mine all happen to be expensive—but don't forget your system's programmed to flag anything before it leaves the premises."

"I knew that," Quinn said.

"I don't know. It's a fucking island," said Prince Caspar Akhtar-Bukhari. "It's in the middle of the fucking ocean. What do you want from me?"

"Yeah, but where?" said Howie Reed, across the table, chewing a cigar. "What ocean?"

Caspar lit a Camel and exhaled twin streams of smoke. "I don't feel like telling you now. So are we going to play some fucking cards or what?"

Howie sighed, sending a tired expression across the table to Scooter Maverick.

The oilman shrugged. "Kid's got a point, Howie. We're here to gamble. No need to measure each other's tackle."

"I'll second that," said Harlan. "Now, gents. We've been playing chump change long enough. What do you reckon we all toss on another four-mil and play a real game? Casper here's got an island, but one of us could still win enough to match him."

"It's *Caspar*," said the Prince, spitting on the carpet. "You fucking Americans. You can't pronounce for shit."

"*Oui*," said Vincent LaFleur, behind a wall of cigarette smoke. "*C'est vrai*."

Caspar wagged his head. "What, you think I understand what you're saying? Speak English, fuckwad. These fucking French, think they're better than everybody. You know, other, richer countries have a language, too."

"True, but at least mine does not sound like you are having a cold."

"Ha!" Caspar stubbed out his cigarette, narrowing his eyes. "Ha! Well at least I know how to conjugate in fucking English."

"Gents," Scooter said, moving his hands as if to smooth over the conflict. "Settle. We're here to play cards, not fight over verbiage."

"Of course, the American comes to battle pretending to be a peacekeeper," Caspar snarled.

"Dude's got a point," said Howie.

"Okay gentlemen," Josh said, standing and holding out his arms to call for peace. "We've established the stakes and had a good bit of name calling. I say we cut the deck and settle this like menfolk."

"Monsieur," sighed LaFleur. "We were all waiting on you."

Josh slapped his knee with a full-bore Southern chuckle.

"Well lick my nuts and call me sugar, y'all shoulda said something."

"I wanna cut the deck," said Leo Stillwater, resident king of the stock market (who up until this point had been rocking back and forth in coked-out catatonia). "Can I cut the deck? Gimme the deck, I'll cut it. Let's go, let's go, let's go."

"Fellas, I think Mr. Stillwater here's got a point. We're all too rich to be bored, aren't we? Four million each."

"Peanuts," Howie said, snapping. An assistant skittered out of the shadows with a big metal briefcase. "Absolute peanuts. Here. Take it. Please." Then, he looked over to the private bar, where Vicky was sipping a vodka tonic. "Hi, dear? Can I get a drink over here? I'm dying of boredom."

"Well, that settles it, then," Harlan said, looking around the rest of the table. "Howie here knows how to gamble, what about the rest of you?"

One by one, the men produced briefcases full of cash. When they were all on the table, Harlan turned to Vicky. "Darlin', who do we have to suck off to get some chips in here?"

Vicky flipped him off, producing a phone from behind the bar, and made the call. "Two minutes. Anybody else want a drink? 'Cause you hyper-entitled douche-waffles can make them yourself. I'm punching out."

The six men looked at each other, then shrugged.

Vicky shook her head, finished her drink, collected the cash-filled briefcases, and threw open the door just in time for a croupier to arrive with a caddy full of chips. "They're all yours, Stew. I hope you like hearing idiots talk." She turned back to the table and bowed. "Your money's heading to the safe." Then to Josh: "It's been a slice, sugar. *Adios.*"

Harlan tipped his Stetson, and she was gone.

"My, she is a pistol," said Scooter.

"You have no idea," Harlan said, thinking: *Right on time.*

"Hey," said Leo Stillwater. "Anybody wanna get naked?"

"Not me," said Tommy Carlyle. "I mean, sure, I counted a bit of blackjack in high school. But I was never into cards."

"Except for Pokémon," Ruby said.

"Except for Pokémon," Tommy agreed, sighing wistfully. "Strategy, evolution, tiny monsters at your command? Who wouldn't like that?"

"Oh, just the cool kids."

"Yeah, well the cool kids have clearly never beaten Brock's gym with a fire-type. It's amazing. Like taking down a glacier with a Zippo."

"Not helping your case," Ruby said.

"Not making a case," Tommy said. "It's a fact."

Ruby drummed her fingers against her arm, about to say that being impressively nerdy was not the same thing as being impressive, when the second egg-timer dinged.

"And we arrive at step two." Tommy hit the enter key on his keyboard and leaned back with a satisfied flourish.

"What did you just do?" Ruby said.

"Behold," he said, motioning to the display of the OmniView on the wall, a flashing prompt in the middle of the floor plan read: CRITICAL! ELEVATOR MALFUNCTION.

"I'm not saying violence isn't the answer," said Goon Two.

"Good," Goon One said. "That'd be hypocritical as fuck."

"I'm saying biting the principal is an entirely different issue."

"Oh, like you never did that when you were a kid." Then, off Goon Two's expression. "What? What? Oh, fuck off."

They strolled along the corridor containing the entrance to the safe. One more floor, another half hour, and the swing shift would take over. Then, they could grab a beer and head to their respective homes.

"You know," said Goon Two. "It might be hereditary."

"Dude, you don't know what you're talking about. It was a fluke. The kid's fine."

"He bit the principle, who was trying to stop him from murdering a nine-year-old."

"Bully," Goon One corrected. "A nine-year-old bully. Totally different. What? Ugh. Seriously, what? I have a point here."

Goon Two was stopped in front of the elevator which led to the safe. Above the door was a flashing orange strobe.

"That's not good."

Goon One furrowed his brow. He swiped a keycard and pressed the button that hailed the elevator. Nothing happened. He tried two more times, then took a step back.

"Huh."

Goon Two was already on the phone.

"Maintenance," Brie said into the burner phone. Then, not to sell the act, but just for kicks, she added: "Please hold." And put down the cell to enjoy her latte.

She'd been waiting in the casino Starbucks for nearly a half-hour, so it gave her a twinge of satisfaction to make security staff wait. There are few things as pleasing as fucking with a douche in a hurry. If everything had gone as planned, then they'd be in stage-five wig-out right now. She smiled, finished her drink, and picked up the phone.

"Hi, this is Mary, how can I help you?"

She listened as a frazzled-sounding man relayed the situation in machine gun monologue. Apparently, he'd already hit terminal wiggage. So really, she couldn't help it when she said, "Thank you. Please hold."

Then, she collected her things, took her time returning her mug to the barista, and put on her best phone voice.

"This is Darlene. I can be there in two minutes."

CHAPTER 22
TWO GOONS, A TYCOON, AND THE HUMAN PINBALL

Brie arrived at the elevator and flashed her ID at the two bewildered-looking goons. She tossed her duffel on the floor.

"Sorry about the wait, fellas."

Goon Two was scowling at his watch. "You said two minutes. That was eight minutes ago."

"Uhuh," Brie said. "Well, there was traffic. Not to mention I've had to jumpstart about a dozen lifts around the city today. I've been given more shit than a sanitation plant, and I'm way overdue on my evening frapp. So I guess you're just gonna have to deal with it, munchkin."

"Sorry."

"He's a little stressed," said Goon One. "Hey, lemme ask you something. Is it weird if a kid bites the principal?"

"Sorry," Brie said. "My expertise only covers problemed lifting devices. But, off the books? Yeah, that's weird." She tilted her head to the elevator. "This the patient?"

"Yeah," said Goon One.

Brie gave the door an appraising once-over. An RFID-engaged

entry system with no visible overrides? Not bad. "I don't suppose either of you gents has a key?"

They nodded.

"I tried like five times," added Goon One. "It's not working."

Brie looked at her overalls, the elevator, then the men.

"No shit," she said. "Cough 'em up."

The goons gave her their security badges. Brie tried each of them, but only coaxed tortured beeps from the RFID panel. "Yup, she's pooched, fellas. Override panel's at the bottom, right?"

"Yeah."

"Well then, I'm gonna have to crack her open." She unzipped her duffel and produced a drill.

"Woah, hang on a sec," said Goon One.

Goon Two nodded. "You're not—"

"Seriously?" Brie said. "You guff me for tardiness and now you're telling me to wait? You need to make up your mind, nameless goon."

"Let me radio it in—"

Brie feigned the sigh of someone at the tightening end of her rope. "Look. Layman's terms: Elevator, brokey. Drill fixy. Me do drill thing now."

"That elevator leads to a safe filled with—how many millions of dollars, Chris?"

"Lots," said Chris, formerly Goon Two.

"Lots of millions," said Goon One. "I need to radio it in."

Brie rubbed her brow with a long sigh. "I'm not asking you not to. I'm just trying to do my job. And that involves cracking open this door and getting to those overrides."

"But—"

"Your lots of millions are protected with a fingerprint entry system, right?" Brie gave them both an *I am too tired for this shit* expression.

"Yeah, but—"

"And do I look like I have a third thumb on me? Any reports of someone with a recently severed digit in your ranks? No? Good."

Before they could argue, she took the drill and started working on the top left of the door, where a safety latch kept it shut. Coils of metal fell to the floor, and in the time it takes to flip an omelet, the drill plunged through the latch. She removed it, then slid the door open.

The elevator was wedged between floors, leaving a five-foot opening to the shaft. Brie went back to the duffel, produced the magnetic winch she'd been practicing with back at the mall, and slapped it on the bottom of the elevator.

Then, she produced a harness from the bag, stepped into it, and hooked it to the rig.

"You just have that stuff?" said Goon One.

"An ounce and a pound, and whatever," Brie said. She took a steadying breath, leaned back, and dangled into the chasm.

"I really feel like I should radio this in," said Chris.

"Go ahead," Brie said, twirling slowly on the line. "And fellas?"

Both goons looked up from their phones.

"When I get back, there'd better be a frapp with my name on it. Or somebody's going to have a very rough morning. Hand me my bag."

The elevator shaft was circular, about twelve-feet across, smooth concrete the whole way down. There were no vents or lights to guide the thirty-foot descent. Brie set the winch to SLOW, and dropped steadily. It was like the world's slowest Big Drop. Strangely, that made it even scarier.

About ten feet in, the wedge of light coming from above no longer reached her. The remainder of the way would be passed in complete darkness. Brie wished she'd brought a flashlight or a miner's lamp—maybe even one of those *Mission Impossible* headbands with the mini light built in.

The air grew cooler the deeper she went. Darkness, damp and heavy with the smell of mechanic's grease, swallowed her feet. It was like sinking into a pool of cold tar. The churning of a nearby generator filled the void with a kind of white noise, and for a while the only discernible sounds were Brie's breathing and the whir of the winch as it spooled her further into the black.

Halfway down, the sound of groaning metal came from above, followed by a heavy *thunk*. Before she could realize what happened, Brie was in free fall. She dropped a good five feet before the line caught with a banjo twang, and her harness jerked her up with a yelp.

Brie gripped the line, her pulse screeching in her eardrums, an electric shot of adrenaline sent her nerves tingling. There was no slow-mo, life-before-one's-eyes respite. Just white slate; her breath caught in her throat.

Holy fiery fuckballs, I'm going to die.

"Shit," she gasped. She looked up at the tiny wedge of light. The elevator had moved. How? Tommy said it would be at a dead-stop once he hacked it. Could someone override it? Was the elevator actually defective? Oh, wouldn't that be hilarious...

Before she could think further, the movement rippled down the rope and sent her swinging in a loose figure-eight. The winch continued unspooling, sending her in a wider twirl with the slack of the line. Her shoes scraped the edge of the tunnel, then she swung back the other way.

"Oh, no, no, no!" Too late. She slammed into the opposite side hard enough to knock the wind out of her, cracking the back of her head on the concrete. Stars spotted her vision.

In the dark, she couldn't even prepare for the next blow. She slammed her knees against the wall, then her elbows, then swung back. Brie heaved herself up on the line and brought her legs in front of her, then bent her knees to soften the impact. She kicked off and up before the pendulum could catch her again, and bounced in the harness. She was still twirling, but had offset the swing.

"This is *so* not what I signed up for," she grumbled. "Oh sure, Quinn gets to steal a diamond and Harlan gets to dick around in the casino, but Brie? Let's make her play the human fucking pinball."

Her knees and the back of her head throbbed. You had to hand it to physics for being able to suck the joy out of even an elaborate safecracking operation. If it weren't for the revenge driving her, she'd probably just climb back up the elevator shaft and tell the goons to fix this shit themselves.

Light came from the bottom of the tunnel. Brie lowered into a ten foot opening at the base of the shaft, which was lit with columns of florescent tubes in the underground bunker fashion. The floor was white tile. Across the ten-foot hallway was the safe: a great iron door shaped and sized like the front of a freight train, with a six-foot spindle in the middle. To the right was the glowing fingerprint keypad. Etched in the metal was: HEMINGWAY 1961, NO. 0381.

She grinned. Finally, a worthy challenge.

The H-1961, affectionately called the Wax Puppy in the thief community, is so named because it's sensitive. Basically, if you give it so much as a poke in the wrong direction, it will figuratively blow its head off and seal itself. Then, the only way to open it is a key that only works if you know the combination to set its teeth in the right position. Until now, Brie had thought it was just a myth cooked up by bored safecrackers—the thieving equivalent of the Lock Ness monster.

The winch reached the end of its tether, which was troublesome, as Brie was still suspended five feet above the floor. She looked up, pressed the button to advance the lead, and when nothing happened, she sighed.

"Great." She tossed her duffel into the hallway, then produced a pocketknife from her coveralls. It wasn't like she was going to bring the contents of the safe up on the rope. Besides, the prospects of cracking a legendary safe were nearly good enough to compensate for what was going to happen next. She cut the rope.

What happened next—well, it fucking hurt.

Even for a man who'd lived over a hundred years to steel his patience, Gavin Whelan was beginning to find enduring Harry Langtree's sexploit stories painful.

"And then, she takes out a cucumber and a jar of wasabi, and says 'Do you know how it feels to have this on your nipples?' " Here, Langtree rubbed his nipples for effect. "Then she takes the cucumber and—"

Whelan's phone rang. He held up a finger to pause his and Harry's conversation, thinking: *thank the gods*.

"Yes?"

"Cassiday's at the safe," said one of his security personnel. "We're right on time."

Gavin looked at his watch, then grinned. "Excellent. Let's move to phase two."

"You want me to trip the system? The *threat* prompt's flashing."

"No," Whelan said. "Override that, I'm on the way."

He hung up and stood, straightening his blazer. "Mr. Langtree, I apologize, but something's just come up that requires my attention."

Langtree finished his third scotch, standing. "Something I can help with? I mean, the system—"

Whelan waved him down with a grin. "Just another meeting. Thanks for stopping by, Harry."

With that he was through the door.

In the lobby, Gavin's secretary Chelsea was pacing with her hand to her headset. "Pressure sensor triggered a minute ago. I've got a team on the way."

Whelan nodded. "Tell them to bring tactical gear. I'll meet them there."

"Vector Alpha Six, Tango Alpha Three. Full tactical at the base of the elevator. Code Brown. Repeat, Code Brown."

Gavin frowned. "You still haven't changed the name?"

Chelsea shrugged. "For the *Everything's Gone to Shit* code, it's kind of evocative."

Well, she had a point. Gavin put his fingers to his temples and concentrated. He visualized where he needed to be, closed his eyes, and with a puff of blue smoke, he vanished.

Chelsea sighed, wistfully. "Three years, and that shit still gives me the wiggins."

Back in Whelan's office, Quinn stared at the door, just a little dumbfounded. He blinked. He panned from the door to the diamond. Then, back to the door. Then to the diamond. He waited, then he wagged his head and chuckled. A grin spread over his face.

"Well, that was bloody easy." He strolled over to the diamond. He'd been expecting theatrics, and had been working up to a point in the conversation where he'd stand and stride around the office.

Now, alone, it seemed almost unfair. All that prep, all that drying out for nothing. He reached out, and when his fingers were a hairsbreadth from the stone, a fork of electricity jumped off the diamond. Quinn leapt nearly three feet in the air, his hair standing on end, fingers sizzling.

"BLOODY FUCKING HELL." He landed on the floor, putting his fingers in his mouth while he scowled at the gem. "Electrified? Really?"

Then it dawned on him, the true reason Harlan had chosen him over all other sleight of hand experts: not his skill, not his speed, but his bullheadedness, and capacity to withstand pain.

"Oh, you fucking wanker."

He staggered over to the wet bar, flattening his hair. He ripped the cork off the bottle of whiskey and poured out a full tumbler's worth. Not only would he have to grab the diamond and withstand the full extent of the current running through it—he'd have to take it twice when he replaced it with the fake.

He downed his drink, belched, and eyed the diamond with a new level of hatred.

"Well, let's get this over with."

This would not be fun.

This was going to be fun. Brie produced a tube of superglue, an iPhone, a packet of quickset gelatin, a rubber mixing canister, and a small thermal printer from the fake bottom of her duffel. She crouched in front of the fingerprint keypad and twisted the cap off the superglue.

She waved the glue over the combination pad, and the vapors made rings of fingerprints appear like shaking a polaroid. While the ridges developed, she tore open the pack of gelatin and dumped it into the mixing bottle. She added a splash of water and shook, creating a milky, viscous liquid.

She set this to the side and angled the iPhone over the keypad, using the macro setting to photograph the crystalline prints. When she got a shot that would work, she created an inverse of the image and hooked the phone up to the thermal printer. The negative of the prints came out on a strip of clear plastic.

She grabbed the bottle of gelatin, shook another two times, then coated the face of the negative and set a timer on the iPhone for ninety seconds.

Faking a fingerprint was the easy part. Biometric scanners are notorious for their remarkable capacity for being fooled. Generally, with a couple of false starts, you could dupe most of them with a little eye shadow and some Planter's glue. But the good ones don't just read fingerprints, they also read electrical signals from the fingers making them. In that case, glue was about as useful as a ham in a vegan eatery. A gummy bear, however, is a fine alternative.

Because gelatin conducts electricity in the same way as a live finger. Brie had learned long ago that bringing gummy bears on a job was generally a bad call, as she'd eat them before she got within spitting distance of the safe. So it had to be gelatin, tasteless and pure.

The timer on her phone blipped, and she peeled the perfect sheet of fingerprints off the negative. Then, she took the sheet—what was essentially a unflavored Fruit Roll-Up—and draped it over the keypad.

This next part was the tough bit: the fingerprints sat over the numbers she needed to press, but she had no way of knowing the sequence. She'd have to guess. They lay in an L-shape, three down the far left, and one on the bottom right. She eyed the pattern, considering. Any of them could be a double-tap. But most people suck at remembering combinations over four digits. So, probably four. That narrowed it down a little.

She looked. She thought. Then, a number she'd seen scribbled throughout the pages of her mother's journal leapt into her mind: *1947*. All the big business with her mother's version of Whelan had happened in 1947. It was the year he'd taken over the casino. The year his business partner was murdered suspiciously. It was, in fewer words, important. Worth the risk.

So she pushed down on the spoofed prints and took a long breath.

Drumroll, she thought. *Drumroll, drumroll…*

Beep-beep! went the keypad as the light went green.

"Yahtzee!" Brie did a mini booty-dance of victory around the front of the safe, then spun the spindle and the door swung open.

Inside, sitting on a pallet of shrink-wrapped money, Gavin Whelan grinned, giving the thief a slow clap.

"Saw you coming."

Brie eyed the tycoon, who looked about twenty years younger than the last time they'd met. "…Have you Botoxed?"

Behind, the elevator arrived with a ding, and about twenty armed guards rushed out with their weapons pointed at Brie.

"Oh," she said, giving a sheepish kind of shrug. "Gulp?"

CHAPTER 23
COMMUNICATION BREAKDOWN

"Uh-oh," said Tommy Carlyle, furrowing his brow as his fingers ran across the keys.

"Uh-oh, what?" said Ruby.

"Something's wrong." Tommy did a three-beat slam on the enter key. "Yeah, something definitely."

"Something what?"

"Oh my god," Tommy said, eyes growing wide. His gaze panned up to the schematics running on the project. "Oh my god! No way. No, no, no…"

Clack-a-clack-a-clack-clack-clack…

Ruby smacked him in the back of the head, which surprisingly, did nothing to stop his brow-furrowing. "What?!"

"The elevator's moving," Tommy waved with his non-typing hand to the display that showed the elevator moving. "That can't happen. I wrote the code myself. That means… That means… Oh my god."

The hacker looked up from his display, face twisting with the kind of grim admiration normally reserved for a particularly fetid roommate's dump.

"I'm being hacked." Then, with a frowning nod, "Props."

Meanwhile, over at the Olympus, Steve Halverson grinned, chucking a bottle of Beck's to Gibbons. "Ah, I love this part. They never see it coming."

Phil chuckled. "Everyone loves an unexpected blindside."

"Let's just take a moment," Steve said, smiling. "Just imagine Carlyle's face right now. I bet it's priceless."

"Probably looks like he just bit into a pee-soaked pepper."

Steve gave his partner a disparaging frown. "You're lucky they don't pay you for your analogies."

Tommy made a face as if he'd just bitten into a pee-soaked pepper. "Where are you coming from?"

Typing.

"What are you distracting me from? Where are you going?"

More typing.

"Oh, crap."

"Should I even bother with the 'Oh crap, what?' " said Ruby.

Tommy turned the laptop just in time to show all of their photographs appearing on-screen. "Only if you care about whether the authorities know who you are?"

"Oh, *crap*."

Tommy nodded. "I got this. Just sit tight, okay?"

Ruby was already standing and pacing, which to no small extent harshed the hacker's cool. "Yeah, we can all sit über tight in prison."

Tommy commenced typing like a new kind of madman. "You know, I really thought the two of us had developed a rapport."

"Your point?" Ruby sighed, pinching her brow.

"Do I seriously have to fend this attack off while explaining all the ways you're not helping?"

He typed. He typed some more. He typed more than anybody.

"You know, you're not helping," sighed Halverson, taking a sip of his beer.

"What are you talking about?" Gibbons said. "I opened your beer, didn't I?"

"Yeah, not how I meant."

"Well, not knowing how to express gratitude is one of your issues. You know, this is part of why your marriage is on the fritz."

"Just because your name is Phil doesn't mean you've got a doctorate," Steve said through clenched teeth. "Now pipe down, I'm trying to concentrate."

"Fine, but only proving my point," said Gibbons.

"Pipe down, okay?" said Mister Weasel. "I'm holding him back. And if I swing this right, we'll also have all the Olympus's secure emails we could ever hope to look at."

Ruby shook her head. It wasn't that the hacker didn't understand the stakes, it was that the only way to reset them was typing that bothered her. Usually, this kind of heroics required guns and spunky attitudes.

"If they get those pictures to the cops or Interpol or something…"

"Of the two of us, who's actually *been* to prison?" Tommy took a steadying breath. "Now, please. Concentrating…"

"Well, I sure hate to nag, I'm just kind of attached to my freedom and anonymity, here."

Tommy chuckled. "Anonymity is the thing we sell you to give us your identity."

Ruby gave him an *I will kill you* expression. "Not helping."

"Well, at least this is the biggest of our problems?" Tommy said, completely oblivious to who was outside.

The last egg-timer went off.

Outside, Agent Max Reyes climbed out of his Prius in the escort of Sophie of the Mistress Shangrila. Around the block, a posse of ninja babes cocked their weapons, emerging from a fleet of unmarked vehicles. (And honestly, that part made Max feel at home.)

He made a series of hand gestures to Sophie, who'd relay them to the ninja squadron. A fist with the thumb out, asking for a horn-honk; three left-handed thumbs over the shoulder; an index to the sky, then the rock horns back and forth.

Max nodded, as if he'd just relayed an entire tactical plan, which he had.

Sophie shrugged, as if to ask *What the fuck?!*, which she was.

Reyes sighed. "We flank them in a horseshoe. Two teams hit the back, the rest of us go in the front?"

"Oh," Sophie said, nodding. "Cool."

She made an equally complex, but different set of gestures, then racked the slide of her shotgun. "Let's move."

Holding a riot grade shotgun with 40-gram beanbag rounds, Reyes led them across the road. The remaining ninjas circled around the back of the building.

It all deserved a soundtrack. But at this point, blaring the Stones would kind of ruin the element of surprise.

Brie was taken to a room that was all cinderblock and bare bulb. The goons dumped her in a metal chair. Then, before she could react, another one slapped a pair of zip ties around her wrists. Whelan came in with a grin.

"You know, a smarter thief would've left town."

Brie chuckled. "Didn't really leave me much choice, did you?"

"I know all of this must seem, well, evil—"

"Ha!" She couldn't help it. "I mean, at this point, I expected flowers and maybe a pony."

"You can't honestly say you didn't see this coming."

"Oh, no. I did. This part, I was actually banking on." Brie wagged her head. "You're missing the *why* of why I'm here. Someone like me doesn't just let themselves get caught, now does she?"

"It's noble," Whelan said. "Paul was noble, too."

"Don't you dare talk of him like you knew him."

"No-no." Gavin shook his head. "You see, I *did* know him. I've known him for years. The fool thought he could keep you hidden. He didn't think that might come back to bite him, which it did, which—I mean, thank you. Really, you've taken a load off me."

"And again," Brie said, testing the hold of the zip ties. "We're coming up on that *fuck you* part of the conversation."

Gavin took the seat across from her. Over his shoulder, he snapped, and a goon wheeled over a closed-circuit TV. Another goon handed him a laptop. He opened it and began typing.

"You know, there's a thing in *The Art of War*." He hit a few keys, connecting the computer to the TV. Static flashed over the screen. "'Take what your enemy holds dear, and they'll be amenable to your will.'"

The screen flashed, and then she was looking at Kevin, strapped to a chair. The woman named Jezebel strode around him, naked, a knife trailing along his collarbone.

"It's not a bad weakness, Brie. It's an excellent one. It's the one everyone would expect you'd have. Including me." As if on cue, Jezebel slashed Kevin's clavicle, and while there was no sound, Brie could see her brother cry out.

"Motherfucker!" She slammed the chair against the ground. The zip ties cut into her wrists as she howled.

"Oh, Brie," Whelan said, softly. "It's not your fault. It's *instinct*. It's why I knew I could bring you here."

"Is this where you make a villainous bargain? Because, frankly, I'm not feeling all that amenable."

Whelan slammed his fist against the table. "It's *not* villainy. It's necessary. There is a world you don't know, Brie. A world I'm a part of. A power. And I'm not going to let an angry little girl take that from me."

"Are you sure?" Brie said. "I mean, not to be a ball buster, but I'm kinda seeing the cracks in that facade."

Whelan grinned. Didn't fake it, wasn't playing around— he meant it. "Do you want to know what I'll do to you once I really start to crack? Do you? You wanna *find that out*, huh, Brie?" He took a breath, composed himself. "Who are you working with?"

"You don't actually think I'll buy that, do you?" Brie scoffed. "I tell you, you let me walk? Really?"

"Oh, you won't." Whelan nodded to the monitor. "But he could."

Brie watched her brother sway in his chair, blood running down his shoulders. Every tendon in her body was screeching for escape—to leap across the table, gouge out the tycoon's eyeballs and turn his smarmy face into purple mush.

"Just let him go," she said. "You've got me. You can have me, just let him—"

"You still have something I want, Brie. So, I'll ask one more time. Who are you working with?"

Josh glanced at his watch, making no effort to conceal the movement. Not that he needed to look—after this many years pulling jobs, he had what he thought of as a sort of super-thief Spidey-sense. He could feel it. Something was off. And yup, look at that: Brie should've cracked the safe and tripped the OmniView ten minutes ago.

Well, that's not good, he thought. He gave his cards a perfunctory glance.

"Will you make your fucking bet, already?" said Prince Caspar, slurring and quite drunk. "Look. Randall's checking his watch."

"Another moment, *s'il vous plaît*," said Vincent LaFleur, raising a finger to mark his point. "Patience is the mark of a wise man."

"Ha! Pfft! It is the mark of an *old* man. Now place your fucking bet before I take you back to my island and feed you to sharks that are poked with sticks on a regular basis. Fucking French."

"You've got that?" said Josh, losing his grip on the predicament for a moment because—well, how often do you hear that from people?

"Pretty elaborate to just have floating around," said Howie Reed. "And I've got rocket launchers and robotic suits of armor at my penthouse, so coming from me that's saying something."

"Where'd you get the sharks?" said Scooter.

"From the fucking ocean," Caspar said, rubbing his temples. "Asshole. Where did you think?"

The oilman chuckled. "Somebody's testy."

"I am *nobody's* testes. Shut your dick trap, old man. French-man, play your cards."

LaFleur sloshed back his cognac and stood. "Monsieur, you are a child, a pampered one, and I am done with it."

"True, true, and good," said Caspar. "Now sit, and make a fucking bet before I cut a Z in your forehead with a machete."

"Why Z?" said Harlan.

"Because… fucking Z. It's an arbitrary fucking letter, you nimrod. Frenchman, play your cards."

"It's the only card you have left, Brie."

On the screen, Jezebel circled Kevin menacingly, trailing the knife across his shoulders. He arched his back, then his head slumped forward.

"You bitch!" Brie said.

"She's going to start really hurting him soon," Whelan said, folding his arms as he leaned back in his chair. "All of this stops if you just tell me what I want."

"Okay," she said, taking a series of sharp breaths to steady herself. Blood trickled from gouges the zip ties had left in her wrists. "Fine. I'll tell you."

Whelan smiled. "I'm glad we're starting to understand each other."

"It's Bert, Ernie, and the Cookie Monster."

The smile wilted like a week-old banana. "Sarcasm?"

"It's a coping mechanism."

The tycoon ran a hand through his hair and stood. "I'm disappointed, Brie. I thought by now you'd take your actions seriously."

"You think I'm not? We both know how this ends. I tell you, you kill us. I don't tell you, you kill us. I'm not about to make it easy for you."

Whelan stared at the floor, shrugged, and sighed.

"As you wish. But for the record, I did ask nicely." He produced his mobile, hit the speed-dial, and said, "Do it."

On the screen, Jezebel raked the blade across Kevin's throat. Blood spurted from the edge of the blade.

"NO!!!"

"I will not play my cards," snarled Vincent LaFleur. "In fact, *mes amis*, I think it is time to call it a night."

"Oh, come on!" everybody cawed.

LaFleur raised his hand to silence them. "Enough. I have lost three and one-half million dollars. I am quite drunk. I am done." To Harlan: "*Monsieur* Randall, you are not what I expected, but thank you."

"You really have no idea," said Harlan. He eyed his watch again, then the security camera in the corner. Thirteen minutes. Whatever was going on—well, whatever. Someone needed to trip the system. He'd waited long enough.

So, he stood. He removed his sunglasses, his hat. Then, he ripped off the prosthetic nose and sideburns. He grinned, rubbing the glue off his face as the table let off a collective gasp.

"What the fuck?" said Scooter Maverick.

"What the *fuck*?" said Howie Reed.

"*What* the fuck—" said Caspar Akhtar-Bukhari, who wheeled around to see Harlan and blinked. "What the *fuck*?"

"*Ouate de phoque?*"° said Vincent LaFleur.

"That is definitely *not* what I meant by getting naked," said a traumatized-looking Leo Stillwater.

"Sorry gents," Josh said. "I haven't been totally honest with you.

° "Seal cotton" (Really.)

Actually, haven't even been partially. Now, if you'll excuse me, I've got a casino to rob."

Then, he grabbed his chips and bolted for the exit.

Harlan spilled into the casino, dumping the chips as he tumbled in a backward somersault into the hallway. He recovered, then took off like a sprinter through the main gambling hall toward the entrance.

He was almost at the foyer when a string of mean-looking goons in suits intercepted. Josh skidded across the marble floor as they caught him in a horseshoe, each of them flexing their knuckles.

He planted his hands on his knees, panting. Then, he nodded. "Would any of you be open to a bribe?"

Below, Steve Halverson and Phil Gibbons were in the middle of a vicious round of Rock, Paper, Scissors—the loser of which had to write the report on the attempted breach of the casino's safe.

"No, paper beats rock."

"How? Have you ever thrown a rock at paper?"

"It's not called *Sense, Paper, Scissors*," Steve said with a sigh. "I didn't make the rules."

Gibbons frowned. "Two out of three."

"That *was* two out of three."

"Three out of six."

"That's literally the same fraction."

"That's not how it works!"

Steve chuckled. Gibbons always went rock on the final throw. "Okay, fine. Three out of six. Which, by the way, reduces to two out of three."

"That's not how it—"

Just then, an alarm siren wailed like a seagull in a trash

compactor. An array of lights strobed over the huge displays across the wing, and the great metal door sealed itself shut.

"What the shit?" said Phil.

"Something must've tripped the OmniView," said Steve.

"And *why* does lockdown seal us all in here?"

"Security measure. It's like the compartments on the Titanic that prevented it from sinking."

"And nobody remembered how that worked out?" Phil sighed. "What are we supposed to do from here?"

Steve shrugged. "Relax. Probably just a latent reaction from the safe—"

"Holy shit," Gibbons breathed.

"What?" Steve said, wheeling back to the security feed, where Josh Harlan was being dog-piled by a team of goons. "Holy shit!"

Then, the entire floor froze, all the technicians giving a collective "Holy shit!!!"

And then it was chaos.

Chaos was exactly what Max Reyes was preparing himself for as he and Sophie burst through the door to the abandoned mall. They came in, full-on action hero stances, guns panning around the entrance.

"Let's go," he said.

Max had the GPS tracker on his phone, leading Sophie past the fountain, heading toward the back of the building.

"Big space for seven thieves," she said.

"Yeah. If you knew Harlan the way I know him, that wouldn't shock you."

"Oh, I do, and I'm not shocked. It's logistics, Max."

Max couldn't help but give her an enamored grin. At least now he could figure out why he'd caught a thing for her. They had more than a little in common. Then, he caught himself and went with tactical speak. "Signal's coming from the back of the building. I lead. Watch my six."

Sophie chuckled and gave the agent an affectionate junk-squeeze. "You watch it."

Then, she took off. The ninja babes spilled in behind, flanking off in teams to cover the place. Max cleared his throat and trotted after Sophie.

"So, did you want to get dinner, or something? I mean, some-time? Sometime after this... Sometime?"

"Nah," she said, flashing him a grin as they cleared three rooms. "Dinner is awkward. You sit across from somebody, watch how they eat. It's messy. Not enough fun."

"Oh," Max said, trying desperately to will himself back to some form of professionalism. "Okay."

"I would go for a drink and a rough shag, though."

"Oh," Max said. *Concentrate. Protocol. Concentrate. Proto*—"Okay?"

They reached the point of the beacon—which was the brainstorm room, which was dark and empty.

Reyes looked around the place, feeling the prospects of his evening collapsing. It had been cleared out days ago.

"Oh, no."

CHAPTER 24
WOK-Y, TALKY

About a week ago, a reservation was made at the Wynn Casino and Resort for a luxury cabana often rented out to NASCAR drivers. The reason they rented the cabana was that, along with two stories of sleek modern furnishings and swanky accoutrements, it contained a fully decked out mechanic's garage. It also had a slushie machine that you could attach a bottle of booze to, which—let's face it—was just awesome.

The reservation was made for Reginald Ignatio, a ridiculously wealthy monster truck driver from New Orleans that liked to wrench his own rigs between races—a character born entirely of Josh Harlan's imagination.

The top floor had three bedrooms, two baths, a jacuzzi on the balcony, and a fully functioning arcade. The downstairs had a kitchen, a bar that spun on a twelve-foot circular platform, and past that was the living room: an atrium opening up to the second floor, two couches angled around a coffee table—and it looked remarkably similar to the brainstorm room back at the mall.

In fact, if a certain writer-type had been a jerk and decided to fudge the narrative, one might assume that Tommy and Ruby had never moved here to begin with. It goes to show, those folks are shifty, and should not be trusted for an instant—but enough about that.

"Oh yes!" said Tommy Carlyle. "Boom! Owned, biz-itch! I hope you like the taste of Mister Weasel's patent pain. Yes!"

He tossed the MacBook on the couch and commenced a Snoopy-dance of victory around the room. Ruby chuckled and rubbed her temples.

"So, you did it?"

Tommy grinned. "Not only have I digitally put some wannabe Raphael Gray in his place, we now have access to every transaction record, invoice and video loop ever burned on the Olympus's server." He chuckled, so pleased with himself it would make a French waiter look like a Tibetan Monk. "I even got the emails! I don't want to use the word genius... but if you want to say it about me, I'm okay with it."

"Oh my god, you're hopeless."

"I'm thirsty is what I am—you want a boozy slushie?"

Ruby gave him a look that said: *seriously?* "Seriously? We're in the middle of a job, here."

"No, we're at the end of a job. Well, the end of my part, anyway. I say we drink."

"You don't want... I dunno, like one of those token-nerdy energy drinks or something?"

Tommy shrugged, eyeing the mountain of crushed Red Bull cans piled around his feet. "Honestly? I feel like it's probably a good idea to even out at this point."

Ruby gave a tired sigh. "Strawberry or cherry cola?"

"Why not both?"

"*Why* both?"

"…Because it's delicious?"

Ruby walked off, shaking her head. "You're a toddler."

"Thanks," Tommy said. Then, curiosity finally got the better of him. He plopped back on the couch, grabbed the MacBook, and started surfing the pilfered data. He skipped over all the official-looking stuff, throwing it on a USB to give Josh later, and went straight for the emails. He flipped. He scanned. He read.

"Oh, scandal!"

"What?" Ruby said from the kitchen, making a significant amount of noise for mixing a couple of drinks.

"Head of security is boning Whelan's secretary. I don't want to get into details, but there's like an entire paragraph here about some seriously creative uses of Jell-O. Oh. Cool. Secret stuff!"

"What?"

"They're drugging the bar. They're putting Ecstasy in the drinks… Some boring stock figures, some shady business deals— hey, there's an allusion to murder… A whole buncha stuff about the slot machines that's got to be in code, although I can't figure what—this guy's dirty," he said. "I mean, not like *Hustler* dirty. But he's got dirt."

He typed, digging further. Ruby padded back behind him. Tommy smirked—the agent was right. "Then there's a lot of talk about his woman Jezebel. You know, the one who tried to kidnap Kevin?"

"Mhmm?"

"Wow," Tommy said. "I don't know if it's euphemism but— *woah*. Apparently, she's a—"

He caught movement from the side of his vision. He turned, and connected face-first with a mini fridge, being brought in a great overhand swing by Ruby, as if it were little more than a tennis racket. Then he was out.

"My, that *is* unexpected," she said, hip cocked, a smile splitting her face. She twirled a lock of her hair as it changed from blonde to black and grew three inches. Her features shifted. She grew taller, curvier. "Surpriiise?"

Before she turned to leave the room, Ruby Cobb had transformed into an entirely different person.

Jezebel.

Brie howled. She shrieked until her throat was raw and her limbs went numb in their restraints. She slammed herself back in the chair over and over and over.

Hands grabbed her by the shoulders, slamming her back against the chair. Whelan grabbed her by the jaw and snapped her back to attention. "Well, this *is* deplorable of me. Your brother is bleeding out. I have a medical team waiting. But you need to give up," he snarled. "So *give up*."

"Harlan," Brie choked. "It's fucking Harlan. And he's going to take you for every penny you're worth. Now don't you dare try to con me again, you fuck-waffle."

Whelan blinked. "What?"

"Oh, please. Why else would you commission Queen Bitch to kidnap him?" Brie said, a smile curling on her face. "Never con a con, you tool."

Whelan's mouth opened and closed, trying to find a response. "But..."

The door flung open. A skinny man in glasses staggered in, then whispered something in the tycoon's ear. Brie nearly chuckled when she watched Gavin's face slacken.

"When?" he said.

"Five minutes ago," said the technician. "They're bringing him in now."

"Surpriiise," said Brie.

"Go!" Whelan waved his hands at the surrounding goons. "Get to the safe and put the money on a truck. Go, go, go."

"Five minutes," said Glasses Guy.

Whelan nodded, then followed him to the door. "Tug? Smiley? Stay here."

"But, Gavin," Brie said. "I thought we were having a moment."

"And it's been a pleasure, Brie." To the goons: "Kill her."

In the corridor outside, Whelan and his goons took a right, headed toward the shipping bay of the casino. Three of the henchmen hung back to stand guard. Meanwhile, a large Asian man in a suit entered from the hall on the left.

The goons flanked him in a triangle.

"Woah, hold up. This area is off limits."

The Asian grunted, fishing into his jacket pocket. He flashed a badge. "Max Reyes, FBI. Here to collect a prisoner."

Goon One furrowed his brow, looking to Goons Two and Three for support. "We didn't call you—did we call him?"

"Don't think so," said Goon Two.

"You didn't need to," said the big guy. "I've been working a sting. The woman in that room is my suspect. When your system tripped, your boss called. I'll take her from here."

Goon One eyed him, suspiciously. "I'll call it in."

"The longer you leave her in there, the more time you're giving her to escape. Open the door."

"It's protocol to radio it in," said Goon Two.

"Fuck your protocol. You guys think you're hot shit, but when a federal agent tells you to open a door, you cram your protocol where the sun don't shine and listen. Now. Open the door, please."

Goon One gave the agent a challenging glare, keyed his radio and said: "Dispatch, this is Tango Beta Three, I've got some prick who says he's FBI…"

Chirrp. *"Hold your post, Tango. We'll verify."*

And here, the agent grinned. He produced a cast-iron wok from inside his jacket. "You made the right call."

He brought the wok in a back-handed tennis swing, catching Goon One under the chin and knocking him clean off his feet with a *bwoong!* Blood and a couple of teeth flew through the air.

Goons Two and Three scrambled for their weapons, but the furious wok came at them.

Bwoong! Thump. Bwoong! Thump.

Jimmy Wok straightened his jacket with a grunt. He looked at the pile of dispatched goons with a frown. "Too bad there weren't more of you. I'm just getting warmed up."

Then, from the hallway behind came dozens of footfalls.

Jimmy turned to find a cluster of about thirty more suits rushing him. They fell in a circle. He adjusted his grip on his Taylor & Ng, cracked his neck, and grinned.

"Shoulda brought more."

Brie flexed her wrists against the zip ties while Tug and Whitey circled her, both wearing pleased expressions. Clearly, they'd been waiting for this moment. She chuckled, flashing a grin at both her captors.

"Ou, he seemed pissed. Do you think he was pissed?"

"Probably," said Whitey.

"Yeah," said Tug.

"Well, that's too bad," Brie sighed, shaking her head. "I thought people liked surprises."

Whitey nodded with a smile. "I gotta say, babe. Your glib demeanor in the face of imminent death is troublesome."

"Yeah," said Tug.

"Just trying to keep it light."

"Well, that's a bit of a problem. You see, Tug here can't enjoy himself if his victim isn't scared."

"Yeah," Tug growled.

"And if he can't enjoy himself, he starts getting grumpy."

"Yeah."

"So, I'd suggest revising that."

Tug nodded.

"Well, if I'm revising last words," Brie said while Whitey moved behind her. "I feel like a joke would be good. Right?"

"No," said Tug.

"He's not gonna like that," added Whitey.

"Oh! Oh. I've got one. What did the Left Goon say to the Right Goon?"

The henchmen gave each other a confused expression.

Brie grinned. "'Shit! Fuck!'—and honestly the last part is always a tossup between 'Ass' and 'Dick'."

Whitey and Tug chuckled. This chick was tiny, zip-tied to a chair. Brie could tell they thought she was stalling—which was the real joke, because she wasn't. Tug produced a tire iron and started patting it against his palm, walking slowly toward her.

Closer. *Thump, thump, thump.*

Closer, thought Brie.

And Tug came a step closer. He wound back with the tire iron, and Brie shifted in the chair, kicking the goon in the balls so hard he shrieked, doubling over on the floor.

"Shit! Fuck! Dick!"

"And here I thought he was an *ass* man," Brie said with a grin.

Whitey lunged at her, and she stood, spinning. The chair caught him by the legs, sending him crashing into the table.

"Arrrgh!"

Behind, Tug pulled himself up with a growl. He came at her in a low tackle. Brie ran across the room, up the wall about five feet, then kicked off. She came down on Tug, the chair exploding on his back.

"Gaaahh!"

Brie rolled backward and came up standing, the arms of the chair still zip-tied to her wrists. Whitey recovered, producing a pistol. He came at Brie, aiming, and she swung the piece of chair. It caught Whitey's forearm with a bone-shattering crack, and he cried out as the pistol fired.

In the small concrete room, the sound was deafening. A feedback pitch whined in Brie's ears as she sidestepped. The goon cradled his broken arm, howling, and she whopped him in the side of the head. With a yelp, he was on the floor and oozing fluids.

Behind, Tug groaned, producing a gut-hook knife from his ankle, and staggered to his feet. He wagged his head as if to clear water from his ears. Brie swung the other chair leg in a screaming arc that terminated with the side of his face. His nose shattered. Blood spurted. He hit the floor like a dead fish.

"Told you," Brie said.

She grabbed the knife and cut the zip ties. Then, she righted the turned-over table, leapt onto it, and started working the vent off a two-foot air conditioning duct in the center of the ceiling. It broke free. She tossed it to the floor, wiggled her shoulders, then jumped and caught the edge of the duct. She pulled herself in, thinking: *cat burglar, escape artist—same thing.*

Inside the duct was freezing. She shimmied her way along to an intersecting passage that she guessed would lead her out of the room. It had been a long time since she'd used an air duct to commit a burglary, but she'd cased enough places to know how to navigate.

This had to be the most badass half-hour she'd had in ages. Sure, she was professional, but she couldn't help feeling just a little proud as she crawled toward the duct on the opposite side of the wall. She grinned.

Then, the metal beneath her groaned. She froze, watching the rivets connecting this patch of ductwork to the next twist and pop.

"Uh-oh," she said.

Below, Jimmy Wok stood in a field of dispatched henchmen, facing off against the last of the bunch: the one guy who was actually his own size. The goon brandished an electric cattle prod, its end arcing with a tiny lightning bolt.

Zzzzt. Zzzzt. Zzzzt. The goon grinned, bouncing his eyebrows.

Jimmy gave a pleased-sounding growl. Mass-whoppage, and finally a challenge. He flipped the wok a couple times, and the two giants came at each other with full-on warrior cries.

That's when the duct work collapsed, crushing Jimmy's conquest underneath. Jimmy skidded across the floor.

"The fuck?"

Brie slid out of the ductwork and brushed herself off. "Oh, hey Jimmy."

Jimmy's brow stitched with equal parts confusion, disappointment, and relief. "What were you doing in the air duct?"

"Uh, escaping?" She looked around at the hallway, which looked like a men's clothing department after an earthquake. "Somebody got their clobber on."

"Good day." Jimmy grinned.

"Okay," Brie said. "Let's get out of here."

At the same time, Gavin Whelan, Steve Halverson and Phil Gibbons stood by the receiving door of the Olympus's shipping bay. A team wheeled the contents of the safe over on two shrink-wrapped pallets. The steel shuttered door rolled open to a moon-lit service alley.

"So, if we've got Harlan and Cassiday roped in, why are we getting rid of the money?" said Gibbons, rubbing his head.

"Security measure," said Halverson. He sucked coffee from a styrofoam cup.

Phil didn't seem so convinced. "Is this like the Titanic thing?"

Gavin rubbed his eyes, somewhere between exhausted and livid. "They aren't working alone. Cassiday came in far too easily, and Harlan—how did he get in here?"

"He was in disguise," said Steve. "Security found a bunch of prosthetics in a private poker room."

Gibbons produced a small metal tube with a USB key on the end. "They used this to hack into our network. That's how they bunged up the elevator."

Whelan nodded. "They have a team. Cassiday was the distraction. Harlan was the backup. They think we'll be so busy catching them that the safe will be unattended."

"What now?" said Phil.

"Now, we get that money out of here. Start sweeping the floor for the rest."

"Round 'em up and call the cops?" said Steve.

"No," Gavin said. "These thieves we'll take care of the old fashioned way."

"Like the Titanic?" said Phil.

Headlights filled the alley. A Brinks truck pulled ahead, then backed into the loading bay. The truck's doors flung open, and a hefty black woman in her early fifties climbed out, followed by a scrawny man in his forties. Both wore light blue under bullet-proof vests and looked like they were irritated with something—general existence, perhaps.

"Which of y'all motherfuckers called this in?" the woman said. "Pulled me out of a perfectly good bubble bath."

Whelan came forward, flashing his best businessman's grin. "That was me, ma'am. I'm the owner. Apologies for the inconvenience."

"Fuckin' better be. I was about to have a date with Mister Buzzer. Now you got me all stressed and grumpy." To the cash. "This the shit?"

Gavin nodded.

The woman turned to her partner. "Load it up, Frank." She whipped out a clipboard and came back to Gavin, clicking a pen and pointing. "Sign here."

Whelan took the pen and eyed her. "You're not the usual driver."

"No, I'm not. Fuckin' on-call bullshit. You want credentials?"

Whelan shrugged. The woman produced her ID badge and handed it to Halverson, who'd come over with a wireless console. He swiped it. Then, he went over to Frank and repeated the process.

"They're legit."

Whelan signed the form and handed the clipboard back to the woman. "Can't be too careful."

"Oh, sure. 'Specially when your driver's black and a woman, right?"

Whelan held up his hands in a make-peace gesture. "Oh, no. I didn't mean—"

"Y'all never mean it. That's the fucking problem, ain't it?" she huffed, shaking her head. "Stereotypes and shit. Frank didn't get that shit, and he's an ex-child molester."

"Hey!" said Frank.

"I don't mean it. Just proving a point." To Whelan: "Now, you just sit your pretty boy ass back there while we load up, and this nightmare of an interaction's over."

Gavin went to apologize again, then thought better of it and backed off.

The woman nodded to Steve and Phil. "You too, Glasses. And you, Cue Ball. Do it right I might even give it a rub, see if a genie pops out."

Frank directed the team operating the forklift as they moved the money onto the truck. They cleared out, and the Brinks drivers climbed back into the truck.

"Y'all have a good day now," said the woman. With that, they drove off.

Whelan, Halverson and Gibbons headed back for the casino.

"Scan everything," said Whelan. "They can't have gone far. Get a town car ready and call Tiny."

"It's his night off?" said Steve.

Gibbons nodded. "He'll be pretty pissed."

"Exactly. Get him here."

Just then, a horn honked, and another Brinks truck pulled in. The doors opened, and the usual driver climbed out.

"Sorry I'm late. Scheduling mix-up."

The three men looked at each other.

"Oh, for fuck's sake," said Gavin.

CHAPTER 25
QUINN UNDERWATER

When Quinn Donovan was little, his mother would sit with him each night as he fell asleep. "You're special, my little chestnut. You're the chosen," she'd whisper. "Chosen by gods. There's a plan, you see? So when you're right buggered, just say these words…"

When the goddess rolls, her dice are loaded.

Now, slouched on the bar at the Double Down Saloon, a priceless gem in his jacket, having just betrayed the closest he'd had to friends in years, the words looped in his mind.

He'd thought he'd forgotten; spent so many years drinking away the memories of his mum—who'd spent most of his childhood drinking away the angry hand of his grandfather, right up until it killed her. When they first came back, he couldn't figure where they'd come from. Why should he? She'd died at around the age he was now, and he'd drifted from boarding house to boarding house, eventually picking up the sleight of hand from one of his headmasters. There was a lifetime of rough memories between those soft, tender nights and now—too many, really—to prepare him.

So he sat. He smoked a cigarette, and swayed to "Wish You Were Here" on his stool: melancholy, confused, and sheep-buggeringly drunk; scarcely aware of his surroundings. It was just him, a glass, and Roger Waters.

He'd nicked the stone—what else was there to do? Quinn only knew how to run. And, realizing this, he decided that he rather hated the only thing he knew. He should've stayed. Could've helped. Too late, now. He was here, next to his Bungered Bag (the contents of which were a passport, change of drawers, and a bottle of Bushmills he'd swiped from a bordello). He liked Vegas, but not enough to stay. He eyed the plane ticket on the bar, and sighed the sigh of a very lonely, very tossed-about man.

"Hey, Quinn." A hand on his wrist. He turned and found Yolanda, a soft smile with a hint of sadness. "I thought I'd find you here."

"Here to kill me then?" he said. "Because returning your sacred crystal pleasure-stick is quite a definite impossibility."

She chuckled, kissed him on the cheek and patted his back. "No, sweetie. You never had it."

"How's that?"

"I swiped the original out with a fake. It's with a fence in Berlin."

"Cheeky monkey." Quinn sighed.

Yolanda eyed him, signaling the barkeep for a drink. "You look sad."

Quinn finished his drink. "Just moody is all. Remembering somebody I lost."

"Sorry."

Quinn shrugged. "She used to tell me things. I was special. I was chosen—whatever that means." The bartender came back with her drink and splashed another few fingers in Quinn's glass. The magician nodded and sloshed it back. "I'm leaving town."

"I know," said Yolanda. "It's why I'm here. You've got a talent, Quinn. Lot of people would be interested in it. I'd prefer if I had it in my wheelhouse. You wanna job?"

"What, go legit?" Quinn scoffed. "I'm not sure I'm capable."

Yolanda shrugged. "I might be legit, but that doesn't stop me from doing some proper thieving when I need to."

The magician grinned. "When the goddess rolls, her dice are loaded."

"Huh?"

"It's a thing me mum used to say. I figure it means that if you're good enough, even losing is winning."

Yolanda gave him a once-over, grinned, and kissed him.

"I'm at the Chicken Ranch until the day after tomorrow. Security consult. You can stay with me if you want. And when it's over, we can go anywhere."

Quinn thought, *Shall I tell her now, or after we shag?*

"You like diamonds, yeah?"

Brie and Jimmy stood at the corner of East Tropicana and Ocean Drive, the blue hint of dawn climbing the horizon. It was about two blocks away from the Olympus, where they'd escaped through the kitchen, encountering only a sous chef on smoke break along the way.

"I can't believe you didn't bring handcuffs," Brie said. "How are you supposed to be a convincing FBI agent without handcuffs?"

"I'm not supposed to be convincing," Jimmy said. "You said it yourself, Brie. *Just come in a brain them.* Exact words."

Before she could argue, a Brinks truck pulled up on the curb.

The side door flew open, and Kevin, still in his fake uniform, appeared.

"Get in."

Brie and Jimmy did, and the truck sped off.

"How'd it go?" asked Kev.

"Pitch-perfect," Brie said. "He caught me at the safe, used that video he took of you to try to con me. I threw him off enough that when the alarm sounded, he panicked. You?"

"Look behind you."

Brie and Jimmy turned to find the two pallets stacked with bills they'd been leaning on. Brie nodded. "I'd call that a success."

"How were the disguises?" Billie said from the driver's seat. They were headed down Las Vegas Blvd. to the Wynn to meet up with Ruby and Tommy.

"I'm gonna have to exfoliate for a month to get the glue off, but they ruled."

Billie chuckled to herself, weaving through the sparse traffic. "I got you covered. You think you go a lifetime in the effects biz without learning how to prevent breakouts?"

"I'm confused," said Jimmy. "I thought Kev was too drunk to remember what happened when the hot chick kidnapped him."

"He was," said Billie.

"Bug in Whelan's office," added Brie. "Harlan told us the whole thing before we picked you up."

"Hey, speaking of," said Kevin. "Where is he?"

"He didn't catch up with you?"

"I thought he was meeting up with you on the way out?"

"I thought he'd already left. Have you talked to Tommy?"

Billie hit the speed dial on her cell. "Third time. He's not picking up."

Brie considered the options, then it dawned on her. Her sense of jubilation deflated like a slashed tire. "Crap."

"Crap," said Kevin.

"Crap," said Billie.

Jimmy sighed, exhausted with how little these people properly communicated. "So, where is he?"

Josh Harlan swirled his wine with a grin across from Gavin Whelan and the goon named Tiny. They were in a restaurant called Khoi, on the second level of the Olympus, a half-eaten platter of sashimi on the table between them.

"You know, a smarter villain would've cut me loose to lead them back to the money."

"And risk you escaping?" Whelan said. "I don't think so, Josh. Cassiday already got away, and I'm not about to let the same happen to you—and why does everybody keep calling me a villain?"

Josh chuckled. "You did buy dinner."

"You deserve it," Gavin said, grabbing another strip of tuna from the platter. He chewed. "You got me, Josh. Catching yourself? Disguises? I must say... Very clever."

"Well, brawn'll only get you so far. Honestly, I'm a little disappointed you're not more broken up about it, but I'll take a compliment."

"Well, if it's any consolation, I'm going to take you out to the desert and murder you after this."

"Thanks. That helps."

"I want you to know something." The tycoon leaned in, placing his chopsticks delicately on his napkin. "I don't actually want to do it. You? Cassiday? I'm not happy I have to kill you. You just haven't left me much choice. It's necessary, you see?"

"Sure." Josh shrugged. "Bad dude's gotta do what he's gotta do."

Whelan shook his head. "Regrettable. Such brilliant minds to waste."

"It is a bummer. But at least this sashimi's incredible."

"You should know, if you tell me what I want to hear, I won't hurt your team. You and Brie, well, I need to close off loose ends. But the rest can go."

"Cool," Josh said. "Hey—does this wine taste funky to you?"

"Shit's working, boss," observed Tiny.

"I mean, not *bad* funky. Just like it's been left out or something. Tiny? Has anyone ever told you you've got an impeccably shiny head?" Josh said, his mouth feeling rubbery. "Seriously, there should be an award for that or something. Oh, I'm drugged, aren't I?"

"Scopolamine," Whelan said with a grin. "The best kind of truth serum. I lined your glass with it. When you wake up, you won't remember this conversation—at which point, I'll be killing you in the desert, so it doesn't really matter... But I'd hope there's at least some consolation there."

"So, if we're asking why people call you a villain... I mean, *truth serum*? Really? 'Oh, don't mind me. Average Joe, here. Just holding this truth serum for a friend.' " Harlan wagged his head and erupted in a giggle fit. "I mean, did it hurt when you fell out of the *Bond* movie? By the way, you look *good*, Gav. Like, I don't know if you botox or whatever, but keep it up, Benjamin Button... He's—"

"I know who he is," Whelan snapped. "Where is the diamond?"

"With the Irish guy you fell for being a rep from OmniView... I mean, SpyTech. Whatever. The point is, the Irish guy has it."

"And where is he?"

"Somewhere. Probably a where involving a bar if I can guess right—Your eyes... they're very blue."

"You don't know which bar?"

"Nope. I was supposed to find out, but things got kinda messy and now he might as well be in Fiji—I mean, like ice, or an ocean... Like a husky. They're like husky blue... Is that a thing?"

"Naw," said Tiny.

"Don't think so," said Whelan. "And the money? Your crew?"

"Well, I don't really know where they went." Josh frowned. "They were supposed to go back to the safe house. But then again, they were supposed to meet me before they did that. So now, they could be anywhere. I mean, they could be at a bank, at a strip club, at Denny's getting breakfast... I honestly couldn't tell you."

Here, Josh grabbed a sliver of Yellowtail. "Hey, can we get some miso soup? That'd be awesome right now. Oh, and calamari. And some cilantro scallops. And maybe dumplings? Can I have water? I'm really thirsty. ...Is this the drugs?"

"What was the plan for where they went?" Whelan said.

"What about vermicelli? No, wait. That's Vietnamese."

"Can I hit him, boss?" said Tiny.

"Woah, I know it's faux pas to mix up cultures, but hitting seems a little overkill," Josh said. He blinked, trying to clear the creeping blur from his vision. "They were *supposed* to go back to the brainstorm room. That's where we have our meetings and stuff."

Whelan grinned, sipped his wine. "And where is the brainstorm room?"

Josh shrugged, draining his glass, completely forgetting it was drugged. "Which one?"

Tiny's chest puffed up like a blowfish. Under the table, he put a gun against Harlan's knee.

"Woah, hey!" Josh slurred. "I know what that is, and I'm not convinced by it, you hear me? You're not going to shoot me in the middle of a casino on opening night. You walk alone, buddy... You walk alone."

"What does that mean?" said Tiny.

Josh went to answer, when Whelan cut him off—which was rude, if you were asking Josh, which if you were, he'd tell you things... Probably not the things you were asking for, but *things*. Such is the snag with truth serums: they don't actually make the subject tell the truth. And while we're on the subject of the pitfalls of said drugs—passing out is a big one.

Which is what Josh did.

Dawn. Jezebel walked beneath the great pillar of the Stratosphere in the direction of the Olympus, thinking: *I could've killed him. I could've popped the geek's head like an overdue zit. Instead I brain him with a fucking mini fridge. What is with me, lately?*

Maybe she *was* going wobbly. She'd never admit it to the ghost, but the way she'd been bothered with Paul Cassiday, everything she'd kept from Whelan about the thieves' plan, and now—even in the face of nearly being discovered—she'd elected to let the hacker live.

She fumed. She frowned. She strutted.

Everything had gone so fucking sloppy after killing Brie's foster father. She didn't even know whose side she was playing anymore. This was not godly behavior. Sure, gods might do a lot of shit out of petty, but going soft on the mortals was not among said shit. What? You pretend to be one for a while, conjure an entire friendship from thin air to get your freedom—and this was what happened? It wasn't fucking fair. It didn't make any sense— and considering she was one of the immortals who'd voted in favor of sense, she was furious.

Ahead, a half-dozen strung out strippers mingled with a crunch of off-duty clappers, trading lies and swapping jokes. For a moment, the goddess considered taking the form of a puma or a crocodile—any form with teeth or claws big enough to flay the skin of those who would not be missed, but then she thought better of it; a tiny voice whispering in her head: *they deserve to be here, as much as the sun or the cacti—and don't forget what happened the last time you took the sun and killed all those awesome overgrown lizards.*

Why? *Why?* When she was the cougar, she didn't start craving Fancy Feast. When she was the fly, she didn't think like a fly (which, if you're wondering, is pretty much a series of *Bzzts*) A million creatures; millions of years, and for some stupid reason, it was the human who'd fucked it all up.

She took a wide curve around the street people, walking out into the middle of the road—when without warning, the sky darkened. Clouds boiled overhead.

A voice, clear as if it were right beside her: "When the goddess rolls, her dice are loaded."

The air around her snapped and crackled. The hairs on the back of her neck stood on end. The ground beneath her lit up, and a huge bolt of light exploded. Jezebel was tossed a good two-hundred feet in the air. Thunder ripped down the street, shattering windows in the buildings all around.

She hit the ground, sending a cloud of powdered asphalt into the air, and car alarms for three blocks in every direction blared like a chorus of tortured geese.

As the dust cleared, the street people gathered around her in a horseshoe.

Slowly, very slowly, Jezebel pulled herself out of the woman-shaped crater and cracked her neck back into place.

"You okay?" said a man in a bowler hat.

"Hold still," said a tawny woman with frizzy hair. "I'll call 9-1-1."

The group—about twenty or so—all commenced pulling out their phones and dialing. Jezebel stood, wagging her head, trying to clear the noise from her eardrums.

"What the fuck was that?"

The man dropped his phone, staggering back. "You were, uh… You kinda got struck by lightning."

She looked around, shrugged. "Nifty."

Then, she felt a strength return to her. Something she hadn't felt for a very long time. She grinned, then spun around and disappeared in a cloud of blue smoke.

PART IV
UNBOUND

"Which is justice, which is the thief?"
— *King Lear*, Act 4, Scene 6

"Strike harder, squeeze him, don't leave any slack! He's very
clever at finding ways out of impossible situations."
— Power, *Prometheus*

CHAPTER 26
REVISIONS

Sunlight spilled over the mountains as Billie pulled the F800 through the parking lot of Wynn. Kevin stared out the window, frowning. Jimmy was flipping his wok in his hand. Nobody spoke. Brie rubbed the scuffs on her wrists from the zip ties, ruminating.

It was all her fault. She should have just left town, like Paul said. If she'd done that, if she hadn't tried to fix things... Well, none of this would be happening. He'd still be alive. Harlan and his gang would be on a plane headed to Fiji. She and Kevin would never have had to wind up here. It was hindsight, she knew, but if she'd just known better...

It was like when you tried cutting your own hair and kept screwing up and cutting, over and over until you'd accidentally ripped off Sinéad O'Connor. You couldn't blame anyone but yourself. Now, she could feel everyone silently seething. *How? How could I have been so stupid?*

"I'm sorry, guys."

"Why?" said Jimmy.

Kevin kept his gaze out the window. "It's not your fault, Brie. You can't be in charge of everything."

"I don't want to be in charge of anything. It's just... If I'd known... Well, none of this would've happened."

"We all knew what we were getting into, sugar," Billie said. She pulled them into the cabana's garage and killed the engine. "Things go wrong. Sometimes, nobody can help that."

They climbed out of the truck. Jimmy looked around the fancy cabana and said, "Why didn't we just *start* here?"

"Part of the plan," said Kevin.

Billie, who'd been shown the place after Josh introduced her to Reyes, headed through the entrance to the brainstorm room, where Tommy Carlyle groaned beneath a mini fridge on the floor.

"Oh my god, Tommy!" She rushed over and heaved the fridge off the hacker, wiping a streak of blood from his forehead. "Are you okay?"

"Fine." Tommy nodded as she helped him to his feet. "Fine. How'd it go?"

"Money's in the garage," Brie said. "What happened?"

"Dunno," the hacker sighed. "I cracked the servers and was reading some emails—next thing I know, I catch the end of a mini fridge. Where's Harlan? Quinn?"

The four all bowed their heads.

"Harlan got nabbed by Whelan," Brie said. "We don't know what happened to Quinn."

"I'm gonna sit down, now," Tommy said. He thought it over. "Crap."

"Yeah," said Brie.

"I mean, do you think he's got an exit strategy? Did he tell you anything before—"

"It happened too quick," Brie said. "Where's Ruby?"

"Ruby would be why I was brained by a mini fridge."

"No?"

"Uh, yeah? She was the only other person here when I got hit."

Brie wagged her head. "Why would Ruby betray us? No take. Nothing to run away with... I mean it doesn't make sense."

"We've got bigger problems," Billie said.

Kevin nodded. "What do we do?"

Brie thought it over. "Well, Whelan's going to want his cash back. He'll use Josh as ransom."

"If we give the cash back, he'll be pissed," said Tommy.

Brie nodded. "That's our payout. I don't know about you guys, but I've come too far to just give Whelan what he wants."

"So, Quinn?" said Jimmy. "He's our odd man out. Maybe a trade?"

Brie shook her head. "Quinn might as well be halfway around the world by now. No, we should focus on Harlan. If he's gonna be the ransom, that's our best shot."

"Well, what do we do?" Tommy chuckled. "We don't have an upper hand, here. Whelan's either going to get his money back, or kill him. And if we're not giving him his money back—"

"We don't need to give it back, we just need to make him think we are," Brie said, nodding. "It's gonna be a con."

"But by now, he'll know who we are," Tommy said. "He's got the most advanced security in history. We can't lie to it twice."

"Don't worry about security."

"You want me to make more disguises?" said Billie.

"No."

"Oh, thank god."

"I want you to build another truck," Brie said.

"What?" said Billie.

"What?" said Kevin.

"What?" said Tommy.

"I don't get it," said Jimmy.

"We're gonna do a Violin Scam," Brie said. "Billie? How fast can you make it happen?"

"With some help? Three hours at best."

"I'll buy you a pizza?"

"Okay, two," Billie said. "But that still leaves us with what to fill it with?"

Brie grinned. That part she'd already figured. "Jimmy? Tommy?" she said. "Hit every board game store you know. You've got three hours."

They nodded.

"You wanna drive?" said the hacker.

"You drive," grunted Jimmy. "I hit."

They headed off for the exit. Brie turned back to Billie. "How easy can you rig the thing with explosives?"

Bille furrowed her brow. "I've got you and your brother?"

"Yeah," said the Cassidays.

"Four, maybe four-and-a-half hours."

"Great," Brie said. "If I'm guessing right, we've got two."

Billie chuckled and led them back to the garage. "You know? You and Harlan have a lot in common."

"Well, that was different," Quinn Donovan said, lying in a pretzel with Yolanda, both glistening with sweat.

Yolanda sighed, pressing her breasts against him while she twirled his hair. "Something you could get used to, I presume?"

"Love, for all the ways I could get accustomed, you're always a surprise."

"You're talking about that wasabi and cucumber thing again, aren't you?"

Quinn cradled her in his arms. "No—yes... I mean, it was lovely."

"You're thinking about Harlan and his mooks again, aren't you?"

Quinn tried to think of the best answer. On one hand, he could tell her the truth—on the other? Well, there was still much celebratory snogging to be done. "No? Yes. I mean—"

Yolanda kicked him off and drew the covers up to her ears.

"We never get a moment to ourselves when you think like this."

"Well, it's getting better, innit?" Quinn sighed. "I mean, the last time we were in bed together, he—"

And then, the door exploded inward.

"Bloody fucking hell! Can I get a sodding minute here?"

They turned and found a woman in skintight leather, dark-hair and sharp features, standing in the entrance on a cocked hip.

"…You're not my boss?"

"Quite the opposite," she said. Then, she strode across the room, grabbed the bag containing the diamond, and caught Quinn by the ear. "Time to go."

"Fucking hell, fucking hell, I—"

"Sorry," she said with a shrug.

Yolanda went to argue, but the pair disappeared in a puff of blue smoke.

"Now that *is* different," she said.

Billie Black pulled on a painter's mask and started working on the truck's cobalt stripe and logo. Brie walked across the workshop into the new brainstorm room, where Jimmy and Tommy had just entered, carrying about ten plastic bags each.

"You got the stuff?"

"Five-hundred boxes," Jimmy said.

"Are you sure this is gonna work?" said Tommy.

Brie shrugged, nodding to Jimmy. "It did on us. Slice?"

The two men looked at each other, made a *Well, duh...* gesture and each grabbed some pizza.

"Done," Billie Black said, emerging from the workshop and unzipping her overalls for ventilation—which Tommy zeroed-in on, a cord of cheese dangling from his open mouth.

"*Amazing,*" he said. Then, wagging his head: "Uh... I mean... Sorry?"

"For what?" Billie winked.

"Uh..."

With that, she took another slice and headed back to the garage.

"Dude, you're totally whipped," said Jimmy.

"Am not! I'm a professional—"

"And how many coffees have you professionally bought her?" Brie said, raising a brow as if to say: ...*Well?*

"Like six?" Tommy said. "And we make them here, okay? I didn't buy anything. Can we talk plan, please?"

"I'll second that," a voice came from the entrance.

They turned to find Jezebel, leaning on the doorway with a grin. "And this is yours, by the way," she added, tossing Quinn Donovan into the room.

"What the bloody hell was that?" he said.

"You," Brie said, eyes narrowing.

"Me," Jezebel beamed. "And I'll take a slice for my trouble."

Now, this was going to be tricky. It would require a certain amount of finesse—something, being a god, Jezebel hadn't had a lot of experience with. So, she took a slice of pizza from the box Brie was holding and said, "Thanks."

Which of course, only prompted Brie to ask, "What the fuck are you doing here?"

"Returning your magician as a peace offering, of course."

"And you've got about three seconds to tell me why I shouldn't kill you, bitch."

Kevin and Billie came back from the garage to see what was happening.

"Well, to start with, you've seriously gotta stop calling me that," said the goddess, then she nodded. Her features shifted. Her hair went blonde. She dropped about a half a foot. Then it was Ruby Cobb standing in front of the thieves.

"What the fuck?" they said in chorus.

Finesse: not a strong suit for Jezebel. She shifted back to her natural form. "So, I've got a lot to explain, and not a bunch of patience. Sit?"

Everybody just stayed frozen in place.

"Okay," she sighed. "So first thing's first. I'm a god. Surprise?"

"Ruby," Brie breathed. "What the fuck did you do to her?"

"Nothing really. I *am* her. She's me. The Cliff's Notes: I've been here the whole time."

"That's impossible," Brie snapped.

"Really? I can change for you another couple times if it'll help, but that's not what we need to talk about."

"No, I'm pretty sure it is."

"Agreed," said Kevin.

"I'll give you another private conversation later, handsome." Jezebel winked. "What we need to talk about is that diamond Houdini over here stole."

Quinn, who was naked save for his top hat, looked at the bag containing the diamond, which was covering his junk. "It's a big bloody expensive rock, so what?"

"We've got other plans," Brie said. "So if you're here to give us a giant speech, we're gonna need to reschedule."

"Not gonna happen, B. This stuff is important. That gem? Big mystical backstory. Back in the days of King Solomon, dude mojos himself into having power over the gods. He bound me to the diamond and—"

"Wait, I thought we were in a heist movie?" Billie said. "This is way outta left field."

Jezebel rolled her eyes. "You're not in *any* movie, toots. This is real life. And hold onto your butts, 'cause it gets weirder. So the big S decides he wants a whole legion of immortals working for him. He calls up a demon, builds a castle, gets brutally murdered, and I stay stuck to the stone. Fast-forward a couple millennia and the stone winds up here. A few centuries after that, it's in the hands of a dude named Bugsy Siegel, and a fun and flashy city is born."

"Thanks for the history lesson," Brie said. "But who cares?"

"Well, to start with, you probably should," said the goddess. "You see, it's all about you and your brother, B. How the diamond works is, it's meant to follow a lineage. Back when Solomon had it, he knew he couldn't live forever, but his legacy could, so long as they had the stone. The only way to break the heirship is to steal the thing and say some magic words."

"So, what?" Kevin said. "You're saying we're the heirs of King Solomon?"

Jezebel chuckled. "Mmm, nope. That'd be ridiculous. You two are the great grand-children of Benjamin Siegel—illegitimately, I mean."

"That's actually pretty badass," said Jimmy, who was the only person in the room who actually knew enough Vegas history to see the significance.

"That's impossible," said Brie. "Our grandparents were farmers. I mean, they're from Boulder."

"Actually, it's totally plausible," said Tommy, working out the timeline in his head. "Say your grandma came to Vegas one night, got a little drunk and had a one night stand with a casino guy. That's literally all it takes."

"Eww," said Brie and Kevin.

"What? Grandmas have one night stands, too."

"I don't even wanna know how you know that," said Billie.

"Well, ick-factor aside, I really don't care," Brie said. "Magic diamond, gods, whatever."

"B, you gotta think about it," said Jezebel. "All the shit that's gone down? It's because of that diamond. That's why your foster dad was paying off Whelan. That's why he was hiding your identities. The diamond belonged to you, and Gavin would do whatever he needed to make sure he wouldn't lose the stone. That's why he sent me out to kill Paul. But what he didn't expect was Quinn here being an heir, too."

Brie's jaw tightened. Rage burned in her eyes. She moved across the room, put an elbow into Jezebel's neck, and slammed her against the wall. "I'm a hairsbreadth from crushing your windpipe, bitch. So you better start elaborating on that last part."

"You're adorable," Jezebel said.

She grabbed Brie by the wrist and tossed her across the garage like a wet rag, where she collided with a tool shelf and landed hard on the table beneath.

Kevin went to lunge forward, but Billie held him back.

"You're gonna need to get it together, B," Jezebel said. "So your life unraveled a little. Sure, it hurts. But worse happens to other people all the time. Now, you can whine and mope and call me the bad guy, but I didn't choose to do what I did. Try to think big picture, pumpkin."

"I'm a little busy picturing how I'm gonna kill you," Brie said, recovering.

Jezebel gave her a patronizing grin. "Doll, I'm a god. You couldn't kill me if you tried. There's no scheme you can cook up that I can't zap my way out of, and point of fact: I'm not even your enemy. So get over it, 'kay?"

Satisfied, the goddess turned to the gang. "As for the rest of you—"

Thunk! Jezebel hit the floor like a sack of bricks, revealing Brie, brandishing a tire iron.

"Zap outta that."

CHAPTER 27
A DARK DAY FOR EVERYONE

Josh awoke in what could only be the trunk of an Audi—which was odd, because a moment ago, he'd been ordering a sashimi platter to enjoy while stonewalling Whelan. Clearly, he'd missed a few steps. Tires hummed on asphalt. Stars spotted his vision. His hands were zip-tied behind his back. His head felt like it was about to split open, and his mouth felt like it was lined with cotton.

Dammit, he thought. *I didn't even get take-out.*

He'd been drugged before, including once in Beijing with a week's worth of opium; on top of that, he'd had enough black-out nights in his time that waking up in a trunk didn't cause panic. Instead, he went with problem solving.

He knew it was an Audi because the engine sounded like one. Probably a sleek black town car, which the tycoon surely had a thing for. Escape was out of the question, since they were probably going over sixty miles-an-hour, and the last time he'd tried jumping out of the trunk of a speeding car, he'd broken his leg in three places. Which direction they were headed didn't matter: it would be remote, probably with a pre-dug grave. Classic desert execution. If he tried making a break for it when they took him out of the trunk, he might make it a few hundred yards before they put a bullet in him.

So, that left only one option.

Josh shifted his weight and got his thumb under the latch of his watch. He popped open the clasp and the watch slid down his wrist. What with the zip ties and the dark, he couldn't do much better than hope it was enough.

The watch, a silver Rolex, was actually a GPS scrambler. He'd picked it up from Miss Galaxy the night he and Brie had gone over the plan. It connected to a computer, so you could freeze the signal transmitted from the tracker in his wrist. So long as the watch was on top of the tracking chip, he could bungle the feed. Hopefully, moving it a few inches would let the signal through.

Reyes was going to be so pissed.

Brie walked a slow circle around the goddess. After she'd knocked Jezebel out, the crew didn't know what to do besides put her in a chair and bind her with zip ties and enough duct tape to line an aircraft carrier. They were in the maintenance closet of the cabana—a five-by-eleven concrete cell full of electrical breakers and cleaning supplies.

Brie wasn't sure where to take this. It was nearly eleven-thirty. By now, Whelan surely had Josh on his way to murder or torture. The others were outside, finishing work on the second truck, and if the plan was going to work, they needed to get moving. The window of time was closing off.

But on the other hand, they couldn't risk leaving the goddess here. Jezebel might claim to be switching sides, but it didn't change the fact that she was a loose cannon. If she managed to escape—well, she could shape-shift, teleport, and apparently had no issue killing people when requested; screwing up their plan would be easy. Brie's mind was in a tug-of-war, and the pressure to do *something* for either situation left her spinning. Too much to do, too little time.

"I'm sorry, you know," Jezebel said, coming-to.

"Well, thanks. That helps a bunch."

"I don't understand what I'm doing. I haven't been able to make my own decisions for kind of a long time. And honestly, I've never apologized to anyone before. I gotta say, it's kind of uncomfortable."

"Well, here's your first lesson in apologies: just because you make one doesn't mean it's going to be accepted."

"That doesn't seem fair."

"Yeah, well, worse happens to other people all the time, miss goddess. Maybe you should get over it."

Jezebel flexed against her restraints. "I don't think you get how big this is. I've been around forever, and ever since I made Ruby—ever since I met you—I've started feeling things. That's not supposed to happen."

"No, what's not supposed to happen is finding out the woman who killed your dad and the woman who's your best friend are the same person. Especially when it turns out that your best friend never existed. Which, by the way, is weird."

Jez nodded. "I guess we've both got adjustments to make."

"How, though? I've known Ruby for years. You've seriously been fucking with me for that long?"

"No, when I say I made her, I mean I made everything. Her whole life. Childhood, high school, first date—the whole deal. When I was her, I was living her. But that life never actually happened. Think on it for a minute, B. Do you actually remember meeting Rubes?"

Brie frowned. She ran through all the times she'd had with Ruby, and the further back she went, the more the memories seemed to blur together—then suddenly she'd be remembering something that happened a month ago. Like she couldn't place it. Like—well, like it had never happened.

"Okay, that *is* weird."

Jezebel shrugged. "Gods have that effect. And by the way, they also don't feel things the way you do. We don't feel sorry. Sorry's not in our vocab. The time we've spent together—real and fake— it's... changing me. When I say I'm sorry, I actually *feel* it."

"Congratulations," Brie said, wishing she'd brought the tire iron with her. "I'm so happy for you, but I kinda don't have time to sit here and have a love-in. Your ex-boss has Josh, and we've got to go save him before he gets turned into bratwurst or something."

"Harlan?" Jezebel chuckled. "You want to save Harlan? He's the moron who pulled you into this—and you want to help him?"

"Pretty much," Brie sighed, leaning against the wall. "Harlan's a douche. But he's *our* douche."

"You mortals are hilarious." Jezebel snapped her restraints and stood. "Can I help?"

Brie backed toward the door, thinking: *Yup, totally should've brought the crowbar.* "*You* want to help?"

"B, look. I know I can't make it right. But I *can* help you take Whelan down. He killed Paul."

"No, you killed Paul."

"And if I could take that back, believe me, I would." Jezebel pulled the duct tape off her wrists. "Gavin's treated me like a puppet for years. I'd like to return the favor. It's simple, B. You want justice, and I want revenge, and he'd never see it coming. It's mutually beneficial."

Brie knew it was a crap idea. But, short of repeatedly braining the goddess with a tire iron, she was pretty sure she couldn't stop her. She drew a deep breath, pinching the bridge of her nose.

"We do this, you need to prove your word."

Jezebel nodded. "What do you need?"

"Nobody else dies."

"I'm not sure I can guarantee that."

"Well," Brie said. "You're a god, aren't you? Figure it out."

Agent Max Reyes lay beneath a satin duvet at the Temple of the Mistress Shangrila, smoking his first cigarette in eighteen months, pouting.

I am a cosmic failure, he thought, playing the ember of his smoke around the lip of an ashtray. Somehow, Harlan had used the one thing Max had up his sleeve against him. Now the grifter was as good as gone.

His tenure with the FBI would come to an unceremonious close; no medals or commendations or back-patting. He'd become the punchline of water cooler bull sessions at Quantico ("Duped him like that fucktard Reyes," they'd say.) and he'd die cleaning a toilet at JC Penny's. All because he'd allowed himself to be tricked into thinking he was in control.

Now he was smoking again, his moral compass spinning like the blades of a blender, in a Nevada whorehouse, wondering if he'd have done better as a beat cop. And if that wasn't enough, because he was distracted by the case, he couldn't even pitch a healthy boner (an issue that had plagued and ultimately demolished his first marriage). Not even the understanding embrace of Sophie, chief ninja-babe of the bordello, would sooth his bruised ego.

It was a dark day in the world of Max Reyes.

"It's okay, Max," Sophie said, running her fingers through his hair and stealing a drag from his cigarette. "You've had a rough day. Everybody pushes rope now and again. Don't beat yourself up."

"I can't even beat myself off," Max said. "I'm sorry. You don't need to hear this." He sighed. "Sometimes, it just seems like the world is out to get me."

Sophie put a hand on his cheek. She moved the ashtray off his chest, straddled him and kissed his eyelids. Then, she held his face against her cleavage to shut him up. "Darling, relax. We don't even know that Harlan's left town."

"Mmhmm mmm mnn mmmmh."

"It's okay," Sophie sighed, smoking the cigarette. "Just breathe."

"Mmmh mhhm."

"I'll give you that. This thief is super annoying. When we do catch him, would it bother you terribly if I killed him? For the pain he's caused you, I mean… And stuff."

"Mmmh mhhm!"

"You're right, that's a bad call. I'm just saying, could be fun?"

Max ripped himself out of Sophie's cleavage with a gasp. "Can't breathe."

"Oh, shit. Sorry," she said, nuzzling the nape of his neck by way of apology. "Why didn't you say something?"

"I was trying."

"Well, that's what I'm saying, hun. You're trying. That's all we can ever do. You need to work on being kinder to yourself. As Lao Tzu said: 'Failure is the foundation of success.' "

Max sighed. "Can you just suffocate me to death with your boobs, please?"

"With pleasure." Sophie grinned, cradling the back of his neck, when an electric chirp came from Max's bag.

Reyes reached over and fished his phone out of the bag. He swiped across the screen and furrowed his brow. "Huh."

"What is it?" Sophie rolled off to get a better look at the screen.

"It's Harlan's tracker. It moved." Max scrambled out from under the duvet and jumped into his pants. "About a mile west of the Hoover Dam."

"Another scam?" Sophie said, grabbing her jeans off the floor.

"No way. He already gave us the slip, right?" Max panned around the room looking for his shirt. "There's no reason he'd reactivate the tracker, unless—Oh crap."

Sophie handed him his shirt and stood. "I'll get the girls."

Brie came back through the door and sighed. Counting on luck was not her style. Weird, she could handle. Slapdash, she could also handle. But both of them together? There were so many places this plan could go south—but there was no time to revise. It was a gamble, and considering she was the daughter of a cardsharp, that bothered her quite a lot.

She came into the garage, where Billie, Tommy, Quinn, Kevin and Jimmy all stood in a horseshoe around the completed armored truck.

"Well?" Kevin said.

"Same plan as before. Only, now we've got backup."

"Wait, you mean she's helping us?" Tommy said. "Do I have to point out that's the person who knocked me out with a mini fridge?"

"You really think we can trust her?" said Billie.

"No," Brie said. "I really don't. But we're out of time here."

"Brie, I don't think it's a good idea," said Jimmy. "And coming from me, that's a lot."

"You're right, Jimmy. It's a stupid idea. Unfortunately, stupid's all we've got. You and I go with Jezebel."

Jimmy nodded with a grunt.

"The rest of you ride with Billie. After we get Harlan, we'll need to get out of there in a hurry, so keep the motor running."

"I'm riding with you," Kevin said.

"No," Brie said. "It's too dangerous."

"I know. You're not going alone."

"Yes, I am. After everything that's happened. After Paul—I won't risk losing you, too."

"Same goes for you, sis." Kev took her by the shoulders and squeezed. "You're not the only one who lost him. I'm not riding sideline for this. You need a good driver in case things go sideways. And besides, somebody needs to make sure you don't get killed."

Brie shook her head. "But—"

"I'm riding with you," Kevin said. "We do this together. You know arguing with me is pointless."

"Kid's got a point," Jezebel said, entering the room. "Besides, we're short on time, aren't we?"

Tommy glared at her. "And how exactly were you planning on helping? Drop a fridge on the bad guy?"

Jezebel chuckled. "Anybody know the tale of Prometheus?"

"Save the history lesson," Brie said, producing her cell. "We've got a douche to save."

Josh kneeled in front of a pre-dug hole in the desert, staring down the barrel of Whelan's .45. Tiny leaned on the shovel, a grin spreading across his face.

Whelan pulled the trigger.

The hammer clicked.

Whelan's brow furrowed. He tried again.

Josh grimaced, closing his eyes.

Click. Click. Click.

He opened one eye, arching his brow.

Whelan sighed, checking the rounds in the cylinder, then spun it and tried again.

Click. Click. Click. Click. Click.

"Am I dead?" Josh deadpanned. "Is this hell?"

"Shit," Whelan said, tossing the gun over his shoulder.

"Because, honestly? I thought it'd be hotter... Although it *would* make a good purgatory."

Whelan grabbed Tiny's Desert Eagle and racked the slide. "Apologies for the wait," he said, affecting his best host's tone. "I'm sure this will make up for it."

He aimed, grinned, and Josh's phone started playing three bars of the "Imperial March" from *Star Wars*.

"Shit, could someone get that?" Josh sighed. " 'Cause it's just gonna keep ringing."

Whelan motioned to Tiny. The goon came over and fished the phone out of Harlan's pocket.

"Thanks, big guy."

Tiny growled, then answered the phone. "Yeah?" He paused. To Whelan: "It's for you."

Gavin frowned and grabbed the cell from his henchman. "This is Whelan."

"You know, traditionally, you're supposed to call me. I mean... Assuming you want to get your money back and whatnot."

"Brie," Whelan said. "And here I thought you'd be halfway across the Pacific by now."

"Well, I was gonna. But then my friend showed up with this ginormous diamond, and I figured that's gonna be a bitch to get through customs."

"You don't say."

"I never understood why people say that," Brie said. "I mean, given how it usually follows somebody saying something, it's just kinda antithetical, don't you think?"

"I think we should skip the quips," Whelan said. "Especially since I've got Josh at gunpoint. I'm a patient man, Brie. But, frankly, I was looking forward to shooting him."

"Really? And Josh is usually so charming."

"No need to be coy, Cassiday. We know how this goes. I tell you I'm going to kill him. You offer to return my property in exchange for his life. We decide on a place, then I give you an absurdly short amount of time to get there to keep you from coming up with a plan, and tell you to come alone."

"Hoover Dam Bypass Bridge. Half an hour. Or, we could just blow up your casino with the four sticks of C-4 I had hidden in that duffel you confiscated."

Whelan chuckled. "You're bluffing."

"I sure could be. But we never did finish our conversation. For all you know, I've just deployed a bunch of ants I control telepathically into your casino to do it for me," she said. "Obviously, I didn't. But I did spill a bunch sugar on my way out. Because ants—"

"Hoover Dam Bypass. Half an hour. Bring the cavalry." Whelan disconnected, then turned to Tiny. "Get Halverson and Gibbons on the line. Tell them to check Cassiday's bag for explosives and report."

Josh, who'd only heard the one side of Whelan's conversation, said, "Tell them to look for ants, too."

Whelan rolled his eyes. "Let's go for a drive."

"Now can I call shotgun?" said Harlan. Then, off their expressions. "Okay, fine. But no trunk this time."

CHAPTER 28
THE GOOD, THE BAD,
AND THE GODLY

Noon. Two Ford F800s named Christine and Igor sped along the Arizona highway, headed toward the Hoover Dam Bypass Bridge: a nine-hundred foot archway slung over the Colorado River. Billie, Tommy and Quinn drove Christine, the original armored truck, and pulled off at the entrance for the bridge. Igor (so named because of its stout and burly appearance) pulled onto the bridge.

Kevin was behind the wheel. Brie rode shotgun. In the back, Jimmy Wok sat next to an eagle, feathers dark as onyx, roughly the size of a German Shepard, bobbing its head to the bounces of the truck.

"I'm seriously uncomfortable with this," Jimmy said.

"Aaaaarrrww!"

"No offense."

The great bird nodded, chuffing its feathers.

"Guns time, Jimmy," Brie said.

Kevin slowed the truck. "Are we sure we want to save Harlan? Last chance for a U-turn."

"Nobody gets left behind," Brie said. "I don't actually believe there's honor among thieves, but Paul did."

Jimmy handed her a shotgun. She pumped a round into the chamber. The eagle snapped its beak in approval. She nodded to Kev and passed him an enormous pistol. "We do this. For Paul."

Her brother nodded. "For Paul."

"I really don't like guns," Jimmy said. "Why can't I just make a face-shaped dent in my wok? I'm totally planning on getting a new one after this."

"Caaawwwww!"

"What? Don't judge me. Edgar Allen Poultry."

"So, the bird's plotting to take the sod's liver, then?" Quinn said. "Bit harsh, innit?"

"That's just the myth," Tommy said. "Prometheus steals fire from the gods, gets chained to a rock and has a big eagle eat his liver for eternity. It's a cautionary allegory about pride."

"Well, I get *that*." Quinn rolled his eyes, unscrewing the cap on a bottle of Jameson's. "But I think she's being a little more literal."

"Honestly, I'm still dealing with the fact that gods are real."

"Bloody nutty, right?" Quinn pushed the bottle in Tommy's direction. "Pull?"

Tommy looked at the bottle, then shrugged and took a swig.

Billie stared out the window, watching as Igor made its way onto the bridge. "Did anybody catch what their signal was gonna be when they make the switch?"

"Nope," sighed Tommy.

"Don't think so," added Quinn. "Oh wait! Waffles. ...No, that was what I wanted for breakfast—I reckon they'll fire a flare or something."

"Because you think they just *happen* to have a flare gun with them?" Tommy said, rubbing his eyes.

Billie yanked the bottle out of his grip and took a swig. "I shoulda known. Something always goes wrong around this point."

"Uh, no," Quinn said. "I suggested that because I saw Brie take a flare gun out of the big lad's car before we left? Jesus, just because I'm drunk doesn't mean I'm useless, you know."

Billie and Tommy blinked at each other, unsure whether to be embarrassed or impressed. Billie handed the Jameson's back to Quinn, who gleefully took another three belts before belching like an ogre. "Well?"

There was an extended silence.

"Flare gun," Tommy said.

"Awesome," Billie added.

"Brilliant," Quinn deadpanned—which was honestly the most surprising thing he'd ever done. "I'll definitely count on you two when everything gets cock-up."

"Speaking of," Billie said. "Tommy? Don't you think it's about time to make that call?"

Tommy grinned, producing his phone. "Thought you'd never ask."

"Balls," Quinn sighed. "Liquor I can handle, but you two make me sick."

Kevin pulled the truck to a halt about two yards from the Audi parked in the middle of the bridge. Strangely, though the bypass was a tourist mecca, and it was well into the day, the road was empty. He threw it in park and looked at his sister.

"You remember what he used to say, right?"

Brie nodded. "Never order a plate you can't finish."

"Well, are you sure…"

"Oh, this plate? I'm starving for it." She threw open the door. "Stay behind me. Jimmy?"

"Uhuh?" said the big guy, who squirmed as the giant eagle nipped at his arm.

"You and me are up front. I'll do the talking, so just stand there and be scary. And Jezebel?"

"Ccrrwaaaapp—Cawww!"

"Yeah… Whatever."

With that, she climbed out of the truck and slung a duffel bag over her shoulder. Kevin followed. Jimmy threw open the door, and before he could move, the great eagle flung itself out the door and flapped into the air.

"I fuckin' hate birds!" he howled.

Whelan and Tiny climbed out of the Audi. The tycoon walked into the space between the vehicles. Tiny moved around back, popped the trunk, and pulled Harlan out.

Brie, Kevin, and Jimmy met the tycoon and his henchman in the middle of the bridge.

Gavin nodded at Kevin. "So… you're fired."

"You pay crap anyway."

Whelan shrugged, then eyed the shotgun Brie had at her side. "You know, unless you didn't bring the money, you won't be needing that."

"Oh, this?" Brie said. "Just a little insurance policy. You see, the last encounter I had with a shifty businessman, he tied me to a chair in his basement. Makes a gal a little twitchy."

"Fair enough," Whelan said with a shrug.

"We left off with you saying Paul was noble," Brie said, taking a step toward the tycoon. "You were right. But me? Not so much."

Here, Whelan produced a pistol and shoved it against Harlan's neck. "I hope this isn't your preface for a trick. Because… Well, I really want to kill him."

Harlan grinned and said, "Hey."

"Hey," Brie replied. To Whelan: "And no, I just wanted you to understand that I'm not the same person you killed. I want you to know, after all this? I'm gonna find you, and I'm gonna make you all kinds of dead."

Whelan mocked a shiver. "Oh, I'm terrified. Really. You've got me at a disadvantage here." He pressed the pistol deeper in Harlan's neck. "Tiny? Would you be kind enough to advise Miss Cassiday as to what happens when I'm crossed?"

"Mo-fuckah loses his shit."

"And when I lose my shit?"

"People get hurt. Mister Whelan got a temper, dig?"

"Yeah. Shocker," Brie said. She nodded over her shoulder. "Throw it, Jimbo."

Jimmy pulled open the door of the armored car, revealing three rows of duffel bags. Brie tossed the bag she'd been carrying to Tiny, who unzipped it and checked the bills.

"It's good, boss."

"Uh, guys?" Harlan said. "You seriously had better not be giving up seventy-two million bucks on my account. I mean… I'm worth about sixty. But—"

"Shut up, Josh," Brie said.

"Okay, but you're making a mistake."

"It's more complicated than you think," Brie said.

Josh nodded. "It usually is."

To Whelan, Brie said, "That bag is yours either way. We circle each other. Halfway, you give us Josh and I toss you these"—she held up the keys to the van—"then, we watch you leave."

"No." Whelan shook his head. "You give us the keys, we give you Harlan."

Josh rolled his eyes. "Oh, for fuck's sake."

He walked over to Brie, took the key, then walked back to Whelan and slapped it in his hand. "Okay? Can we get this over with? Thanks."

Whelan toed the duffel. "Why did you put it in bags?"

"Have you tried getting across the border with two pallets of bills?" Brie chuckled.

"Can't throw that in checked baggage," added Jimmy.

Josh came back and Kevin cut the zip ties off his wrists. "Well, gents, it's been a slice. But I've got a thing with a private jet."

Whelan chuckled, tossing the keys to Tiny. "I'll take the Audi."

"Man of the people," Josh sighed. To his cohorts: "Shall we?"

Just then, a '97 Buick station wagon pulled up behind the Audi.

"Stop!" Steve Halverson said, climbing out of the passenger's seat. Phil Gibbons came out of the driver's. "Stop, stop, stop."

Whelan wheeled around. "Phil? Steve? What?"

"Don't let them go," Halverson gasped, hands on his knees.

"The explosives? You didn't get them off site?"

"There were no explosives," said Gibbons, sweat beading on his brow. "They fucked us."

Gavin wagged his head. "But if there wasn't a bomb—"

"There was worse than a bomb," Steve said, catching his breath. "Cassiday's bag was full of bricks of C-4. But when bomb squad moved in, they cut open one of the casings. They were bricks full of ants."

"Fire ants," Gibbons added.

"They were all over the place. Some idiot dumped a bunch of sugar in the kitchen. Then Health and Safety come in following up on an anonymous tip…"

Whelan shook his head. "The point?"

"They shut us down, boss. The dude called a facility evacuation."

"And you let him?" Gavin's left eye commenced twitching.

"Code 857-C," Harlan beamed. "In the case of an outbreak of foreign species, the property must be evacuated. And by the way, surprise!"

Whelan turned on him, furious. Over his shoulder, "Is this true?"

"Federal law," said Gibbons.

"We tried to stop them," added Halverson. "Then they threatened to court-martial us. The point is, don't let these fuckers go anywhere. We can pin liability on them…"

"I can do better than that," Whelan said, racking the slide on his pistol.

Just then, a black carbon shuriken flew through the air, catching Phil Gibbons's hand and impaling it against the door of the Buick, where he proceeded to screech like a mashed cat, blood bubbling from his palm.

"Gavin Whelan?" a voice came from behind Igor. "Put your weapon down and show some hands."

A neat-suited figure came out, brandishing a standard issue Beretta M9. A group of twelve slender shadows fell in behind as the man walked toward them.

"Max Reyes, FBI. I lost my badge, but you are totally under arrest. Now, put down the fucking firearm."

The ninja babes surrounded them in a chorus of clicks as they cocked their weapons. Josh had to admit, the agent's act had improved a lot since the last time he'd seen him. He'd always expected Vegas to grow on him, but now Max was practically dripping it on the pavement.

"Well, it's about time, Agent. Did you stop for burritos or something?"

"He took a detour," Sophie called from the ring of ninja babes. "Thanks for setting us up, by the way."

"Get out. You two played rumpy-pumpy?" Harlan bounced his eyebrow, impressed. "Good job. Honestly, I didn't even know he was capable—"

"Can it, Harlan," Reyes said with a smirk. "Now everybody put their fucking weapons on the ground." He panned to Brie, Kevin and Jimmy. "Everyone. Let's go. On the ground."

The thieves held their ground.

"Him first," Brie said, motioning to Whelan.

"I'm sorry," the tycoon said, coming forward. "Reyes, was it? Why should I believe you're FBI? I'd like to point out, you're surrounded by con artists and came in with an army of hookers."

"Escorts," Reyes corrected. "They're escorts. And also highly-trained assassins."

"Point taken," Whelan said. "But without a badge—"

"Okay, here's a different way to look at it: Whoever I am, you're surrounded by highly trained escort-assassins. They're here to collect Harlan, but I'm here to arrest you. Apparently. Honestly, it's a bit of a surprise—thanks, Josh."

"My pleasure," said the grifter.

"Fine," Whelan said. "Let's assume you *are* FBI. What exactly am I under arrest for? These thieves stole my property, I'm only retrieving it."

"Oh, I got that," Reyes said. "It's just this thing about holding somebody at gunpoint being illegal. So, to start, I'll go with that. There's also some alleged stuff: embezzling, property fraud, tax evasion... Not to mention the resisting arrest I'm going to slap on top."

Whelan raised his hands in defeat. "And if I put this down, I presume we can negotiate?"

"We are negotiating. But it'll definitely go better if you drop the firearm."

"I understand, Agent." Whelan crouched slowly, putting the gun in front of him. "Now, I'm sure we can work something—"

"Aaaaarrrrgggh!!!" cried Phil Gibbons, still pinned to the driver's side of the Buick. With his free hand, he flung open the door, reached in and came back with a Glock-17.

"Aw, crap," Josh said.

Gibbons opened fire, howling like a madman, panning the pistol in a wild arc. Halverson ducked behind the passenger's door. Whelan and Tiny hit the concrete, shielding the back of their heads.

"Grraaaaaaaaaahhhh!!!!!" *Boom, boom, boom, boom, boom-buh-boom.*

Josh and Reyes lunged toward Brie, Kevin and Jimmy, and the gang scrambled behind Whelan's Audi. Bullets ricocheted off the armored truck.

"Aaaaahhhh!!!!!!" *Boom. Ping-ping!!! Boom, ping!*

A windshield shattered. Tiny grabbed Whelan by the collar and dragged him to the side of Igor for cover.

Thunk, ping! Boom! Buh-buh-buh-buh-boom! Chikt-chikt.

Silence.

Max, Josh, Brie, Kevin and Jimmy all brushed the popcorn glass off their shoulders and stood. The ninja babes all came up from defensive positions and put their sights on the Buick.

"Everyone okay?" Brie said.

"Shit," Sophie stammered, hand on her solar plexus by the edge of the bridge. Blood trickled through her fingers. Surprised, she looked at her chest, then fell to her knees and folded over.

Whelan and Tiny peeked around the side of the truck. Then, a shrill warrior cry came from the ring of ninja babes. Bullets rained over the Buick and the armored truck in a deafening hail.

Reyes slipped out of Harlan's grasp, lifting his gun arm and firing as he waded across the bridge toward the Buick, where Halverson and Gibbons crouched, using its doors as shields. Each shot hit Gibbons in the forearm—which was still pinned to the front of the door.

Max fired until his clip emptied about three yards from the station wagon. Phil shrieked, his arm now a bloody chunk of swiss cheese. Max slammed a new clip into his service weapon, racked the slide, and aimed.

Then, with a deafening boom, his left shoulder exploded with a spray red. Max yelped, spinning, and hit the pavement.

Tiny came out with the smoking barrel of a Desert Eagle.

A thunderstorm in gunfire: The ninja babes opened up again. Jimmy and Brie took opposite ends of the trunk of the Audi, each firing at the side of Igor. Josh leaped into the middle of the insanity, reaching for Reyes's pistol.

Tiny emptied his clip, then tossed the Desert Eagle aside, walking out into the field of fire with no regard for the ninja babes, who were still focused on Halverson and Gibbons, the former of whom tried to use his shirt sleeve as a white flag. Erin, the ninja babe second in command to Sophie, responded by shooting off his index and middle fingers.

Jimmy caught a bullet in the armpit, yelping as the force threw him to the ground.

Josh pointed the gun at Tiny, when with a *thuppt* like striking a match, Whelan appeared, putting his revolver against the grifter's temple.

"You earned this, Josh."

"Harlan," Brie bellowed, training the shotgun on Whelan's back. "Down!"

Blam!!! Blam!!! Blam!!!

And, like a smudge on a film strip, Whelan disappeared.

Josh fell to the ground, covering his head. "Fuck! Really, definitely, fuck!"

Brie pumped the shotgun, when the air whooshed beside her. "What the…?"

"Sorry, Brie," Whelan said, planting an elbow in her nose.

She howled, throwing a pained left hook that caught the tycoon's gun-hand. The pistol skittered across the asphalt. Whelan whipped a knife out of an ankle holster, then drove it between Brie's ribs. "I'd like to say I regret this, but—"

"Squaaawwwwkkk!!!!"

Whelan went to turn, when the dog-sized eagle caught him by the gut and threw him against the side of the Audi.

"Gaaaah!"

"Ever hear the tale of Prometheus, fuckstick?" Brie groaned.

The eagle snarled and pecked at the tycoon, chunks of flesh and tattered button-down flying. He moaned, clawing for the pistol. He reached it, then aimed at the vicious bird.

It cawed and brushed the gun away. Whelan cackled, blood bubbling from his mouth. Then, he disappeared in a cloud of blue smoke.

Back in the middle of the bridge, Josh pushed himself to his knees, wagging his head. "Was that a bird—"

Then Tiny caught him by the shoulders in a low tackle, running him across the bridge and slamming Harlan against the rail of the walkway.

"Aiight," he said, leaning Josh over the rail. "Now, I'ma show you how I scare people."

Vrrrmmm! Behind, Halverson and Gibbons had climbed into

the Buick, and were pointed directly at Josh and Tiny. The goon wheeled around, then leaped out of the way.

"Josh!" Brie screamed. But it was too late.

"Uh-oh," Josh said. The front of the car caught him and sent him flying off the bridge. "Woaaaaaaahhhh!!!"

"Screeeeeeeaaaaaacccchhh!!!!" went the eagle as it dove over the side of the dam after him.

"Motherfu—" Jimmy cut himself off, sending a salvo of shotgun pellets at the side of the truck. Tiny dove for cover.

"Boss?! Boss!!!??"

Halverson and Gibbons spilled out of the station wagon and scurried over to the henchman. Then, Kevin leaned on the side of the Audi, aimed, and blew a chunk off Steve Halverson's shoulder.

The ninja babes ran out of ammo. Brie pulled herself to her feet and pumped a fresh round in her shotgun just as the armored truck peeled off.

"We need to get to the river," she said, producing a penknife from her pocket and flicked it open. Then, to Kevin. "Tell the gang to call an ambulance."

Then, she climbed into the Audi and hotwired it. Kevin and Jimmy climbed in while she throttled the gas pedal.

CHAPTER 29
EAGLE'S TORMENT

"Call HQ," Whelan said, holding the gash in his abdomen. "Tell them to power up."

"But they cleared out the casino?" Halverson grunted, blood streaming down his shoulder. He pulled the armored truck onto the freeway back to Vegas, struggling not to use his ruined hand.

"Then get them back. I've had enough fuckups for one day."

"I'm sorry, boss," said Gibbons, going pale in the passenger's seat.

Whelan glared at him. "Is that supposed to change something?"

"We gonna let 'em get away?" said Tiny.

"I can't do shit until I fix this," Gavin said, motioning to the angry wound below his ribs.

Tiny shrugged. "But how? Ain't nobody in there to juice."

"Exactly. Nobody's in there, so we don't need power."

"You serious?" Steve sighed. "Recovering from that'll take a week at best."

"And he's being generous," added Gibbons.

"One more word out of either of you, and it'll be you who makes the difference," Gavin hissed. "Drive."

Brie, Reyes, Jimmy and Kevin stood in a horseshoe on the bank of the Colorado River. They were about a mile west of the bridge. Brie held her side as the gang watched the river, looking for Harlan.

Jimmy shook his head. "He's gone."

"Fall like that?" Reyes said. "Nobody could survive it."

Just then, Billie, Quinn and Tommy pulled up. The hacker was first out of the truck.

"Where?" he said.

The three shook their heads.

"No sign yet," Brie said. "He could've drifted a lot farther."

"You're hurt," said Billie, climbing out of the driver's side.

Brie nodded. "One of the many."

Quinn staggered out of the back of the truck, staring at the river. Without a word, he passed his bottle of Jameson's to Brie, who swigged.

Reyes sighed. "That's it, then. You all should get out of here before the uniforms arrive."

He tilted his head to a furl of dust moving up the road toward them. The gang shared a collective frown, watching the red-and-blues flash.

"Brie needs a doctor," Kev said. "She's got to go with them."

Brie nodded at Reyes, who was still attempting to keep pressure on his bummed shoulder. "You too."

Behind, Erin and the rest of the ninja babes pulled up in an unmarked SUV. "Anybody hurt?"

Jimmy, Brie, and Reyes all nodded.

"Get in," said the mistress.

Kevin helped Brie over to the SUV. "This is my sister. I'm coming with."

"Don't worry," Erin said. "You're not losing her. We've lost enough sisters today." To Reyes: "You okay?"

Reyes shook his head. "I'm sorry, Erin. There was nothing I—"

"Did she die saving you?"

"Not a chance."

"That's our girl. Get in. All of you."

Max and Jimmy climbed into the SUV just as the EMTs arrived, scrambling out with a pair of binoculars and a crash cart.

Brie nodded to Billie. "Throw it."

"There!" shouted one of the EMTs. " 'Bout a yard out. He's drifting."

He pointed to the middle of the river, where a body bobbed along with the current.

"Go, go, go!"

Another three dove into the river and paddled out to Harlan.

Erin slammed the door on the Range Rover. "We've gotta go."

Reyes nodded, cradling his bleeding shoulder. "If they can save him, they will."

"That's nine-hundred feet," Brie said. "He's gone, Max."

The SUV pulled onto the highway.

The armored truck pulled into the roundabout of the Olympus, where a medical team waited with a stretcher. They hauled Whelan out of the truck and wheeled him away.

"What about me?" grunted Phil Gibbons.

"And me," said Steve Halverson, raising his ruined hand. "I'll never get to flip off a bartender again."

"Will you bitches stop being bitches for a minute?" Tiny said. "At least we got the cash back."

"We should probably pull it in back," Phil said. "No telling what else they had up their sleeve."

Steve nodded and threw the truck in reverse. "It's gonna be a long weekend, the amount of paperwork those fucks just caused."

"Doesn't matter," Tiny sighed. "We got what's ours."

He climbed into the back of the truck and unzipped one of the duffels to sniff some cash, a habit that over the years, he'd discovered could sooth most of life's woes.

"Says the guy who doesn't do paperwork," grumbled Halverson. The truck beeped as he backed it into the alley.

"Paperwork sucks," added Gibbons.

Tiny ignored them. He pulled a stack of bills out of the duffel and breathed deep, then frowned. "That's not right. Smells like paper."

"Money *is* paper, idiot."

"No, I mean it smells like the wrong paper—Aw, shit."

"What?" said Steve. "What?"

"Oh fuck," said Gibbons. "Is that Monopoly money?"

Tiny tossed the multicolored bills across the truck, ripping open another bag and finding more of the fake cash. He dug deeper as a muffled bleep came from under the bills. Then, he pulled out an elegantly printed business card.

Nice try, fucksticks!

Beneath that was a row of gray bricks connected with a string of copper wire.

"Mothafu—"

The truck exploded in a massive fireball, shattering windows on the first three levels of the building. Flaming bits of Monopoly money rained over the alley like flash paper.

A pair of medics clamped Whelan into the Virtruvian machine. He howled when they lifted his arms, pain shrieking up from his abdomen. The front of his shirt was slick with blood. One of the medics scissored it open and sized up the wound. She frowned and twisted to her partner. "Suture kit."

"It's fine," Whelan groaned. "Don't."

"You'll bleed out," said the other medic.

"I'll do a lot more than that," the tycoon said, nodding across the room.

At the console, a third medic powered up the machine. "Full power in five…"

"Clear out," Whelan said.

The first medic threw open the suture kit. "But—"

"Clear out!"

The machine started humming. Blue light emerged from the cuffs on his forearms and ankles. The machine reached a fever pitch. The lights started flickering. Streams of blue shot down his arms.

Then, the lights went out. An orange bulb started flashing over the door as an emergency siren wailed like somebody repeatedly hitting a sea lion with a hammer. Then a flicker, static as the tone cut out, and the machine fluttered.

Thump. Thump. Thump-Thump.

Jackson 5's "You've Changed" rocketed over the PA.

"Prometheus steals fire from the gods," a woman's voice came from the shadows. "Didn't exactly work out for him."

"What?" Whelan wagged his head, trying to will his eyes to adjust to the darkness.

Jezebel came into the glow of the machine with a grin.

Whelan struggled against his bonds. The machine sent a throbbing pulse through the air. "You?"

"Me, baby. And I'll tell you this: liver tastes like butt."

"But, Cassiday," Whelan huffed, the strings of blue wrapping around his arms as the machine started squealing. "I thought... It should be—"

"Me?" Brie's voice crackled over the speakers. "Oh, don't worry, Gavin. I'm here. I wouldn't miss this. She'll just enjoy it more."

Whelan snarled, writhing against his shackles.

"Shh." Jezebel put a finger to his lips. "Don't kill the mood, pumpkin. Although, I did have a question. Say we reverse the way the slots work—what do you think'd happen?"

"No," Whelan cried, the light building at the center of his chest. "No—"

"Gavin," Jezebel chuckled. "After all these years, all the shit you put me through—you think I didn't work this out?"

The light jumped down the tycoon's throat, sending a shockwave through the room that toppled servers, exploded lights, set keyboards on fire, and actually turned up the music. Jezebel shielded her eyes as the room filled with blue, then the light gathered around the top of the machine and shot up through the ceiling.

Silence.

Whelan lay limp in the Virtruvian machine, shriveled and leathery like a mummy.

The goddess nodded. "Happy comeuppance, boss."

Light cascaded from the top of the Olympus in a sprawling mushroom cloud. Although next to nobody would notice, in the hours that followed, dogs yipped gleefully, cats and smaller dogs frisked around their houses with newfound frenzy; three-dozen husbands shagged their wives with more energy than they'd had in decades; folks nursing hangovers started dancing, and everyone, throughout the greater Paradise area, felt at least a few years younger.

They'd never know what caused it—and indeed, most would head home from their vacations never giving it a second thought. The effects had only added a few hours to the lives of everyone in the city, but one thing was certain: It definitely didn't suck.

Brie hung up the phone and turned to the band of thieves. "Done."

The rest of the gang cheered. Quinn passed around a bottle. Jimmy grabbed Brie in a bear hug. Billie jumped into Tommy's arms, wrapping her thighs around his back. Kevin grinned and high-fived Reyes.

Brie slipped out of Jimmy's arms and grabbed the bottle from Quinn, who responded with a bemused, "Oi!"

"Shut it," she said. She raised the bottle. "To Harlan."

"To Harlan," said the gang.

"To Sophie," added Reyes.

"Sophie," the gang agreed.

"If he were here," Tommy sighed. "He'd say something snarky. So given that he's not—let's enjoy the moment and feel bad later."

Brie nodded, handing the hacker the bottle. She knew all too well how he was feeling. "I've come to the conclusion the two aren't mutually exclusive."

"And if Sophie were here," Reyes said. He bowed his head, thinking. "...Well, actually she wouldn't be. So I guess that's my cue."

With that, the agent exited the Wynn.

"Gee, he sure knows how to kill a buzz, doesn't he?" said Kevin.

CHAPTER 30
CLOSURE

Paramedics wheeled Josh Harlan into Sunrise General Hospital, a tube hanging out the side of his mouth. They traded a few bits of jargon, when the grifter coughed violently, then scrambled to pull the tube from his windpipe.

The lead EMT held him down. "Calm. You fell almost nine-hundred feet and hit water."

Josh wagged his head and spat out the tube. "And you're asking me to be calm about that?"

"He's back," the EMT called to the group following the stretcher. "Prep an ICU." To Harlan: "You should know, you're insanely lucky."

"Yeah, real luck would be not falling off the side of a fucking bridge, wouldn't it?"

"Buddy, you fell almost a thousand feet, didn't drown, didn't break your neck—didn't break anything, actually. Do you have any idea how unlikely that is?"

Josh considered. "Does it change anything if I told you a dog-sized bird saved me?"

"I'm going to medicate the shit out of you," the EMT said with a chuckle.

"Swell," Josh grinned. "Oh, hey—before you do, could you do me a favor?"

"We don't really do favors."

Josh nodded. Professional dignity, always the toughest nut to crack—especially when it came to folks who worked with the public. "What if I offered you three grand?"

"Are you bribing me?"

"Damn betcha. So what do you say?"

"I'm very sorry, Agent," the EMT said with a frown. "Harlan drowned after he hit the water."

The agent nodded, solemnly.

"Even if he hadn't, both tibias were shattered, his fifth and eleventh vertebrae were mashed potatoes—there was nothing we could do."

Reyes rubbed his nose and sighed. "I understand. Thanks for your time."

The EMT nodded and headed back down the hall.

Max walked out the sliding doors of the hospital and lit a smoke. Well, that was it, then. He'd go back to his hotel, pack up and start the paperwork. He'd tender his resignation from the bureau later—maybe take a year or two off, travel, do a bit of soul-searching... Open a chip truck, and work himself to death. That, or he could take a spot on a local PD's homicide team. At this point, either would do.

It was odd, he'd never really liked Harlan—definitely never enjoyed his company—but now, without the running commentary of smartass bullshit... The world seemed almost uncomfortably quiet.

Max pitched his smoke, rubbed the back of his neck, and headed for his Prius. He'd never admit it, but melancholy clenched his guts like a bad Cobb Salad—and the agent hated Cobb Salads.

He climbed into the rental and peeled off. He speeded back to the Venetian. Just because he could.

Because he'd spent the last three years in prison, Tommy Carlyle thought his first attempt at asking someone out should be special. It should be witty, but not sarcastic. Funny, but not hammy. It should seem natural, but cordial. Laid back, but exciting... But for the past two hours, the best he'd come up with was a lame "gotta catch 'em all" joke that would barely work for a Hallmark card. Doubt brooded over him like a tiny raincloud.

"Dude, just ask her," Harlan had told him, then talking about Tommy's barista. "You overthink way too much."

At that point, Tommy was flying a helicopter away from a squadron of Sandanistas who were setting up an anti-aircraft rocket to blow them out of the sky (they'd just stolen some secret missile codes from their headquarters), so he was a little distracted.

"Fine, so what, then? I mean, it's always a big thing and now I'm supposed to add not overthinking to my list of what not to do?"

"No, you're supposed to lose the not-to-do list all together. It's a date, Tom. Not a bomb defusal." Josh yanked the controls from him and pulled the chopper in a wild barrel roll. The missile screeched by them.

"Don't do that! I don't know how to recover from that—this is my first time!"

"Go with your gut, Carlyle!"

"My guts are shitting themselves!"

"Exactly!"

Now, he sat on the edge of his bed at the Wynn, smiling.

Fucking Josh: the Fonda to his Jimmy Stewart. In a way, it was a slight homage to his friend—who'd always nagged Tommy for needing to put himself out there more.

He fidgeted uncomfortably. He could almost hear the grifter chuckling from beyond the grave. He bobbed his head to an imaginary beat while he fiddled with his phone. Figuring out an opener was like slipping into a razor wire man thong.

"Hi Billie. Wanna grab coffee?"

Nope. "Wanna grab a drink?"

Nu-uh. "Billie! Hey, I was wondering, did you…"

Too much enthusiasm. "Oh, sorry Tommy," he said in falsetto. "That's so sweet of you. I'd love to, but I've got plans with a guy who isn't a total dork. He's got long hair, wears a leather jacket, probably rides a bike—Oh, for fuck's sake."

He bit his lip, unlocked his phone and tapped the numbers.

"Surprisingly, we're *not* behind," said Stacey. "Oh, and Gus called. He said he's gonna be late on rent. Waiting on a check or something. But he said to tell you he promised, end of the week, it's in. Also, he apologized kind of a lot. Also, he cried a little. He asked me not to tell you, but well… It's just too funny."

Billie was back behind the chair, finishing an up-do on a Barberella-styled blonde in a chrome torpedo-boobs Madonna bra and a pair of thigh-high patent leather boots. Remarkably, the actor's name was John, and he was actually a forty-five year old man. But for the early bristles of a five-o'clock shadow, you'd never know.

Normally, Billie would be pleased with such a transformation —especially since she'd done it in about thirty minutes. But since she'd billed the production company for two hours a head, she frowned.

"How about a shave, John? You want an espresso?"

"Thanks Billie, but I've got lunch with the big T."

"The one with the hair?"

Before John could answer, the phone rang. Stacey came back with the cordless and handed it to Billie. She took it, headed back through the entrance to the front of the shop and started fiddling with paperwork behind the register—a habit she'd developed before Stacey had been around to take the calls. In case it was a miffed client, Billie had always pretended to be her own secretary. Oddly, she'd always called herself Stacey.

"Gus, it's fine if you're gonna be a little late. You don't need to keep calling."

"Uh, hey Billie. It's... Tommy?"

"Oh, hey Tommy. What's up?"

"Well I was just wondering... Uh..." The hacker sounded hoarse, as if he'd just beaten a cold or something. "Does Gus ride a bike?"

"I don't think so." She started leafing through the day's mail. "You called to ask me that? How do you know Gus?"

"I uh..." Tommy sputtered. "Well, it's stupid. I'm staying in town another couple of days. And I just was, uh, wondering... If, you know—I mean if you've got nothing else happening— would you...?"

"Oh my god."

"What?"

"Oh. My. God."

"What? What?"

Billie held up a neat white postcard, reading with a grin. "Have you gotten any mail today?"

"I haven't checked—"

"Check," she said.

"Billie, what is it?"

"Just check the mail."

"Hey, somebody left something under my door. It's—oh my god."

Jimmy Wok came out of KitcheNova carrying a large paper bag. He felt good—excited, even. There were few things as satisfying for the big guy as purchasing a new pan, and in the bag was a handmade 18" carbon steel *chukanabe* with a reinforced tempered handle and *JW* etched in its center. The pan came with a lifetime warranty, and Jimmy couldn't wait to see what the policy was on face indentations.

He climbed into his BMW M6 convertible and slipped the key in the ignition, when a flash of white caught his eye on the windshield.

"The fuck?" He reached around and grabbed the paper. It was a postcard-sized cut of thick cardstock, velvety between his fingers. He turned it over and read:

Congratulations!

You've been selected to embark upon a super mysterious adventure.
Antics, surprises, and probably a lot of money await.
Yeah, admit it: You're wildly curious—which is good!
Unless you're a cat—then it's bad.
Head to the private jet terminal at McCarran International...
November 22. 7 p.m. (Because who likes waking up early?)
...to get some answers.
Or, you know, keep on being boring and stuff. Up to you.
Seriously though, show up.

—You know who I am.

Kevin pulled his souped-up Silverado into a parking space at his building. It was a gated two-story walkup. He slipped his key fob over a black box, and the gate beeped opened. Inside was all palm trees and eucalyptus.

"I presume the fence is to keep the hookers out," a voice came from behind.

Kevin sighed. *Just when I think the weird shit is over.*

"You again."

"I guess now that address I gave you makes a little more sense." A cigarette glowed in the shade of a palm.

"Talking to a guy that's been dead for a bazillion years does not make a lot of sense," Kevin said. "What—does the afterlife fry your brains or something?"

"Ah, so ya know who I am. That's convenient."

"I'm trying to get back to normal. So please don't tell me you're here to screw up my life again."

"Money's all about who you know, kid." The shadow grinned. Kev wasn't sure how, but he could feel it. "I just came to tell ya, thanks."

"You're not going to haunt me for forever, are you?"

Silence.

Kev took a step toward the palm. "Hello? Creepy old dude?"

He reached into the shadow, but came back with air. The smell of roses hung on the breeze. Kev looked at his hand, then the space where the ghost had been, then back and forth a few times.

"Huh."

"This is bloody bollocks, you know?" Quinn Donovan huffed, a cigarette hanging from his lips as he clambered up the slope of the dune.

"Quit whining," Jezebel said. "You have booze, don't you?"

They were in the middle of the Mohave, about a mile south of Boulder. Nothing but cacti, tumbleweeds, and scorched earth in every direction. The sun hung above like a great glowy wanker. Sweat trickled down Quinn's back. He was half-past hungover, and while he *did* have booze, it didn't quite make up for the goddess dragging him out to the middle of the sodding desert at the hottest part of the day.

"Well, I just don't like the mystery is all. Not having me out here to kill me, are you?"

"Against the rules," she said. "Unfortunately."

Quinn took a belt from the whiskey. "You know, if I'm to spend an extended life in your escort, the least we could do is *attempt* a mutual fancy."

"I'll think on it," she said, nodding toward the horizon. "A little further."

They crested the dune, coming up on a sprawling valley. Dust cyclones danced along the huge column.

"Oh, lovely," Quinn said. "More desert."

She led him down to the mouth of the valley, where a pair of sand blown rocks sat like martian chez-lounges. She sat cross-legged on one, and Quinn tossed himself on the other with a relieved sigh. His feet had burned the last mile.

"So, what now? Teach me to teleport and whatnot?" he said. "A gauntlet ensues?"

Jezebel shook her head, staring out at the valley. "This wasn't always a desert, you know."

Quinn swished the bottle. "Oh?"

"When the diamond first arrived—when I got here, it was a meadow. Lush, green, teeming with life. It was beautiful."

"Like an oasis."

"It was *the* oasis. Before everything, this place was called Oasis. Anyway, after a time, some people showed up. The first people."

"I think we call them a nation now, love."

Jezebel rolled her eyes. "Nations are made of people. Anyway, they dig up the diamond, and I make a deal with the chief. I tell him he can have good crops and wellness for all, but the catch is, he can't get angry when the fortune ebbs and flows. That's how it works. Sometimes, you're up. Sometimes, you're down. But if I'm on your side, you can always count on it falling in your favor."

"There's always the same amount of luck," Quinn said. "If you're getting good, you can count on some sod getting bad. Vice versa, but the amount is always the same."

"Smart," nodded the goddess. "I like that."

"Some writer bloke made it up," Quinn replied. "I paraphrased."

"Well, that's the gist of it." She sighed, hugging her knees. "I'm a god, but I don't make the rules. Luck is finite. So, I tell the chief all this, and he goes 'I understand.' "

Quinn looked out at the desert. "Bloody bungered it, didn't he?"

Jez shrugged. "Things were good for a while. A long while. Crops were good. People were healthy. Everything was grand. Then, one year, they hit a drought."

"And everything went tits-up."

"Understatement of the millennia. The chief came to me and said: 'What have you done? How can you let this happen?' So, I explain again what our arrangement was. 'Not good enough,' he replies. 'You are god, right? Fix this, like a god.' Which I can do at a cost, so I say: 'There will be issues.' And he just sort of nods and goes: 'Whatever. Do it.' "

"Wait a tic," Quinn said. "He said literally *that*?"

"I'm paraphrasing."

"So don't get greedy is the moral?" Quinn said. "Let me opt out now, then."

"Just listen. I agree, and things continue as they had. Then things start going wrong. Slowly at first: a sick cow, some dead corn. Nothing major. Then, all the crops die. All the animals get sick. The water starts to dry up. People start talking mutiny. They bash his skull with a rock, then start fighting over what preserves they have left before anybody can even leave. Let's be nice and call it a bloodbath. Anyway, after all that—everything dries out and dies. Oasis disappears. Now we've got this."

Quinn looked out at the desert. "So, can we change this?"

"Sure," said the goddess. "We can make it right."

"But it'll only continue to happen until you're free, won't it?"

"Probably."

Quinn stood, pulled the diamond out of his backpack. "Well, fine then. Let's free you. If I smash this, it's over, right?"

Jezebel nodded. "I go back to the land of imagination, life goes on as it has since we gave you the world."

"But you'd be free, yeah?" Quinn eyed the diamond as sunlight shimmered off its angles.

"I would," Jezebel said. "I haven't been free in—wow, I don't even know anymore."

Quinn placed the diamond on the stone he'd been sitting on, then produced a mallet from his bag. "Well love, I don't need a genie. Let's fix this sodding desert and free you."

He wheeled back and closed his eyes. Then, he swung.

About halfway down, it felt like he'd hit a force field. He opened his eyes and found Jezebel holding his arm.

"Not yet."

Quinn dropped the mallet. "But… You've been a plaything for centuries. A slave. You don't deserve that. Nobody deserves that. It's what's right."

"Maybe," Jezebel said. "But, well... I dunno. Being around you folks has changed me. I don't know why, and I'm not sure how. But I feel in a way I never could as a god... I'm—I'm just different, I guess."

"So you want to keep doing what you have?" Quinn took another swig from the bottle, and the goddess swiped it from him.

"No," she said, producing a white card from her pocket with a grin. "I want to see what happens next."

The hardest part of grief is allowing yourself to feel it. In the face of loss, it's easier to turn away—to get your groove back; find your balance. Somehow, we're taught that grief is a thing to get over: an obstacle to beat. Not something to live with, but rather through. But loss is not a gauntlet. It isn't something you get over; it's a weird gift you're given. Not a lesson, but a new lens with which to view the world. To quit rambling and get to the point, this is what Brie Cassiday was beginning to feel.

After having vengeance—or at least a little wrath—once she'd done what she'd felt was retribution, Brie went home. And that was when it came crashing back: a black hole, opened up in her gut, at moments so bad she thought it would double her over. Not because there was anything different, but because most of life wasn't. It wasn't a change. It was a hole.

She thought: *What gives? I'm supposed to go through some stuff. Do some other stuff. Finally face the first stuff and come out the other end with some closure. That's how it always goes in the movies?*

No doubt, she'd been through stuff. Definitely, she'd done some other stuff. She'd faced the very thing she'd thought would end her, and here she was: No lessons. No closure. It would be nice if all that led to another realization, but this isn't that kind of story. The lesson, as far as she could gather, was this: losing Paul was something she'd never get over. She'd just live with it.

And that lesson would take a lifetime. Hell, it might never come. There are just some ends you can't close off. Ask the writer-types: it's kind of a bitch.

So, for whatever reason we *ever* look at family photo albums—she didn't.

Instead, she stood in her apartment, staring at lame penned caricature of her, Kevin and Paul, drawn on a day where they'd all decided to play on the Strip the way tourists do. There was a curl of a smile on the big guy's face; a grin she'd miss as long as she lived.

A grin, she realized, he always made right after he farted.

CHAPTER 31
OVER THE HILLS AND FAR AWAY

Kevin and Brie were in a booth at Baby Cluck-Cluck's. Neither of them had touched their food. The weirdest thing about it was how they were facing each other. Normally, their booth at BCC involved them bumping elbows and swapping shit-talk. They were both trying to keep it light, but what with the gap of a table between their elbow-jabbing, things were just different.

Kevin stabbed his pancakes. "I'll say this, I certainly get more food this way."

Brie laughed. "I was gonna punch you, but you're further away."

"It's weird, right?"

Brie stared at her food, the goings-on around the restaurant, anywhere but her brother. "I think it'll always be weird. How couldn't it?" She took his hand. "But it will get better."

"How can you know that?" Kev said. He shook his head, stared out the window.

"Because I have to. I don't know how it works, but if there are gods, then there's us—and you can't just lose a person. You said it yourself, broheim."

Kev nodded. "It just hurts, I guess."

"It's supposed to. That's what tells you it meant something."

"I don't mean to interrupt a healthy bro-sis," a man said from above. "But have either of you heard of mail?"

Josh Harlan stood at the nape of their table, a pot of coffee steaming in his grip. "Not to kill the moment or anything, it's just normally at this point, people do the whole fallen-hero bit. You know, what he was good at, how they'll miss him. That thing."

"He always was an incorrigible dinkbag," Brie said, winking at her brother.

"If he hadn't died saving the rest of us, he'd still be that loser," Kevin added.

"Usually people go more for the compliments," Josh said. "Expertise, necessity and whatnot."

"If he hadn't been there, someone important might've been killed," Brie continued.

Kev grinned. "Someone useful."

"Someone missed." Brie held out her mug and nodded to the grifter. "No room, please."

Josh sat beside her and filled the mug. "You are both *so* adorable. Here's the deal, wordsmiths. Apparently neither of you accept USPS, so here goes. I've got a jet. The rest of the gang's already invited. I just wanted to make sure you both could deny it formally."

"Thanks," Kev chuckled.

Brie cocked her head. "Where's the jet going?"

Josh grinned. "Follow me and find out."

"Ouu, *secrets*," said Brie.

Max entered his suite at the Venetian. The door latched, and he let out a long sigh. His arm hurt. Paperwork and banality waited for him back at Quantico, so he thought of cracking open the minibar, getting sloshed, and penning the reports he'd be grilled for. It had been a pipe dream: Freedom? A vigilante, knocking down criminals with the help of a much-bespoke ring of ninja-hookers? He didn't live in a comic book.

He fished a cigarette out of his pack and went to light, when he noticed the banker's box on the bed.

"Huh." He popped the top off the box and found all the paperwork he'd been after at the start of this.

How? How could anybody even know that? The last person directly involved was Harlan, and…

A white postcard lay next to a USB key on the bed. Knowing whatever was written on it was something he'd have to deny seeing for the next twenty years, Max sighed. He picked it up and turned it over. In fancy cursive, it read:

Toodles.

—J.H.

Let him go, or call it in? he thought.

A Cessna 780 pulled up to the boarding dock at McCarran Airport, pointed toward an obviously mysterious adventure. Brie, Kevin, Billie, Tommy, and Jimmy climbed onto the plane carrying duffels.

Each took a seat and waited.

"Thank you for choosing Harlan Airlines. Liftoff is in five minutes," the pilot said over the line. Then, the door to the cockpit opened, and the grifter at large strutted out with a pleased grin.

"I'm not dead," he said.

"We know," Tommy said, sitting next to Billie Black.

Harlan frowned. "You do?"

"Brie told us," said Jimmy.

Josh looked at Brie with a saddened expression. "*Et tu, Brie-tus?*"

"Sorry," she said with a smile. "So where are we going?"

Just then, there was a flash like lighting a firecracker. Jezebel and Quinn stood in a billow of blue smoke in the aisle.

"Please tell me it's somewhere interesting," said the goddess.

"Bloody hell!" Quinn said, swaying on the spot. "Tell me it's the sodding library. I've had enough interesting for today."

"Then grab some of those tiny bottles of scotch and lay back," Harlan said. "We've got about five hours."

"We're not going to the Caymans, are we?" said Billie Black. "Because that never works out."

"Don't be ridiculous," Tommy said. "Our money's there in spirit, but we'd never. I mean... Oh. Oh, no. No, no, no. And furthermore? No. *That's* crazy."

"So let's talk crazy." Josh gave the hacker an affectionate grin. "Who wants to rob the Caymans?"

Slowly, very slowly, each of the thieves raised their hand.

"But this is a bad idea," Billie added.

"You say that, but once you have legit crepes, it'll change everything," Tommy said.

Billie gave him a once-over. "'Kay, but Squirtle is still superior."

"Oh my god. I'm moving. I can't spend this much time next to a newb."

Billie shoved him back in his seat. "Fine. But what if we start talking Doctor Who?"

Tommy thought about it. "Which Doctor?"

"Did you seriously ask that? And I'm the newb?"

Harlan rolled his eyes. "Captain Stillwater? Think we're about ready to go."

"Cool," Leo Stillwater called from the cockpit. "Buckle it up, boys and girls! We're going to the land of freedom."

Harlan flopped in the seat beside Brie, who looked out the window as the plane taxied onto the runway.

"You know, usually at this point in the story, the two of us would settle our differences and make out."

"Really?" Brie said, bouncing her brow.

"It's not a rule. Just a thing that happens."

"Well, then I guess it's good this isn't a story," Brie said.

As the plane rumbled off the ground and pitched toward the Atlantic, Leo Stillwater came over the intercom. "Hey, you guys wanna get naked?"

"No!" they shouted.

ACKNOWLEDGEMENTS

Thanks go to the usual suspects: my ninja-editor, Aidan Cullis, and vice-ninja Jacob Leonard for their careful notes and the general business of making me look smarter.

To Vanessa Ricci-Thode, Ian Wienert, Terry McMillan, and Stephanie Killbank for their insightful reads and help in the refining process. I hope you each found a hint of your feedback in these pages.

My Vegas sherpas: Brian Eddy and Neil School, for giving me some insight into the glitzy city, keeping me from getting mugged, and for feeding me excellent tacos—thanks.

My family, Denise, Alastair, Manal and Melanie Younger. Thanks for putting up with me.

To Stacey Rebertz, Haley Wolk, Carla Vollemecke, Shane Perch, Caroline Fréchette and all the other wonderful friends who keep this ship sailing. You're grade-A.

Extra-special thanks to Ben van Duyvendyk, whose artistic genius and monk-like patience helped make the cover. I couldn't have done it without you.

And finally, to my readers. Keep turning pages, and I'll keep writing them. The gratitude I hold for each of you does not have words—in this, or any other language. Yes, that includes you. Yeah, I'm talking to you. Thanks.

ABOUT THE AUTHOR

DANIEL YOUNGER is Amazon's least-known bestselling author of *Delirious* and *Zen and the Art of Cannibalism*. He lives in Canada (Eh?), where he mushes a pack of wild huskies next to a river of maple syrup every morning. He enjoys spicy food, gourmet coffee, beaver-racing, and acid jazz. You can e-mail him at danieljyounger@icloud.com, or find him causing a ruckus on Twitter @youngerdaniel.

CPSIA information can be obtained at www.ICGtesting.com
Printed in the USA
LVOW08s1634290916

506736LV00003B/726/P